Also by Terry Spear

Red Wolf
Joy to the Wolves
The Best of Both Wolves

Wolff Brothers
You Had Me at Wolf
Jingle Bell Wolf

Billionaire Wolf
Billionaire in Wolf's Clothing
A Billionaire Wolf for Christmas
Night of the Billionaire Wolf

SEAL Wolf
A SEAL in Wolf's Clothing
A SEAL Wolf Christmas
SEAL Wolf Hunting
SEAL Wolf in Too Deep
SEAL Wolf Undercover
SEAL Wolf Surrender

Heart of the Shifter
You Had Me at Jaguar

Highland Wolf
Heart of the Highland Wolf
A Howl for a Highlander
A Highland Werewolf Wedding
Hero of a Highland Wolf
A Highland Wolf for Christmas
The Wolf Wore Plaid

Silver Town Wolf
Destiny of the Wolf
Wolf Fever
Dreaming of the Wolf
Silence of the Wolf
A Silver Wolf Christmas
Alpha Wolf Need Not Apply
Between a Wolf and a Hard Place
All's Fair in Love and Wolf
Silver Town Wolf: Home for the Holidays

Heart of the Jaguar
Savage Hunter
Jaguar Fever
Jaguar Hunt
Jaguar Pride
A Very Jaguar Christmas

White Wolf
Dreaming of a White Wolf Christmas
Flight of the White Wolf

Heart of the Wolf
Heart of the Wolf
To Tempt the Wolf
Legend of the White Wolf
Seduced by the Wolf

WHILE THE WOLF'S AWAY

TERRY SPEAR

Patty Cieplinski—thanks so much for enjoying my books and always being eager to try the new series! I hope that they take you into new worlds of wonder!

Published by Sourcebooks Casablanca, an imprint of Sourcebooks
P.O. Box 4410, Naperville, Illinois 60567-4410
(630) 961-3900
sourcebooks.com

Printed and bound in Canada.
MBP 10 9 8 7 6 5 4 3 2 1

Chapter 1

Eager to get their clandestine meeting started, David Davis got ready for his weekly Skype session with Elizabeth Alpine. It was their only opportunity to visit face-to-face since she lived in Yellowknife, Northwest Territories, Canada, and he was located near Ely, Minnesota, the gateway to the Boundary Waters Canoe Area Wilderness.

They had to do this in secret because her Arctic wolf-pack leader, Kintail, would have done something drastic had he known they were still in touch. To say Kintail had issues with his pack members trying to break free was an understatement.

Not that David would ever consider himself one of their pack, even if they did, technically, save his life. It was either be turned or die of a heart attack during a bear hunt gone terribly wrong in Maine. And he was glad he wasn't dead, no complaints there. But once he was turned, Kintail and his pack thought they owned him.

David had other ideas. And so did Elizabeth, which was why she'd helped him to escape.

She'd meant to escape with him so they could make a home together in Seattle, Washington, where he was a PI, and be free of Kintail and the pack, but Elizabeth's grandmother,

Ada, had gotten sick. Elizabeth couldn't abandon her only family; she would forever have regretted it. Ada had often told David that Elizabeth just needed to leave to be with him and get on with her life, and the pack would take care of Ada just fine.

But Elizabeth wouldn't have been just fine if she had left her grandmother in other wolves' care. Especially with the way Kintail treated his pack. The other wolves might really want to help Ada but be prevented from doing so by Kintail.

David drummed his fingers on the table as he placed the Skype call and waited for Ada to pick up. She was always trying to sneak in some "before time" with him. And sure enough:

"Oh, David, you're looking more handsome every time I see you." Ada smiled. "I want you to come and take Elizabeth away from here *before* I'm gone. Kintail and his men are bound to be watching her to ensure she doesn't leave as soon as I've passed on to join my dearly beloved mate."

They'd been over this a dozen times before. David smiled gently. "Elizabeth needs to be there for you for her own peace of mind and for yours. But as soon as—"

"No. Now. I feel it in my bones that I could go any minute now. Oh, scratch that. You smile at me and look at me with those big, adoring brown eyes, and I almost forget I'm as old as an ancient oak tree. If Elizabeth and I could trade places, I would be racing out of here to be with you. She's a silly goose to waste her life away here without you."

Sometimes, Ada's curly white hair was piled high on top of her head in a chic coiffure, as if she were getting ready to go to a dance. Other times, like today, her hair was long and silky and down around her shoulders as she lay in her big bed. She did seem more tired than usual, but she still had good days too. Besides, David was used to this line of conversation. Ada had been saying she could go any minute now ever since Elizabeth had returned home to take care of her. He smiled wider and gave her a wink for good measure. "You're not going anywhere and good thing too. Who would sing my praises if you weren't around?"

"Are you on Skype already?" Elizabeth asked, hurrying into her grandmother's room with a couple bottles of water. She sounded mildly accusative, but David knew it was a game the two women played, Elizabeth pretending to be late to the session, David and her grandmother getting on just a little early so she could chat privately with him.

"Grandma, you know you're not supposed to be on Skype without me. I never know what the two of you are plotting." Elizabeth's beautiful brown curls were partly up and partly down. She looked like she'd been working in her grandmother's garden again.

He hoped Elizabeth would love gardening in the plot at his cabin. He hadn't planted anything there yet. He wanted it to be her garden. Every summer he kept it weeded, just in case he had to go rescue her and bring her home. In the winter, it lay dormant waiting for the spring. Waiting for her.

"What am I plotting?" Ada said. "Running away with this handsome wolf since you won't? We would make a lovely pair, wouldn't we?" She sighed dramatically. "But alas, he only has eyes for you. You need to go to him."

"I can wait," David said, like he'd said so many times before, because there had never been anyone like Elizabeth and he knew there never would be. "I'll wait forever for you, Elizabeth, honey." And he would. He would wait as long as he had to. But being together like this wasn't the same as *being* together. The last time they'd actually been together, they'd been on the run from her pack leader. But staying in hotels and having unconsummated relations because wolves mated for life hadn't really counted.

Yet they'd known then and they knew now they only wanted each other.

Still, he couldn't help the doubts that crept in. When they were finally able to physically be together, safe from danger, would they still feel the same way about each other? When they finally lived in his cabin on the lake, and he was off working as a PI and she was... She was what? He didn't even know what she would do when he was away on missions. Would the magic still be there?

"She's treated like an omega wolf here," Ada was saying. "I'm not just crying wolf. She needs you and your pack's protection. And she needs it now."

"Grandma, shush. I'm fine. I'm happy to be here with you, and I won't leave until it's..." Elizabeth took a deep breath, but the tears in her eyes said it all.

David hated that Kintail was such an ass. He wanted nothing more than to swoop in and take Elizabeth away from her pack, get her out from under his control. David had been glad Elizabeth had more time with her grandmother before the end came, but he hated that Kintail and the other pack members were still giving Elizabeth grief for having freed David and his friend Owen. It'd been years since then, but Kintail knew how to hold a grudge; losing new wolves wasn't something he would ever get over.

Losing yet another wolf wasn't something Kintail would stand for either. And Elizabeth *would* leave, the first moment she could. It might have been a different story with a different leader. If Elizabeth had been met with kindness, with understanding, maybe she would have stayed. But Kintail was who he was: Controlling. Demanding. Greedy for power. Kindness was weakness, and weakness was death.

That's why Elizabeth needed to be free.

"Okay, so let's go over the new plan of rescue and evasion, shall we?" That was Ada's favorite topic of discussion when they had their weekly Skype sessions.

"If I drove long days and didn't stop for much, I could make it in three days going up and we could make it in three days coming back," David said.

"Right," Ada said, as if she were making the trip herself.

Elizabeth let her grandmother dominate the calls with David because her grandmother loved them, and it always gave her something to look forward to for the next week. David enjoyed talking with her too. He'd loved his own grandparents, but they were gone now, and Elizabeth's grandmother had adopted him, whether he ended up mated to Elizabeth or not. He loved Ada just as much as Elizabeth did.

David continued going over their plans. "And flights are around twenty-two hours, depending on layovers. Some are longer. Layovers are two hours in Calgary and seven hours in Edmonton."

"I don't like that plan. While I want the two of you out of Canada as soon as possible, Kintail and his men will be watching Elizabeth after I'm gone, and they'll be watching the airport to see if you turn up."

Elizabeth's grandmother had never liked the idea of them escaping by plane, but David didn't want to discount it either. Driving would mean a delay in reaching Yellowknife to pull Elizabeth out after Ada's funeral. It was risky to wait.

"True. But I was thinking I could solicit Amelia—Gavin Summerfield's mate—to help us," David said. "He's another PI partner and long-time friend, and she's a pilot. Then we wouldn't have long layovers because we can take a more direct flight instead of having to fly their scheduled routes."

"Oh, yes, that sounds much better. Also, I don't want a funeral," Ada said. "I'm being cremated, and Elizabeth has instructions to scatter my ashes over the roses in the backyard. Well, if the yard isn't covered in snow. I'll try not to leave when it's snowing out." She always said "leave," like she was just planning on taking a trip—which, in a way, was exactly how she thought of it. "Oh, and I'll try to leave when it isn't the full-moon phase."

The phase of the full moon could be an issue for David. Not for Elizabeth. She and her family were royals, having very few purely human roots in their genetic makeup. But David had been turned by one of her pack members, so he'd been born as a human and dealing with a full moon was harder for him. It tugged on his need to shift, though he was better at controlling it than he used to be. He still couldn't entertain the thought of flying during that phase, though, unless either Amelia or her brother, Slade, piloted him. Their father, Henry, flew planes too, but, David figured, as a royal like Elizabeth, Henry would be holding down the fort while either Amelia or Slade helped David and Elizabeth get out.

"If it's winter, you could sneak in at a rendezvous point and snowmobile out of here," Ada mused.

That was the thing of it. They had so many things to take into consideration—time of year, the moon phases, getting to and out of Yellowknife in the Northwest Territories, whether extra help was needed or not.

His three partners wanted to help him, not to mention their mates too. They all knew Elizabeth from Maine, whether personally or through stories of her bravery, and were ready to jump in whenever David needed them.

"You can't get your partners and their mates involved in all this," Ada said, seemingly reading his mind. "We don't want a pack war up here. You'll never beat them, and they'll bury the lot of you. So don't even think of it. Come alone... well, except for Amelia or her brother, if they can fly you here all right. When Elizabeth is finally safe back home with you, your pack members can help, if Kintail and his men are foolish enough to follow you."

"I like that idea," Elizabeth said. "If Amelia or Slade fly in, it won't matter if the full moon is an issue for you. And if I could reach the airport without Kintail being aware of it, we would fly off into the sunset and be gone before they could do anything about it. Hopefully we wouldn't have to involve your pack at all."

David didn't want a pack war either. The thought of putting his packmates at risk ate at him. But he would—for her.

He couldn't understand why Kintail was so adamant about not losing a pack member. If a wolf was unhappy with the pack, let him go. Once her grandmother was gone, Elizabeth had no kin left there, and most of Elizabeth's friends had turned their backs on her.

But letting Elizabeth go wasn't in Kintail's plans. He couldn't have anyone "mutinying" and that's exactly what he would consider it. Mutiny. What if more of his pack members saw that as a sign to leave too?

Kintail would do anything in his power to stop Elizabeth from leaving. *Anything.*

Just as David would do anything to help her break free.

Ada sighed. "I know she will be in good hands with you and your packmates. I'm going to rest my eyes a bit and let you talk in private with my Elizabeth, but no talking over trip plans without me."

He smiled. "I love you, Grandma." And he meant it.

"Oh, how I wish I was younger." Grandma smiled in return and blew him a kiss.

Elizabeth kissed her grandmother's cheek. "I'll come check on you in a little bit." Then she took her laptop out of the bedroom, closed the door, and went into the living room, settling into her recliner. "She loves making plans to get us together. She says when these calls end, she thinks for hours about how to help us. About the life we could have.

She remembers the time when she was a young woman and went with her mate, my grandfather, to see the States. If her memories of my grandfather weren't so tied to this pack, she would leave with me to join you."

"I would welcome her into my home gladly," David said.

"I know. And she does too. You've done her a world of good. Thanks for including her in our chats."

"I wouldn't have it any other way. I miss you though. I can't say that enough." He longed to be with Elizabeth, sharing kisses with her, and more. There was so much he wanted to experience with her. She was truly the light of his life.

"I miss you too," Elizabeth said.

Despite the closeness he felt with his own pack, it wasn't the same as being with a mate. He thought about her constantly. About running with her as wolves and playing chase and tag. About making love with her and having little wolf pups of their own. About being a family, when he'd never thought he would be interested in such a thing. Not until he'd met Elizabeth—and lost her.

They just had to get her out of Yellowknife and out of her pack's reach. Until then, nothing else mattered.

Chapter 2

Elizabeth loved her grandmother and was grateful she'd had her in her life for so long. She hated her pack leader for vowing to kill David, and any of his pack members, if they dared set foot in their territory.

Her bond with David went deeper than any bond with her pack, with the exception of her grandmother. Her feelings for him transcended place and time. In the beginning, she'd worried about their relationship. What if he had only really needed her for the comfort he'd craved when he was turned, going from an ordinary human to an extraordinary *lupus garou*? What if he wasn't as into her as it seemed? That the newness of being together, or the fact she'd helped him and Owen escape, was the reason he'd been attracted to her?

If it hadn't been for Kintail, David could have made the trip to see Elizabeth and her grandmother from time to time. But she knew spies in the pack were always watching, waiting, making sure David didn't show up. And she was certain they would ensure Elizabeth didn't slip away from the pack once her grandmother died.

Only two places offered funeral services in Yellowknife, so it would be hard to keep her grandmother's death quiet when the time came. The pack would eventually find out; they always did. But Elizabeth promised her grandma she would keep it a secret as long as she could. The longer the pack was in the dark, the better chance Elizabeth had of escaping.

Her best friend, Sheri Whitmore, had said she would take care of the cremation when the time came and would spread Ada's ashes in her rose garden, just as she wanted. Elizabeth hadn't wanted to tell either David or her grandmother of Sheri's offer because no one in the pack was supposed to be in on their plans. But Elizabeth loved Sheri like a sister, and she was her best shot at buying some time.

Still, involving Sheri came with risks, not the least to Sheri herself. If the pack ever found out Sheri had helped her, she would end up in the same position Elizabeth was in now. Friendless. Her family under suspicion. *Watched.*

Elizabeth shook off her dark thoughts and refocused on her call with David. She couldn't believe he had waited for her all this time, though she'd been doing the same for him. If he'd had a chance to find a mate, she had wanted him to take it. To find love.

And at the same time, she hated the very thought of that.

"Still no she-wolves on the horizon?" she asked David. She always asked.

"You're the only one for me. To think I've waited this long and then I would just give you up? No way. You need me and I need you."

She smiled. He had never wavered once about waiting for her. Even when his other PI partners had all found mates, he continued to wait for her. She couldn't help but appreciate him for it. She so longed to be with him.

"How is it out there today?" She pictured all the forested land they had around his pack members' homes. He'd taken her and her grandmother on a video tour of the house and shown them the views of the lake and forest, just so Elizabeth could see the area, could envision herself there when she moved to the Minnesota pack to be with him. And Elizabeth loved every bit of it. Her grandmother had been glad to know how beautiful everything was in the area too. She told them she saw it when she worked on their plans after their calls, adding it to the details in her mind, imagining Elizabeth there with him, happy in the woods and by the lake and in the home he'd built.

"Sunny and warm, perfect for us to go swimming," David said. "We will take the canoe out, paddle to the island. We can shift and have a nice run through the woods."

"Hmm, it sounds delightful. And I'd make brownies for dessert."

"Yes, I love your brownies and the way you always made extras for me."

"You were always so grateful for them."

"And for you for freeing Owen and me and for coming with us."

"I miss that. I wish I was with you now."

"I don't miss the danger, but I sure miss you."

"Yeah. Hopefully, we can do it this time without the chase scenes and all. Okay, I need to speak with you about something else. I know we talked about not getting anyone else involved—especially from my pack. But my childhood friend has offered to help me with Grandmother when she passes. I didn't talk to her about it, I swear. She just knows me too well."

He didn't say anything for a moment, and Elizabeth continued. "It might give me a chance to slip away. It might give me a little bit of a head start."

"Would she say anything to anyone about it?"

"No."

"But they would learn soon enough that she had helped you with your grandmother."

"Yeah. They would."

"Can you get someone else to do it? Someone you trust? Someone human, instead of a pack member?"

"It would be hard to explain why I had to ask someone else to do it. And even if I said something about having an emergency I had to attend to, I wouldn't want to leave Grandmother's ashes to a total stranger to take care of."

"I understand."

"You know they're going to be watching me all the time anyway. As soon as I start leaving the house for more than a trip to the grocery store, they're going to know something's up." Then Elizabeth had another idea. "Wait, maybe we've been thinking about this all wrong. What if we let it be known that you have a mate already and there's no way you're ever coming for me, or that I'm ever going to join you either?"

A long silence followed her suggestion. His face went still, but his eyes spoke volumes. Finally, he said, "It's a good idea. That could be our answer. I'll start working on it."

She was so relieved they might have finally figured out a

way for her to leave without anyone being the wiser. "I'll call Sheri with a sob story, make it sound as realistic as I can."

"But we keep on with our weekly chats." He sounded like he couldn't do without them, just as much as she couldn't.

"Oh, absolutely. I'll let my grandmother know what's going on." This would work. It had to. "I can't wait to be with you, David."

"I can't wait to be with you either. I love you."

"I love you too." They ended the call, but Elizabeth didn't feel the same sense of letdown she usually did when they hung up. They had a plan! She checked David's Facebook page and saw right away that he had posted a picture of a woman who didn't look anything like Elizabeth. Fast worker! She hoped that would be the first step in getting everyone in her pack to believe he had wanted someone new in his life. Someone *not* Elizabeth.

Another update popped up. "Candy" was listed as his wife. *Candy?*

Half an hour later, she checked his Facebook page again and found all kinds of pictures featuring David and the blond—Candy—hugging and being together at the lake, swimming, eating a meal together. It wasn't real. But it would be someday, with her.

Then she smiled, realizing who the woman was. She'd only seen her once; she'd dropped by while David was sitting on his deck at the lake doing a Skype session with Elizabeth, and the woman had to come over to say hi. She was Owen's mate, Candice-now-Candy, a romance author.

David must have contacted her the moment they hung

up to come and help him with the deception. Elizabeth was so thankful for David's pack; she couldn't wait to be part of it. She loved all of them. She just wished her grandmother had wanted to go with her and be with them. She would have loved them too.

Speaking of, she heard a bell ring, and she went to see what her grandma needed and to tell her the good news.

"My hot tea?" Grandma asked. "You finished your talk with David, I hear." She still had the best hearing.

"Oh right." Elizabeth turned on her heel and headed to the kitchen. She heated the water in the teapot, then brought in a cup of hot Earl Grey, her grandma's favorite. "Okay, I have to tell you the great news. David found a mate."

Grandma looked puzzled, but she was a crafty old wolf, and it didn't take her long to smile. "Aww, I'm so angry with him."

"Yeah, so am I." Elizabeth left again, then returned with her laptop. She popped open the lid and showed her the pictures of David's "mate."

Her grandmother frowned. "Photoshopped?"

"No. That's Owen Nottingham's mate, Candice, wearing a wig. She's the romance writer. She makes a great actress, doesn't she?"

"I'll say. I would have believed it."

"In his posts, David doesn't call her by her real name, though, just Candy, so no one will really know who she is. And the wig looks real. I saw her once on a Skype call, and she doesn't look at all the same."

"Does she have her photo anywhere else? A Facebook page that shows her and her real mate or something?"

Elizabeth checked Candice's account. "She shows Owen is her mate, but see? She doesn't look anything like the pictures David uploaded."

"You're right. Between the makeup and hair, she really doesn't. And she doesn't look anything like you either."

"Exactly, like he was going for someone completely different."

"When are you going to tell Sheri?"

"After I cry a bit."

Her grandmother laughed. "Make me some roast-beef hash from last night's leftovers, and then you can cry over cutting up the onions."

Elizabeth laughed too. "It's a deal." She went into the kitchen and started making the hash. While it was cooking, she FaceTimed Sheri, tears in her eyes from all the onion chopping. "David found a mate."

"Oh, no, Elizabeth, I'm so sorry. I'll be right over."

Elizabeth hated lying to her best friend. "No, it's"—sniffle, sniffle—"time for Grandma and me to eat dinner. She's upset about it too. I just had to tell you."

"I'm so sorry. You let me know when you want me to come over, then."

"I will."

"How's Grandma doing?"

"Raging at David on my behalf but fine otherwise."

"Well, as much as I hate to hear it, I'm not surprised. If he finally found someone, it's understandable." There was a pause, then: "He's not a royal anyway. Maybe you'll be better off with someone who's..." Another pause, like she wasn't sure what kind of reception this line of discussion would get. She plowed ahead though. "Who's like you."

Elizabeth wasn't bothered by the whole royal thing, not that anyone from the territory who was a royal was interested in her. And she wasn't interested in anyone like that either. But it did worry her that Sheri said "if" he finally found someone. Did Sheri have doubts about Elizabeth's story?

"Right," she said, playing along, hoping that Sheri bought it. "I don't know what I saw in a newly turned wolf anyway. He would have been nothing but heartache, and having kids by him would mean our offspring wouldn't be royals. Why would I do that to my own children?"

"Exactly. I'll let you get to your meal and I'll talk to you later. Feel better."

"Thanks, Sheri." Elizabeth was already feeling much better. She served up the hash on a platter and took it in to her grandma. She was still eating well and had an iron stomach, Elizabeth thought, which she was thankful for.

"Did Sheri take it hook, line, and sinker?" Grandma asked.

"I think so. And because she thinks that will somehow make everything all right with the pack concerning me, she'll spread the word. Not because she's a gossip or anything."

"Hopefully it will throw Kintail and the pack off the track. They'll figure you'll have nowhere else to go. You won't want to join Cameron's pack now since you'd have to see David with his new wolf mate all the time." She held a fork full of hash suspended in front of her mouth. "Whose idea was it?"

"Mine. I suddenly figured out what might work. I don't know why I didn't think of it earlier."

"Well, it's an excellent plan," Grandma said.

They finished eating and watched a wild thriller—her grandma's favorite kind of movie. When it was done, Elizabeth kissed her good night. "Love you, Grandma. Call me if you need anything."

"I will, dear. Love you too."

Three days later, in the middle of the night, Elizabeth heard a noise coming from her grandmother's room and went to check on her to see if she needed anything. She pushed open the door, listening to the quiet darkness within. Her grandmother had died peacefully in her sleep.

Tears ran in tracks down Elizabeth's face as the reality of her grandma's death pierced her heart. But like Grandma had told her, when the time came, she had to bury her sorrow for the moment and put a plan of action in place right away.

Elizabeth dried her eyes and called David, waking him from sleep. "David, Grandma's gone." Her voice cracked with emotion.

"Oh God, Elizabeth, I'm so sorry. How are you doing?"

"I don't know. I mean, I have expected this forever, and yet it's never seemed real to me. Even now, I can't believe it. But"—the tears flowed again, unchecked—"Grandma died peacefully in her sleep, at home, just like she wanted, and she would tell me to get my butt in gear and get going. So that's what I'm going to do."

"I'll get ahold of Amelia right away and get a flight out

as soon as I can. If she can't do it, maybe her brother can. I already have a bag packed. Did you tell everyone in your pack that I had mated Candy?"

"I told Sheri. She would have told the rest of the pack."

"Okay, good."

"I'll call to have my grandmother's body picked up. I don't know for sure, but I don't think they'll do anything...with her..." Her voice went soft, nearly a whisper, as she struggled to say the words. "With her body until morning at least."

"Elizabeth, honey, it'll be okay. I promise." His heartbreak for her came through in every word. "Don't think about that right now. I'll call you back as soon as I know what time we are leaving and when we'll get in, and we'll go from there."

"Okay." She sniffed. "At least the waxing gibbous moon phase is here, so you won't have a problem with shifting for a while. And it's summer." She sighed through her tears. "No moon *and* no snow. I swear my grandmother planned it that way. I love you so much."

"I love you too. Your grandma was a great woman. For the time I got to know her—even though it was just on Skype—I loved her and miss her too. It's time for us to be together now though."

"I know she wanted this for me, for us. I know she did. She knew how much I wanted to be with you. I love you. I'll talk to you soon."

Then Elizabeth ended the call so she could take care of her grandmother, one last time.

Chapter 3

Hating to hear her feeling so destitute after her grandmother died and unable to hug Elizabeth like he wanted to, David was immediately on the phone to Amelia, waking her. He didn't waste time with niceties. "Hey, it's on."

Amelia responded like he hadn't just awoken her from a dead sleep. "Elizabeth's grandmother died."

"Yes."

"Okay, I'm calling my mom to have her get ahold of a couple of standby pilots to take Slade's and my flights for the next couple of days. I've already talked to Slade about going with us so we can switch off on flying. We always have a bag packed for emergency flights so we're ready to leave at a moment's notice. This is definitely an emergency rescue mission. I'll take care of the flight plan. We'll be going to Winnipeg, refuel, and then to Calgary, which is two hours from there. And another three hours from Calgary to Yellowknife. Are you sure that the business with being mated to 'Candy' was enough to have Kintail call off his watchdogs?"

"We won't know for sure until we get there. I'll rent a car and pick her up at some place we can agree on, someplace not anywhere near the airport so they won't think she's taking off. We'll meet you back at the airport after that."

"Okay."

Then he called Elizabeth back. "How are you doing?"

"I wish you were here already. What's the plan?"

"I'm flying out with Amelia and Slade. You need to pick a place where I can come and get you. If you have any indication that they'll be on the lookout for us at the airport, let us know and we'll change our plans in a hurry."

"What if Amelia comes to meet me at a restaurant instead? There's a place called the Wildcat Café. Hopefully, if anyone's following me, they won't think twice about me having dinner with a friend."

"Okay, though it's going to kill me to be so close to you and not be able to see you. I'll stay with Slade." And pray this worked out all right. "What about your car?"

"I could have Sheri drop me off at the restaurant and tell her I was going with Amelia to do something after dinner. I'll call Amelia by some other name though. I hate lying to Sheri about any of this, but I can't tell her what's really going on. I'm afraid Kintail would force it out of her if he suspected anything."

"What if Sheri wants to join you for the meal?" David asked.

"Actually, she could. It might even seem more natural if we all went out to eat together and then I left to do something with Amelia, telling Sheri that Amelia will drop me off at home afterward."

"Sounds good." He told her the flight times to the various airports, then they said another rushed goodbye. But this time the goodbye was tinged with hope because their next hello wouldn't be over the phone.

It would be in each other's arms.

"I'm so sorry about her grandmother, but I'm damn glad Elizabeth is coming back with us. And if she decides she can't live with you, there's always me," Slade said to David, smiling.

Amelia shook her head. "You'd better not even think of it, Slade. I don't want to be on the outs with the whole pack because of you stealing the woman away."

Slade laughed. "As if that would ever happen. I'm just glad David and Elizabeth can finally work something out between the two of them if it's meant to be."

That was the thing. No matter how much David was sure it was, they wouldn't really know for certain it was meant to be until they'd had the chance to be together in a normal setting. At least they'd have a playground—so to speak—in their backyard where they could run to their hearts' content when he wasn't working. And a home they could make their own. And a pack where she knew most of the members already, members who loved her. Maybe he had nothing to worry about. Maybe her transition to his pack, his life, would be easy for her.

Maybe everything would be just fine.

They loaded up the plane, and it wasn't long before they were heading to Winnipeg. Slade took the first shift, being more of a night owl. Amelia and David would get some sleep, but not until after he explained Elizabeth's plan and Amelia's role in it.

"Oh, I bet they'll have bison burgers. I haven't had any of those since we left Alaska," Amelia said.

"Bring us some back, will you?" Slade asked. "I haven't had one since then either."

"Anyone watching might wonder why Amelia is taking a sack of burgers to go," David said.

Slade sighed. "All right. But don't you get yourself kidnapped by Kintail's pack, Amelia, or Mom and Dad will have my head. And David's too."

Six hours later, they landed in Winnipeg, grabbed a quick bite, then refueled. Slade turned the pilot's seat over to Amelia, his eyes already closing as he slumped next to David.

David called Elizabeth to see how she was doing. "Hey, how are you?"

"Nervous. And I can't stop crying. I start to think I'm doing okay, then all of a sudden I'm crying again." She stopped and blew her nose, the sound loud and clear through the phone. "She's already been cremated, so at least that's done. I waited until morning, then told Sheri that my grandmother had died. She had practically adopted her. She's upset because she loved her too. I didn't tell anyone else, but you know how fast word spreads. I know Kintail will hear soon."

"Okay, that's to be expected, even though we hoped he wouldn't learn about it until *after* you were well on your way out of there. What about a bag of your things? Your personal belongings?" David hadn't even thought about that before now. He'd always thought someday they'd be together, and she could bring whatever she needed. Whatever she didn't have, they'd just get in Ely.

"I'm going to need a whole new me. It's not like I can pack a bag and bring it to dinner. Kintail would know for sure something was up. I did mail some documents and things to you just yesterday, thinking it was past time to do it. And I can fit some things into my purse, but when we get to your place, I'm going to have to go shopping."

He smiled. "I'll take you shopping for whatever you want or need." He thought of texting Candice and seeing if she could run to the store for Elizabeth so she would have what she needed as soon as they got in, but decided against it. Elizabeth would probably want to pick out her own things. "This is really happening, Elizabeth. We're on the next leg of our journey." It was his turn for emotions to clog his voice.

"I know," she said softly. "All right, I'm going to spread my grandmother's ashes in her rose garden, though I'm going to bring some of her ashes with me to put in a memorial garden for her. Then Sheri's coming over to have lunch and be with me for a while."

"Don't let on about anything. I know she's your friend, but we have to be careful."

"I won't say a word, but she's going to know something's wrong if I don't have her over. I won't mention going to dinner with a friend until later, in case you don't get in on time. It might seem odd if I kept delaying the time for dinner."

"We need to come up with a story about who Amelia is and why she's meeting with you—" David said.

"I was living in Alaska and met Elizabeth in Yellowknife once," Amelia said.

David put the call on speakerphone. "Did you get that?"

"Yeah."

"And I was going to be in the area again and wanted to see her."

"That should work," Elizabeth said. "We just need to come up with a reason you were in Yellowknife and how we met."

"I'll think about it while I'm flying."

"All right." Elizabeth sighed, more a sound of relief than anything else. "Thanks, Amelia. Love you, David."

"I love you right back."

"Guess that leaves me out of the running," another male said.

Elizabeth guessed it was Slade and was so appreciative he'd come too. "Slade?"

"Yeah, sometimes it seems I'm just invisible when it comes to women," Slade said.

Elizabeth laughed.

Amelia said, "Don't believe him. He's charming and irresistible, but he just hasn't found the woman for him yet."

Well, Elizabeth wouldn't be the one, as she had her heart set on David.

Chapter 4

Elizabeth was excited to see David, but nervous about the possibility that they couldn't pull off their plan without a hitch. She wanted so badly to tell Sheri goodbye and not leave her hanging, but she couldn't. Not without potentially jeopardizing Sheri and also jeopardizing Elizabeth's escape attempt, an attempt that could go so wrong in so many ways.

"Mom and Dad want you to come over for lunch instead of me coming over there," Sheri said over the phone. "But they'll understand if you're feeling down about everything."

"Another time," Elizabeth said. They'd been really good to her, the only ones who had. Sheri's brother, Hans, hadn't been happy with Elizabeth; he was too much of a yes-man when it came to what Kintail wanted, and he didn't like her interest in an outsider. She wondered how he felt now that David supposedly had a mate. "After all that has gone on—between my grandmother dying"—Elizabeth choked on the words; it was all too raw for her right now—"and David mating some she-wolf, I just can't." The lie stuck in her throat.

"Oh, I understand. I'll be over at—"

"Eleven?"

"Oh, sure, you always like early lunches. See you then," Sheri said.

Elizabeth didn't mention spreading her grandmother's ashes in the rose garden, afraid Sheri's parents would want to come over too. She figured she would treat it as though it was a spur-of-the-moment idea.

She quickly packed her grandmother's clothes to give to charity and boxed up canned and packaged food to leave at a food bank. When she dropped them off, she noticed Sheri's boyfriend, Bentley, following her. Apparently planting the story about David being mated hadn't been enough to shake her tail. Ignoring him, she returned to the house to clean. When it went on the market, it would be ready. Furnished even, if anyone wanted a furnished home.

As for her own stuff... She bit her lip, having forgotten for a second she'd be leaving everything she ever owned behind. She would have to pay someone else to come and gather all her belongings and give them away too. Maybe Sheri would do it for her. Sheri could even sell them, if she wanted to, and keep the money for her efforts.

Elizabeth had always envisioned packing her car to the roof with all her belongings, but that just wasn't a viable option. Not if she wanted to slip away before anyone should find out about it.

Kintail knew that as soon as Ada Alpine died, Elizabeth would take off. And he was pissed off she hadn't come to him with the news that Ada had died. In fact, she hadn't told anyone about it. He had to learn about it when Bentley happened to be running out for doughnuts and saw Elizabeth coming out of one of the funeral homes nearby. How would it look to his people if he couldn't control them better than that? After that, Kintail sent Bentley to watch her. He called in to tell the pack leader she'd stopped by a charity organization to drop off boxes of stuff.

What stuff? Her grandmother's clothes?

Why? Why so quickly? The only reason he could come up with was she was planning on leaving. She had to be. He thought of having a man watch at the airport, but they might as well just see what she was up to for now. If Bentley lost her, Kintail would send men to the airport to stop her.

"You know that David Davis has a mate now," Bentley said.

"That's what they say."

"But you don't believe it."

"He might have, who knows? I still don't trust her to stay here with the pack." He hung up, his mind churning. What was she up to?

A few minutes later, Bentley called back. "Hey, Boss, now she's dropping off boxes of food at the food pantry."

"Food?"

"Yeah. Seems like she plans to run. And I was talking to my girlfriend, Sheri, about a funeral service for Elizabeth's grandmother, and she said that there wouldn't be one."

"No way in hell."

"I'm still following her. Looks like she's headed home."

"Stay on her."

"I will." A few minutes later, Bentley called yet again. "She parked in her garage."

"Stay there and follow her if she leaves."

"Will do."

Elizabeth was trying to mess with Kintail's leadership; he just knew it. She'd done it before, and he'd be damned if he'd let her do it again.

He got in his pickup truck and headed toward Ada's house. He would tell Elizabeth how it was. They were going to have a funeral service for her grandmother whether Elizabeth wanted to go to it or not. He had to show that he honored loyal pack members in death, even though Ada hadn't disowned her traitorous granddaughter like he had insisted she do.

He had to prove he was still in charge of the pack where Elizabeth was concerned. What she wanted or didn't want... well, that just didn't matter.

The knock on the door sent panic shooting through Elizabeth. She wasn't expecting anyone, and she was afraid Kintail had figured out what she was up to and had sent someone to stop her from leaving. But when she went to the door and saw it was Kintail himself, she felt her skin chill. She opened the door and let him in. The place was neat, no packing boxes anywhere, but she noticed he was taking everything in like a wary wolf would.

Elizabeth didn't offer him anything to drink or to take a seat or anything. She just stood in the living room, waiting for him to leave.

"When are you going to have the funeral service? You didn't even tell me Ada had died. That's protocol, you know." His lips curled in a haughty sneer.

The coldhearted tone in which he referred to her grandma sent fresh tears down her face. She let them fall, daring him to say something. It was still sinking in, her grandmother's death, and Elizabeth didn't know if she'd ever get over it. The tears, and the fierceness in her voice when she answered him, were both real. "She didn't want a funeral, and no memorial service either."

"That's just not done. How do you think everyone else will feel if they can't say goodbye to her?"

That was Kintail's doing, not Elizabeth's. Her friends had stopped coming by when Elizabeth had moved in after being declared a traitor. Her grandmother made it clear she didn't want to be suddenly seen as a friend of the pack, one that they missed dearly. They were no friends of hers.

"We'll have one in a few days. If you won't set it up, I'll have someone else do it."

"Fine. She didn't want one, but do whatever makes you feel better."

"I hear David finally found a mate."

Her heart hitched, and she didn't have to fake the distress on her face this time either. She hadn't expected Kintail to bring it up; she only hoped her shocked expression was seen as a reaction to her heart being broken and not fear that he was poking around in her carefully constructed story.

"Yeah, so? Once I left, that was the end of any relationship we might have had." She prayed her false bravado worked.

"Forgive me if I don't believe you. Come to your grandmother's service or not. It's up to you." Kintail headed for her door and left without another word.

She hurried to lock the door behind him, feeling like she might throw up. Did he not believe David was mated either?

Elizabeth called David. "Kintail came by."

"He'd better have been offering condolences," David said.

"No, just trying to bully me into having a funeral or memorial service for Grandma. She didn't want one. I told him so. I'm...I'm just afraid he doesn't believe you've moved on with a new mate."

"It doesn't matter. We're taking you home with us no matter what."

"Okay, I'm going to lie down for a bit."

"We'll be there for you, Elizabeth. Just hang on. I love you."

"I love you too."

Exhausted after being up half the night, Elizabeth tried to take a nap after that. But all she could think about was Kintail not believing her about David having a mate. And worrying that she would be stopped before she could reach the airport and the plane and safety. And of Bentley, and maybe others, following her every move.

Before Elizabeth knew it, it was time for Sheri to come over for lunch. That was another reason for fixing lunch for the two of them. To eat up some of the groceries in the fridge. Luckily, Elizabeth didn't have a lot of perishable food. She had been getting only what she and her grandmother had needed every few days in anticipation of just this scenario.

A knock on the door caused Elizabeth to jump again, even though her mind knew it had to be Sheri.

"I should have made lunch," Sheri said, giving Elizabeth a hug, her own eyes misty, looking as sad as Elizabeth felt about her grandmother. Sheri had loved her just as much and didn't have any remaining grandparents, so Ada had been like a grandmother to her too.

"I have too much food to eat now as it is. Maybe you can help me out and take some of it home with you," Elizabeth said.

Sheri's eyebrows immediately rose in a questioning arch, and Elizabeth was afraid she'd said too much. "I just mean, without Grandma, some of this will go to waste."

"Uh, sure." Sheri continued to study her as they sat down to eat their chicken salads. "I heard Kintail was angry with you for not having a funeral or a memorial service for your grandmother with the pack."

"That's the way my grandmother wanted it. You know how she was—angry with him and the others for snubbing me. You know he wanted her to disinherit me."

"That was the worst. And that's what I said to anyone who mentioned it, and that made them shut up."

"Good. Grandma wanted me to spread her ashes on the rosebushes in her garden." Elizabeth wasn't sure if Sheri wanted to help her with that or not, but she didn't want to put her on the spot either. She'd already saved some aside in a plastic bag she'd take with her on the plane.

"Oh. Do you want me to stay with you while you do it, or do you want to do it in private?"

"I want you to stay with me. You've always been my best friend no matter what I got myself involved in."

"Of course. What kind of a best friend would I be if I hadn't?"

"And my grandmother loved you too. She would be pleased if you were here with me, the two of us, doing this together." Elizabeth thought Sheri needed to say farewell to Elizabeth's grandmother almost as much as Elizabeth did. Spreading her ashes together would be a nice way of doing it.

"Yeah, that would be nice." Sheri finished another bite of chicken salad and drank some of her water. "So my pain-in-the-butt boyfriend said you were dropping stuff off at a charity donation site."

"Yeah, all my grandmother's clothes. That's what she wanted me to do."

"Sure, that makes sense. And then he said you stopped by the food bank and dropped off more stuff?"

Elizabeth let her breath out in exasperation. "Some things Grandma ate that I didn't." Elizabeth made a face, as if emphasizing how much she abhorred the food. "What do they think? I'm going to just run off and live somewhere on my own? Try to join Cameron and Faith's pack in Seattle when David is mated?"

David's pack was actually living near Ely, Minnesota, not in Seattle, Washington, but that's where the men were originally from before they were turned in Maine, and that's all Kintail—and, she assumed, Sheri—had ever known about.

Sheri asked, "How'd you find out about it? David's mate, I mean. Did you follow his Facebook page all these years?"

Elizabeth's face heated with worry. She'd never let on that she talked to David at any time after she returned home. Yeah, she hadn't wanted to leave him behind, and Sheri knew about that. And it was some of the reason she had never dated since. But a lot of it also had to do with the wolves in the pack not wanting to date her because of what she'd done. "Yeah, it was stupid of me, wasn't it?"

"No, you had a real crush on him."

More than a real crush.

"If I were you, I would have done the same thing. You never once reached out to him?" Sheri asked.

"No. Don't get me wrong, there were times I wanted to. But what would be the point? He was there, I was here, and that wasn't going to change. At least not while my grandma was alive. And now…now it's too late. He found someone new. Besides, we aren't the same people any longer." Which she hoped wasn't really true.

"Are you sure you aren't thinking of going there anyway? I know how things are for you here. And you don't deserve it." Sheri took another bite of her chicken salad, never once taking her eyes off Elizabeth's face.

"How do you think I would feel being with a pack where all the wolves are now mated, and the one I really had a crush on is too? I would hate to be around him, seeing the other she-wolf. So no, there's nowhere for me to go. You ought to know that better than anyone."

"Yeah, I'm sorry. It'll get better. People will come around once they all learn David is no longer available and you're not leaving us."

"Right. That's why your pain-in-the-butt boyfriend is following me all over town. The mortuary? The food pantry? The charity shop too? It's ridiculous." Elizabeth was afraid their plan to pretend David was now mated and she had nowhere to go hadn't been believed by some of the pack members. She wanted desperately to tell David so he could start thinking of a Plan B, but she couldn't while Sheri was here, or she would confirm any suspicions her friend might have.

"I agree. I'll let everyone know that too. It is just ludicrous," Sheri said.

They finished eating and cleaned up; then they went out to say some words over her grandmother's ashes. Even with Sheri's suspicions and digging for information, Elizabeth felt better with her by her side. She only wished David could have been there. She knew he grieved too.

"Do you want me to stay with you for a while longer?" Sheri asked.

"I've got to run to the bank and get some paperwork done. It's amazing all the things you need to do when someone close to you dies."

"Oh, sure. Listen, if you need any of my help, anything at all, just let me know. I'm always here for you." Sheri gave her a reassuring hug.

Elizabeth hugged her back. "I will, thanks."

Then they packed up some of Elizabeth's perishable food and carried it out to Sheri's car.

Tears filling her eyes, Elizabeth gave Sheri another hug, like she often did in parting or in greeting, but this time, she didn't want to let her go, knowing this would be the end of their friendship. Though if Sheri forgave her for lying to her, maybe she could be her new Skype partner. Wouldn't that be a switch? Trading one for another.

But she didn't want to get her friend in trouble, and she finally released her, tears in both of their eyes, as if Sheri knew what Elizabeth was up to and she felt saddened by the prospect, as saddened as Elizabeth felt at not seeing her friend ever again. Then she belatedly recalled she was going to have dinner with her and the tears were probably for her grandma, not for her. Elizabeth was so torn up about everything and worried about getting out of here without incident, she could barely think straight.

She waved bye, then went inside and grabbed her purse and her list of things to wrap up before she left.

First up, the bank. That much had been true. The amount of paperwork that had to be sorted through was overwhelming. Bentley and another of Kintail's gofers followed her, but overtly this time, like they wanted to unnerve her. They did a good job of it too.

Fine. She finished up at the bank and then returned home and called David. "Okay, I've been thinking about how Amelia and I met. See if Amelia is good with us saying she and I met on a visit to Cameron Falls. We hit it off so much, we ended up taking a hike on Prospector Trail in Fred Henne Territorial Park the next day. She was there with a group to see the northern lights, to take pictures. She's a photographer from Juneau and wanted to see if the lights could be observed any better in Yellowknife."

"But you haven't really left your grandma's side since she's been sick," David said.

"Yeah, I can say we did it before I went to Maine, so before things got bad with her. It wouldn't be the first time I've been up there hiking by myself, so I don't think anyone would question it."

"Okay, let's run with that story. I'll tell Amelia. How are things going for you, honey?" David asked.

She loved how he always used terms of endearment with her. "Good. I have a tail, but I'm not trying to lose them or anything. I'm going to a park I used to visit with Grandma. It'll make me feel better, connected to nature, connected to her. And it will get my mind off worrying if we're going to get away with this. If I could, I would run as a wolf, but I'll save it for when I'm home with you."

"I can't wait."

In the past, running as a wolf had always made her feel better, and thankfully Sheri had always come over to watch Grandma while Elizabeth took a breather.

"I'm going to call Sheri and ask if she wants to go to dinner, that I'm meeting Amelia—or 'Amy.'"

"I'll let her know. We got this. You know that, right?"

"Yeah. Love you, David."

"Love you too."

Sheri answered the phone on the first ring. "Dinner sounds perfect," she said. "Are you sure you're up for it though? It's been a long day."

"I have to do something. Anything. It'll be good to be distracted. I think I'll visit the park now, clear my head. But I'm so happy you're coming tonight… Thanks. I'm going to go to one of the parks that I used to go to when Grandma could come."

"Do you want me to come with you?" Sheri sounded hesitant, like she didn't want to intrude.

"No, thanks. I just want to be there and remember the way it was." Elizabeth could have offered to take Sheri with her, she supposed. But she was a little afraid she might let something slip. It was going to be difficult enough seeing her at dinner with Amelia and not giving anything away. But she was glad Sheri would be driving her because it appeared Elizabeth was going to have a tail wherever she went for now. Whatever would they do once they lost Elizabeth when she flew south to the States? They would have to find something else to occupy their time.

"Oh, sure. Well, if you change your mind, let me know," Sheri said.

"I will. Thanks."

After they worked out the details, Elizabeth drove to Rotary Centennial Waterfront Park. She and her grandma used to come here before she got too sick. They'd sit and talk and look out over Yellowknife Bay, and for a split second, Elizabeth could feel her grandmother next to her, could smell the flowery shampoo she loved, could hear her soft laugh. And then, like a leaf caught in a warm summer breeze, she was gone, leaving behind a soothing sense of comfort.

Not even Bentley, sitting in the parking lot and watching her like a hawk, could shatter the peace that had settled over her. After a couple more minutes, Elizabeth took a walk along the boardwalk to stretch her legs. She hadn't walked here in so long, and it would be the last time she would ever visit. She wished she could take David to see all the beauty Yellowknife had to offer. She would love to do so many things here with him before she left her home for good.

She returned home and cleaned up some more—she just had to keep doing something—until it was finally time for Sheri to pick her up. The ease she'd felt at the bay had slowly eroded, and Elizabeth's nerves were on edge. When Sheri's parents had called to offer their condolences, the sound of the phone had nearly given her a heart attack. And when Sheri rang the doorbell, even though Elizabeth knew she was coming, she nearly jumped out of her skin.

She grabbed her purse—the purse that held the only pieces of her life she could bring with her—and headed for the door, her heart pounding. She needed to breathe deeply and still her wildly beating heart or Sheri would hear it. That was the problem with their wolf hearing. And wolf sense of smell. Sheri could probably smell her anxiousness, but Elizabeth could easily explain that away. Her grandmother had just died, for goodness' sake. Of course Elizabeth was anxious.

She climbed in the car and put on a smile. "Thanks for picking me up."

"I'm so glad we're going out to dinner. You haven't done this in eons. It's good for you to get out and do something you enjoy for a change. How was your trip to the park?" Sheri asked.

"Really nice. I had a lovely time there. I miss my grandmother terribly, but it brought back so many happy memories of being there with her. Of course I had a couple of watchdogs following me this time. It's so annoying. I wish they would just leave me in peace."

Sheri narrowed her eyes. "Was my jerk of a boyfriend still following you?"

"Yep. The whole time and all the way back home too."

"Well, not that it makes a whole lot of difference to you probably, but I told him for sure I was breaking up with him. I told him I thought he was despicable for doing that to you after all you've been through."

"Thanks. He's being a jerk."

Silence filled the air. Trying to overcome her nervousness, Elizabeth concentrated on her breathing, deep breaths in and out through her nose, silently, without Sheri noticing, if she could help it.

Sheri parked at the café and asked, "Has your friend ever had a bison burger before?"

She needed to keep her answers vague. "I don't know. Maybe. They might have them in Alaska, too, or she might have eaten them somewhere else."

"I'm so glad she came when you're free to see her. Does she know your grandma died?"

"Yeah, when she called to get together, I told her."

"I don't remember you ever mentioning her to me before."

Elizabeth's heart stuttered. Why hadn't she thought about that? Of course she would have told Sheri. She told Sheri everything.

Well, nearly everything.

"I saw her before I went with the pack members who were going to Maine. You had just gotten together with Bentley and couldn't spare time for me so I just took a couple of trips hiking." She was talking too much, too fast, but she couldn't seem to stop herself. "You know how I am when I just want to go and walk, even if I can't do it as a wolf."

Sheri pressed her lips together. "Yeah, I'm sorry I was that way. With Bentley, I mean. You were right to be annoyed and go without me. I guess we weren't talking as much then, were we? Stupid Bentley," she mumbled.

"It's fine, don't worry about it," Elizabeth said, the guilt building. Here Sheri was apologizing to her, while Elizabeth lied straight to her face.

"So she's a gray wolf?" Sheri asked as they walked toward the restaurant.

"Arctic, like us. From Alaska."

"Sure. Right."

It almost sounded like she suspected something else was going on. Was she fishing for information? "She's nice. You'll like her. And thanks again for coming out with me tonight. It helps me to get my mind off everything that has just happened."

"Did you want to stay with me at my parents' place for a while?"

"No, thanks, I'm sure I'll be okay."

But as they walked into the Wildcat Café, Elizabeth had no idea if that was true.

Chapter 5

David was dying to go in Amelia's place to the restaurant to be with Elizabeth. Just to pick her up and run like hell back to the airport. He knew he couldn't be seen there though. Not if Kintail's people were still tailing her. But what if Amelia was found out? Could she get hurt—or worse? Could Elizabeth? If either of them were harmed in any way, he'd never forgive himself.

David and Slade watched in silence as Amelia drove off toward the restaurant.

"Amelia's resourceful," Slade said, sensing David's anxiousness. "You know she has been in harrowing situations in the past, and she always manages to get out of them. She'll know what to do. It's just instinctive for her."

Anything could go wrong though. The only good thing was they were eating at a restaurant and Amelia, and Elizabeth, could scream bloody murder if Kintail's men tried to force them out of the place. The worry would be when they left the building. They'd be vulnerable then.

Slade slapped David on the shoulder. "Come on. Let's get something to eat. They'll be just fine. I think the ruse of you having been mated will throw them off completely."

Then why was Kintail having pack members follow Elizabeth?

David pulled out his phone and looked up restaurants at the airport. "You go. I'd better stay with the plane in case any of Kintail's men are hanging around there. They won't know you."

Slade glanced at his phone. "I like the menu for the Copperhouse. They have takeout, and they have wild boar. It includes white sauce, barbecued pulled boar, mozzarella, bacon, onions, bread, and pickles. That's what I'm getting since I've never had it before. They have the bison too. What do you want me to pick up for you?"

"Yeah, get me the same as you. The wild boar sounds good. Thanks, Slade." David watched him go, thankful for his packmates' support. He wasn't sure how he could have pulled this off without them.

A short while later, he got a text from Amelia: I'm at the restaurant, parking out back so no one can see us leave when we get ready to vamoose.

He texted: Okay. Slade's grabbing a bite for us to eat, but I'm staying with the plane.

Amelia texted: Good, because if Kintail's men spot you, this is all for nothing. I'm walking around to the restaurant now.

David: Stay safe.

Amelia: You too.

A few minutes later, Slade arrived carrying two to-go boxes. "Your sister is at the restaurant now," David told him, digging into his wild boar and wishing he was in the right headspace to really savor it. From the look on Slade's face as he chewed, it was damn good.

"Good. Hopefully, they'll make a quick meal of it and be back here before we know it. I'm ready to get in the air. Though I could eat an entire wild boar, it's so good. One perk of flying to Yellowknife."

They ate in a thoughtful silence for a bit, then Slade said, "You know, I've never met wolves who had to go through such ordeals to get their mates. When I meet my dream wolf, I doubt there will be this much drama."

For Slade's sake, David hoped that would be true. But Slade knew if he had trouble, they would all have his back.

David looked down at his dinner and wondered when he'd finished it. He kept glancing at his phone, waiting, waiting for an update. He hoped the story Amelia and Elizabeth had come up with was ringing true with Sheri. He was glad Sheri was there, helping to make it look like they were all friends, if anyone should still be watching. He just hoped they were being careful. One slipup, no matter how small, could ruin the whole thing.

Elizabeth was nervous. She had no doubt she was sending off an apprehensive scent, and knowing that just made her nervousness worse. But Sheri seemed nervous too. She was talking nonstop. She never talked *that* much, especially when Elizabeth wasn't responding, unless she was anxious about something. Elizabeth hadn't even heard half of what Sheri was saying because she was fearfully watching out the window for Amelia. Thankfully, Amelia had sent Elizabeth a picture and vice versa. Wouldn't that have been a disaster? To pretend to know someone and didn't even know what she looked like?

Then she saw Amelia walking in the door with a breezy smile and a casual glance around the restaurant.

Elizabeth half stood up and waved, and the relief in Amelia's face as she waved back and headed over likely mirrored Elizabeth's own relief. They'd gotten this far. They could do this.

Elizabeth introduced them as soon as Amelia joined them at the table.

"So you're from Juneau," Sheri said, rising from her seat to shake Amelia's hand. "Any friend of Elizabeth's is a friend of mine."

"Oh, I'm so pleased to meet you." Amelia gave Sheri a hug, which surprised Elizabeth, and then she gave Elizabeth a hug, which she'd halfway expected since they were supposed to be friends—and hopefully really would be once Elizabeth actually joined Amelia's pack.

In any event, Sheri seemed pleased Amelia had treated her like a friend from the start. Everyone sat down and Amelia looked over the menu and ordered a bison burger. Elizabeth couldn't get anything that heavy down—not when she was feeling like a nervous wreck. She ordered butternut squash soup and a salad.

Sheri ordered the same as Elizabeth, and when they got their orders, Elizabeth glanced out the window, looking for any sign of Bentley and his ilk.

And sure enough, she saw not only Bentley, but Sheri's

brother, Hans, get out of a car and head toward the restaurant. Coincidence? Unlikely. But maybe if they came inside to eat, she and Amelia could slip out while they were waiting on their food.

Sheri gave her brother a dirty look and sent an apologetic one to Elizabeth. Elizabeth surreptitiously followed the men as they were seated at a table much farther away from the door. For once, she was thankful a restaurant she was eating in was crowded, since all the tables closer were full.

"So where are you going, exactly?" Sheri asked, picking at her salad.

"Elizabeth wants to take me on a hike on the Prospector Trail in Fred Henne Territorial Park again. It was one of my favorite spots last time. I'm just so sorry my timing is so terrible." She put her hand on Elizabeth's and gave it a gentle squeeze. To Elizabeth's surprise, the comforting touch felt genuine, like they truly had been friends all this time. She blinked away the tears that sprang to her eyes and smiled at Amelia.

"The timing is actually perfect," Elizabeth said, meaning it in every way. "Just what I need." Amelia pulled away and took a bite of her burger, and Elizabeth thought she caught a little emotion in her eyes too.

"I would love to go with the two of you," Sheri said, "if it isn't an imposition. I haven't gone hiking with Elizabeth in forever."

Elizabeth lifted her spoon to her lips, trying to give herself a moment to respond. The soup was lukewarm now and went down uneasily.

"Listen," Sheri added conspiratorially to Elizabeth and Amelia, her voice a bare whisper, "I don't see any more of Kintail's men here. I mean, outside the restaurant. If we hurry up and eat, I can help you get out of here before my brother and ex-boyfriend get their meals. Believe me, they won't leave without them." Sheri pulled out money and set it on the table, like it was already a done deal. "Are you ready?"

Amelia and Elizabeth shared a look. Clearly, the jig was up. Elizabeth wasn't sure what had given her away, but maybe after years of friendship, Sheri just knew her too well. At this point, it was either trust her or try to bluff their way out—and the likelihood of that working seemed slim to none.

"Uh, yeah, sure." Amelia flashed an alarmed look her way, but there was no going back now. Elizabeth didn't know what her friend had in mind, but she had to trust Sheri was doing whatever she could to help her out, even if it meant she would get into hot water with Kintail, the pack, and maybe even her own family.

They stood up casually and left the restaurant, careful not to look the men's way.

Sheri glanced around at the parking lot. "Which car is yours?"

"It's out back," Amelia said, and she sounded as jittery as Elizabeth was feeling.

"Uh, okay, then. I'll give Elizabeth a ride around back. Since I brought her here, it'll look less suspicious if you leave with me."

"All right." Elizabeth climbed into the front passenger seat and Amelia walked off, heading toward the back of the restaurant. They met up in the alley, at a spot where the restaurant had no windows, just a door that led into the kitchen.

"I wish you would have told me," Sheri said.

"Sheri—" Elizabeth couldn't deal with this right now.

Sheri's eyes filled with tears. "We're sisters. We're best friends." Elizabeth got out, and Sheri did too. "I know you're leaving Yellowknife." She popped her trunk and, to Elizabeth's surprise, grabbed two bags, bags Elizabeth didn't recognize, and motioned to four more she did recognize. They were her bags!

"Hurry," Sheri said breathlessly. "Open the hatchback and move these over."

Shocked at the thought Sheri was planning to leave with them, Elizabeth shook her head. "You can't leave with us." But even as she said it, Sheri was already moving her bags into Amelia's car. Elizabeth grabbed two of hers and did the same. When in the world had Sheri packed her bags for her? While she went to the park? She couldn't believe Sheri had planned this all along and had not let on at all. Then again, Elizabeth had smelled that Sheri had been just as anxious as she had been. Now she knew why!

Amelia sat in the driver's seat, hands tapping the wheel urgently. "Hurry," she said, eyes panning from one side of the alley to the other.

"If you don't take me, they're going to know I helped you. I'm already getting grief for being your best friend after you freed David and Owen. I'm going with you."

This wasn't in the plans. Though Elizabeth knew from her tone of voice Sheri wasn't about to be talked out of it.

"Hurry, then. We have no time to lose. We're wasting valuable time already," Amelia said.

"What's the plan?" Sheri helped dump the remaining bags of Elizabeth's into the trunk, then closed her own trunk and locked her car.

"For you not to be with us," Elizabeth said, choking on the words even as she closed Amelia's trunk. She would never have thought her friend would do this. "You have a life here."

They both climbed into the rental car. Amelia headed down a street that would be out of view of the café and after a few more turns, she drove in the direction of the airport.

"And a boyfriend I have dumped numerous times who won't get the message. Bentley's like Kintail. Once he owns you, it's for life, even if you try to convince him otherwise."

"You have family." That made a world of difference. Elizabeth had no one who would miss her—but Sheri. Well, Kintail would, but for a very different reason.

"Yes! My parents and my brother. My brother is still just as angry with you for freeing Owen and David."

"But David is mated now." Elizabeth didn't know why she even said it. Sheri obviously never bought that story, and it made no sense anyway.

Sheri shook her head at her. "Right."

If Sheri didn't believe it, then Kintail and the others probably didn't either.

They could be in grave danger.

"This is what I know," Sheri continued. "David suddenly has a mate, your grandmother dies, you unload all her clothes and food the same day, and you have plans with a friend I've never heard of before? It all leads to the same place: you getting the hell out. So no, I don't think David has a mate. The woman in the photos is probably one of his packmates mated to one of his PI partners. And on top of that, I had to run some major interference with Bentley, giving him all sorts of excuses for all your running around today to charities and food banks and wherever. You would make a terrible criminal."

"And you would make a great investigator," Elizabeth said. "But if you don't believe it—"

"You should have made up the story about David mating someone a long time ago, like last year or something," Sheri said. "Still, I think there's enough speculation that hopefully it sows doubt. I bought the story at first, so maybe everyone else did too."

"I only just thought of it," Elizabeth said defensively. "And who knew my grandmother was going to pass so all of a sudden like that?" Yellowknife went by in a blur outside her window, and she wanted desperately to take it all in, this last look at her home, but also desperately wished Amelia could drive faster. Amelia was smart though. Getting pulled over could ruin everything. They were so close to leaving for good.

Elizabeth sent a text off to David: My best friend, Sheri Whitmore, is with me. I hope that's okay, and we have enough room for another passenger. She knows everything. She wouldn't stay behind...unless I can convince her of it by the time we reach the airport. We have six suitcases with us. She brought them—four of them mine. I didn't know she'd done that.

David had told her the plane had six seats, but now they would have six suitcases too.

David texted her back: If Amelia is okay with it, we'll manage just fine. Don't worry about a thing. Just get here safely.

Elizabeth: We're working on it.

"I'm your best friend. I would do anything for you," Sheri finally said, her voice soft.

Elizabeth figured she would, but she hadn't wanted her to get this involved in her bid for freedom. She wanted to take Sheri with her and continue their close friendship, but she didn't want to be the reason for breaking up Sheri's family unit. No matter how she looked at it, someone was going to be hurt. Trying to get her mind off the distance they had to drive, Elizabeth asked, "What did you pack for me?"

"Honestly, I'm not even sure. I just grabbed what I could, jammed everything into your bags, and threw them in my car."

"What if I hadn't planned on going anywhere? I would have come home to find I'd been robbed of all my clothes."

"You would have had your pajamas."

"What?"

Amelia chuckled.

Sheri sighed. "I figured where you were going, you wouldn't need them."

Elizabeth's mouth fell open, and she let out a laugh. "Sheri!"

Sheri smiled. "Well, it's true, isn't it?" Her smile faded. "It's okay I'm coming, isn't it? David is okay with it?"

"He is. As long as Amelia thinks the extra weight on the plane will be okay."

"Yeah, it will be," Amelia said, "or I would have told you both to ditch the bags."

Elizabeth explained the plan. "Amelia and her brother are taking turns flying the plane. You're just lucky we're not taking a commercial flight and have to leave you to fly standby."

Sheri gave a big sigh of relief.

Outside, the lights of the airport came into view. Elizabeth glanced behind them, making sure no one was following. A thought brought her up short. "Did you tell your parents you were leaving with me?" she asked.

"They don't know anything about this. I figured they might tell Kintail, even if they thought it was for our own good. Still, all in all, they will be happy for me if I'm happy. I can't believe you planned to leave me behind."

Elizabeth had felt guilty about that. "Sorry, Sheri." To Elizabeth's guarded relief, Amelia parked the car in the rental place, Elizabeth paid for the gas, and then they hurried toward the waiting plane, bags in tow. The sense of unease Elizabeth felt in the car doubled, the hairs on the back of her neck standing on end, but when she looked behind her again, there was nothing. After being afraid for so long, it was hard to shake her paranoia.

David's expression was strained when he first saw her, but then he managed a brilliant and sexy smile. The hug he gave her felt way too brief, and she promised herself a longer one, a much longer one, when they were safely away. He grabbed one of Elizabeth's bags and one of Sheri's. "Are you sure you want to do this?" he asked Sheri.

"Yeah, I'm doing this unless you refuse to take me," she said.

David glanced at Elizabeth. She let out her breath. "She's like a sister to me. If it hadn't been for Sheri's help, I'm not sure we would have made it. I'm good with it if she *really* wants to do this." She stared pointedly at Sheri as she said it, and Sheri gave her a firm nod.

"All right," David said, "join us for a wild ride out of here."

Amelia was already warming up the plane. Slade joined her in the cockpit as David, Elizabeth, and Sheri got settled.

"So where are we flying to first?" Sheri asked.

David smiled. "Seattle, where else?"

Chapter 6

It didn't feel real. The line of her body against his, the joy in his heart, the sense that everything really *was* going to be okay. He'd been waiting so long, and finally, finally, they were together. Elizabeth pressed into his side, and David was overjoyed to be with her at last, giving her a big warm hug and kissing her as if he had never been separated from her.

Elizabeth smiled, looking as overjoyed as he felt. She snuggled closer and offered up her lips for a kiss.

An offer he couldn't refuse.

When they finally pulled apart, there was no denying the spark between them hadn't dissipated with time.

She blushed, belatedly introducing her friend as the plane taxied down the runway. Sheri nodded, then busied herself looking out the window, giving David and Elizabeth as much privacy as she could.

"I can't believe it." Elizabeth kept touching him, rubbing his arm, gliding her fingers along his leg, anywhere she could reach, as if afraid the moment the connection broke, he'd disappear. "After all our planning, we did it." Tears of joy slid down her cheeks, and she kissed him again.

David kissed her right back. "It seems like only yesterday

you were in my arms, just like this. I've missed this, missed you, so much."

The nose of the plane lifted, then the tail, and then they were soaring through the cloudy sky on their way home. Elizabeth settled back under his arm, a small, contented sigh escaping her mouth.

David savored the moment, but as he glanced up and caught Sheri giving them a happy smile, his thoughts shifted. Sheri might be a problem. When her pack learned she had escaped with them too… He just hoped Kintail wouldn't think they forced her to come with them to give them more time to escape.

"So you left your car back at the café?" David asked Sheri.

"Yes. Behind it in the alley. My brother and ex-boyfriend were still in the café when we left. We got into Amelia's car and took off. If they followed, they never knew where we went. I watched the whole way to the airport to make sure we weren't being followed. I think Elizabeth did too." She smiled at Elizabeth, who nodded, her soft hair tickling under his chin. "It will probably take them some time to even figure out my car is back behind the café."

"That's good to hear. I doubt they have any power to do anything about this now that we're in the air." David tightened his arm around Elizabeth's shoulders. "You know we only have one unmated wolf in the pack, don't you, Sheri?" He figured Elizabeth might have told her that all the PIs were already mated.

"I thought *all* of you were mated," Sheri said, sounding surprised and interested.

"I'm still available," Slade said. "What's your ex-boyfriend going to think of you running off like that?"

"It's none of his business. I've been trying to break up with him for years. He just doesn't take me seriously. Which was part of the problem with our relationship. We're done, though, and maybe now he'll actually get the point."

Or not. If he was that hardheaded, David thought, he could see him coming after Sheri. A lone wolf would be easy to deal with. Different pack, different dynamics, different rules. As long as they didn't have the whole Arctic wolf pack from the Northwest Territories coming down to force them to give Sheri up, David was glad to have her stay with them. But he didn't like the issue of her leaving her family behind and not giving them word beforehand, particularly if she was close to them.

"And your parents? Your brother? Will they come after you?" David asked, needing to know just what kind of a bind they could be in.

"Hans, my brother, does anything Kintail tells him to do. He has no mind of his own. In that regard, he's just like Bentley. I love my parents, but I needed to spread my wings, and believe me, under Kintail's rule, no one can do that. When I realized Elizabeth was leaving, I knew I wanted to go with her. I've been planning this one way or another probably for as long as she has."

Smiling, Elizabeth shook her head. "I wish I would have told you. Or that you felt like you could tell me."

Sheri sighed. "I kept worrying I would give myself away and was so afraid you wouldn't take me with you, or I would have talked to you about it all along."

Elizabeth frowned. "Did my grandmother ever hint to you that I was leaving?" She couldn't imagine that she would have, though her grandmother did really care about Elizabeth and Sheri's friendship.

"She didn't need to. I knew you would never give David up, and I knew he wouldn't give you up either. I figured you were keeping in touch somehow. I was really worried you would slip out on me before I could catch you at it. When I went to your house, I fully expected to see a couple of suitcases packed and ready to go. Or find suitcases in the trunk of your car or something.

"Since you said Bentley was following you all over the place, I knew you couldn't just race to the airport or head out of town to the south. When you said a friend was meeting you for dinner, I figured this was it. I told my parents I was having dinner out with you and you needed the company and needed to get away from the house. They didn't question it. Why would they? They know I know you the best, after all. And since they were leaving for Cancun around the time we would be having dinner, there was no better time. So I packed my bags and threw them in the trunk of my car and...here we are."

"Well, you know, if you ever change your mind, we'll get you on a flight back home. You never have to worry about that." David wanted Sheri to know they weren't anything like her pack. That she could come and go freely as much as she wanted to visit with her family and friends or whatever. Though if she returned to Yellowknife, he suspected she wouldn't be allowed to leave ever again.

"There's no going back for me. You're stuck with me. And Elizabeth too. If things don't work out between the two of you, then... Well, I don't know what we'll do, but we're not returning to Yellowknife. Are we, Elizabeth?"

"No. I'll never go back there." Elizabeth sounded adamant about that.

David squeezed her shoulder. She could leave whenever she wanted, too, even though the thought of that all but brought him to his knees. But he would do everything in his power to show her he was the only wolf for her.

"Okay, so what's the deal with your new 'mate'?" Sheri asked.

David laughed. "One of our pack members. That's Candice, Owen Nottingham's mate. She was delighted to help. Owen is—"

"The other one Elizabeth freed. I know all about the two of you. Kintail won't let us forget that Elizabeth freed you both and caused all kinds of trouble for the pack. So Candice is new?"

"Fairly. She's a romance author, and when I asked her if she would help me by pretending to be my mate, she was all for it. Owen took all the pictures while she and I were pretending to be the happy newly mated couple," David said. They had all been laughing so hard, they'd had a difficult time trying to be serious about it. But everyone in the pack had been willing to do anything they could to help bring Elizabeth safely home to the pack.

David got on his cell and texted Cameron and Faith, letting them know he and Elizabeth had successfully made it out and were flying to their first destination—Calgary. And he told them about the additional passenger, Sheri Whitmore, Elizabeth's best friend.

Cameron called David, and he answered the phone. "Yeah, Cameron?"

"Any strings attached that could cause the pack trouble?"

He glanced at Sheri, who looked at him curiously. "Parents and a brother. An ex-boyfriend might be an issue. Of course Kintail could be a bigger one, depending on how he takes this. You know how Kintail is."

"Yeah, he had a fit that he'd lost you and Owen, didn't get Faith, and had me as such a thorn in his side. I'm glad you got out of there without a hitch," Cameron said. "And tell both ladies welcome to the pack. We'll have a celebration tomorrow for them, when everyone's had a bit of a rest."

"I'll tell them." David ended the call. He could tell Sheri was nervous, so he said, "Ladies, Cameron officially welcomes you to the pack, and we'll have a pack celebration after we get some well-deserved sleep."

Sleep. Or maybe not sleep. He glanced at Elizabeth, hoping she would join him in his master bedroom suite and not stay in one of the guest rooms. He'd stayed with her in hotel rooms before, but she might want to take it slower with him at the very first. He would go as slowly as she needed.

"I have a couple of guest rooms," David said, "that you can choose from." He left it open-ended, meaning that Sheri could choose from one while he hoped Elizabeth could stay with him.

"Okay, thanks, David," Sheri said. "You can't know how much I appreciate this."

"You're welcome."

Elizabeth was quiet, just snuggling with him, looking drained.

"I'm going to rest for a while," Amelia said. "Slade, can you take over?"

"Yeah, no problem," Slade said.

Sheri's phone chimed with a text. David and Elizabeth looked back at her. "It's Bentley, asking where we all went. I'll tell him we went to the park to hike and camp, and we'll be back in a few days. Elizabeth needed a break after giving her grandmother around-the-clock care. We used to go for hikes like that, just Elizabeth and me. It definitely sounds like something we would do."

"Go ahead and tell him that," David said. "The only problem I see is that your car won't be at the trailhead."

"I'll tell him we went in 'Amy's' car. But I won't say the make or model. He wouldn't expect me to anyway," Sheri said.

"Okay, that sounds good. And if they happen to find your car behind the restaurant?" David asked, hoping they didn't find it for a while.

"We'll have to take that chance. I would tell my brother to move it, but I'm afraid he would tell Kintail."

"The restaurant employees are bound to notice it at some point," David said.

"It's kind of off to the side where others park to visit another couple of businesses," Elizabeth said. "One is a service station. So it might not be noticed for a while. Besides, they think we're going to Seattle, right, Sheri?"

Sheri's eyes widened. "We're not going to Seattle?"

"Nope." Elizabeth rested her head on David's shoulder again.

David glanced out at the sliver of moon hanging among the boundless stars. "When I would look out at the moon at night, or in the morning, watching it grow in size from the new moon to the full moon in Ely, I wondered if you were ever watching the night sky and seeing the moon and stars way up north in Yellowknife, thinking of me."

"It's funny that you should mention it now when we never talked about it during our Skype sessions, but yeah, whenever I saw the moon, I felt closer to you, knowing we could be enjoying it together at the same time, as if I had my head on your shoulder, and you had your arm around me, just like this."

"We're really not going to Seattle?" Sheri said again, still sounding shocked at the news.

They all laughed.

David could understand her confusion, and it was a good thing. It most likely meant everyone else in Kintail's pack believed he and his partners were still in Seattle too. That would be the first place they'd look. Which was good, since they didn't really try *too* hard to hide who they were. They even had a new name for their PI business near Ely—White Wolf Investigative Services. That might give them away, if Kintail and his men ever discovered they were living in Minnesota and not in the state of Washington.

"Just wait until you get there to see how beautiful it is," David said. "You'll love it." He might have been responding to Sheri, but his heart was talking to Elizabeth.

"Yeah, but that's what I was thinking about Seattle. The Pacific Ocean, the forests..." Sheri sounded a bit disappointed.

David suspected she'd done all kinds of research for information about the area and had been looking forward to living there. "You won't be disappointed, I promise."

When they arrived in Calgary, they all took a bathroom break, drank some bottled water, ate some snacks, topped off the plane's fuel tank, and then they were on their way again.

David called to give Cameron a status report. "We're on the second leg of our journey." It was late, and they wouldn't get into Winnipeg until three in the morning. Amelia was flying again, and Slade would take the six-hour shift to Ely after that. "If Kintail comes after us, we think he'll go to Seattle. It doesn't seem as though his pack knows we're in Ely."

"Okay, good show. But we'll have to keep alert," Cameron said.

David glanced at Sheri, then quickly away again. He knew Cameron was thinking she might be the bigger problem. "I agree. I'll call you in the morning when we arrive in Ely, unless you want me to wake you at three in the morning when we arrive in Winnipeg."

"Yeah, you can wake me. I would rather know you got into Winnipeg all right."

That was the thing about the PI partners. They were like the Four Musketeers, always looking out for one another.

"Will do." David tucked his phone away, pulling Elizabeth closer until she finally fell asleep. David dozed a bit, too, while Sheri slept in the seat behind them. He was restless, though, waking every couple of minutes. He wondered how it would go with Sheri. His pack would welcome her—she was Elizabeth's best friend, after all—but would Sheri feel like it was home? He hoped so. Maybe Slade and Sheri would even hit it off.

But Sheri was going to have to tell her family before long that she was safe with Elizabeth—in Seattle, of course—and not to worry about her.

No matter what, David was glad they had all made it out without any real trouble. He smiled to think of just how angry Kintail would be when he learned of the deception. It served him right for not allowing Elizabeth to see David while she needed to be in Yellowknife for her grandmother.

Chapter 7

"WHAT DO YOU MEAN, SHERI TOLD YOU SHE AND Elizabeth were going hiking and you haven't found any sign of them on the trail?" Kintail roared, furious Bentley botched such a simple task.

"I'm sorry. I texted Sheri, and she said she and another friend—" Bentley said.

"Another friend?" Kintail couldn't believe it. How hard was it to follow one woman around Yellowknife and make sure she didn't run?

"A woman, not a man. Hans and I saw them eating with her, and when we were getting our burgers—"

Kintail's blood pressure had to have risen. "Don't tell me. They gave you the slip while you waited around for your damn food."

"We hadn't eaten all day."

Bentley and Hans wouldn't have starved to death! Kintail ground his teeth. "And the woman?"

"Nobody I'd ever seen before."

"Human or wolf?" Kintail wondered if Elizabeth and Sheri had solicited a human's help.

"Arctic wolf. No one I'd ever smelled before."

Arctic wolf. "Had to be one of Cameron's damn pack. Get to the airport now."

"Yes, sir."

Kintail seethed. *Damn it!* Elizabeth had escaped the pack; he just knew it. The one thing he had sworn he'd never let her do—prove she was smarter than him, that she could do as she pleased. Now he had to read the riot act to Sheri, because he was damn sure she'd helped, along with whoever the hell the other wolf was.

Sheri would regret ever earning his wrath.

As soon as they arrived in Winnipeg, David texted Cameron.

Cameron texted back: All right, good show. We'll be managing the office until you get in. Just enjoy the rest, and we'll have the celebration for Elizabeth and Sheri this evening.

David texted: Okay, sounds good. We'll be on our way in a little bit. I'll let you know when we land in Ely.

Cameron: Sounds good. Night, David.

David: Night, Cameron.

David tried to go back to sleep. He couldn't wait to get home, take a shower, and join Elizabeth in bed. To rest, if she needed it. But if she didn't…

Elizabeth lifted her head off his shoulder and kissed his cheek and smiled, then closed her eyes and rested her head on his shoulder again.

Hours later, they finally reached Ely. Everyone sighed with relief. Hugs were given all around, and Slade helped David load the bags into his vehicle.

"We couldn't wait for the day to come that we could help," Amelia said, "once Slade and I were part of the pack and learned about you and David. We'll see you at the celebration tonight."

"Sounds good," Elizabeth said, Sheri agreeing.

Amelia and Slade headed home, and David, Elizabeth, and Sheri got into his car. Both Elizabeth and Sheri looked all around as he drove them home.

"So what do you think?" David asked.

"Ohmigod, it's beautiful," Sheri said. "So many places to run."

"Absolutely. You'll truly enjoy it here," David said.

"I love it already. Your pictures didn't do it justice," Elizabeth said.

"I know. I couldn't wait to actually get you here so you could see it for yourself. I thought we would have lunch," he said, "and then all get showers and take a nap, if it works for you."

"Yeah, that sounds great," Elizabeth said.

"Oh, yeah, for me too," Sheri said.

When they finally arrived at the log cabin home, Sheri was in awe. "Did you know it looked like this?" she asked Elizabeth.

"Yeah, David showed me videos of it. But it looks so much more real being here."

"It's gorgeous."

He began getting the bags out of the car and the ladies helped him. Then they walked inside his house and David showed them the open living room, kitchen, and dining area, the bathroom and guest rooms.

Sheri hauled her bags to the room farthest away from the master bedroom and began unpacking. "This is my room! Lunch later. I'm getting a shower and going to bed."

"Sounds good to me." David smiled at her, then turned to Elizabeth. "After you," he said, gesturing down the hall to his bedroom. The look she gave him as she led the way made his heart beat in double time. He knew she could hear it because he could hear hers beating just like it.

Elizabeth sighed in the doorway to his room. "It's lovely."

He set her bags in a corner and smiled proudly.

The room was decorated in blues—like she loved—and touches of tan and browns. The comforter and curtains were all blue, and even the wolf paintings of Arctic wolves had a blue cast to the snow around them. The bed was king-size and a cedar chest sat at the foot of it, a blue cushion for seating on top. The furniture was dark oak, heavy like a man would like, but had carvings of wolves in the door panels that made Elizabeth feel as though she had walked into a rustic art gallery. She loved it.

The wolf paintings she'd already noticed on the walls were all portraits of his friends and their mates. One in particular caught her attention. A sleek, black jaguar was seated beside a she-wolf, who sat next to Owen. She assumed it was Candice with Owen, but she wondered about the jaguar.

It appeared as though David had truly embraced his wolf half and his pack, and she was glad to see it. When she first had met him, she wasn't sure he would. It had been a lot to deal with, in the beginning.

A chair sat in one corner; a blue-and-tan-plaid blanket was draped over it.

"I love your bedroom."

"I know your favorite color is blue."

She smiled. "It is. It's beautiful. I like the huge bed."

He glanced at it, then back at her. "We'll have to be sure to stick close together so we don't lose each other in the middle of the night."

She laughed. She suspected that *wasn't* going to be a problem.

He showed her the bathroom, which was in all blues too, though the theme in there was of the woods and lake. There were blue towels, pictures, and the soap dispenser that featured a white wolf. Double sinks in a marble-topped counter, white cabinets, and a mirror that covered the wall. One window looked out on the forest, and it made the bathroom even more elegant, cheerful, and enjoyable.

The toilet was in its own separate little room, and a big walk-in closet opened up next to it.

A glassed-in shower along one wall looked perfect for two. Elizabeth wanted to stand under the warm spray and feel David's arms around her soapy body. The whirlpool tub in the corner would be great for taking baths with him. Her face went hot, and she suddenly wasn't so tired anymore.

Then they returned to the bedroom and the portraits caught her attention again. "A black jaguar?" she asked. He had to be a shifter, though she'd never met one before.

"Yeah, that's Uncle Strom, Candice's uncle. He's actually her adoptive uncle, brother to the man who had adopted her when she was young. Once she was bitten and she saw her uncle, she realized right away by scent that he was a jaguar. He knew she was a wolf, too. Talk about a shock to both of them."

"Oh, I bet. I've never heard of a jaguar shifter before."

"He had been bitten by a jaguar shifter and Candice was bitten by a wolf, so they had two different species in the one family. I guess you don't have jaguar shifters up in the Canadian Arctic."

"Not that I've heard of, but we had some snow leopard shifters pass through our territory on their way to Alaska. That was enough of a surprise."

"Snow leopards? I'd never heard of them before. Which makes me wonder just how many different species of shifters there are."

"Me too."

"Cameron's son, Corey, was the one who bit Candice. Before that, he played hide-and-seek in a camping trailer and ended up in a jaguar-shifter day care in Texas. That was the first time we had learned of the jaguars."

Smiling, Elizabeth shook her head. "He seems like a handful."

"You don't know the half of it."

David drew her close, cupped her face, and studied her blue eyes. "I've wanted to lose myself in your gaze ever since you left. For real, in person, not just on Skype."

After a long, searching look, he bent his head just as

she reached up for him. Their lips met, open and ravenous, tongues twining, stroking, deepening the kiss, bodies pressing together. Heat rising. Heartbeats accelerating. This was what she'd hoped for with David. It was like a magnetic draw, a pheromone conductor, and he instantly gave her an adrenaline rush. She was his and he was hers, and the world was right.

She slipped his T-shirt over his head and tossed it to the floor. He unbuttoned the front of her shirt, fingers working fast, but instead of pulling it off her shoulders like she thought he would, he slipped one hand inside, underneath the lace fabric of her bra, until he was cupping her breast, his hand warm against her flesh, gently squeezing. She softly moaned, loving his touch, good memories flooding back, but she needed his lips again. She found his mouth with a desperate fervor matched only by his. Their tongues teased, rampant need setting her body on fire.

She smelled their sexy, musky scent, her panties already moistened from his touching her so tenderly yet so fiercely. Her blood was on fire as his free hand slid down her back and cupped her bottom. He worked on the button of her jeans, then slid the zipper down. She shimmied, helping him pull them off, kicking off her shoes in frustration when everything got tangled up. She needed to be naked. Needed to feel his body against hers. Forget the shower. When he slid his hand down her back and into her bikini panties, squeezing, she knew she had to have this *now*.

Recollections of all the nights they'd been together in hotels came rushing back. His tenderness and loving ways. His concern about making it good for her while finding his own pleasure. It seemed like only yesterday they had been together like this.

She moved her mouth from his and began kissing his jaw, his throat, his shoulder, his pecs. He smelled the same as before, the same delightful scent of male and wolf, but of his unique scent too. She licked his nipple, and he shuddered. He kissed the top of her head. Then he was reaching for his buckle, and she pushed his hands away, impatient, unfastening it herself and pulling off his jeans, leaving him in just his boxer briefs. She looked down at him in awe, remembering him as she knew he was remembering her. He hadn't aged a day since she'd seen him last, courtesy of their *lupus garou* genetics and extreme longevity.

His head dipped and captured her mouth again, his hands cupping her, pulling her snug against his hard body, his erection a steel rod between them, almost as if his briefs and her panties didn't exist at all. She rubbed her body against his, soliciting a low growl. She loved feeling him against her and wanted him inside her, but like the last time they'd been together, they couldn't go that far, not unless they wanted to be committed to each other forever. And she knew as much as she wanted that to happen, they needed some time to get to know each other. Really know each other for the first time, living together, seeing if they were truly compatible for the long run. There was no divorce for wolves.

But she couldn't keep her hands off him just as he couldn't keep his hands off her. Tongues tasted and teased. His hands were on her breasts, squeezing, enjoying them like she was enjoying his hands molding to her hot flesh. She didn't think she would ever get enough of him. She'd worried it had been just her imagination. That he'd wanted her because she had freed him as a hostage. That he'd felt a little lost because he was a wolf and hadn't known how to deal with it. But she worried no longer. They had a sexual connection that couldn't be quenched easily. A fire that had ignited between them from the minute they'd seen each other and had only burned brighter since then.

He paused to slow down the kisses as if he were afraid they would get this over too quickly and he wanted to savor every moment with her. While she was ready for quick and fulfilling and then being ready to do it again. And again.

She slowed down, though, not wanting to overwhelm him with her enthusiasm or put him off. But slow didn't seem to be working for him, either, and the passionate kisses resumed with him sucking her tongue and her nibbling at his lips, sucking on them, pressing her body against his. Rubbing him to feel his erection straining for release.

He finally unfastened her bra and dropped it to the floor, and then he was pulling down her panties and they fell next to her bra and the rest of their clothes. Then she was pulling off his boxer briefs and running her hands over his rigid erection.

She didn't even know how it happened, but she was in his bed and he was in it with her, kissing her, his hands everywhere, his mouth following, licking her nipples, savoring each morsel, then moving lower, nibbling and kissing his way down her belly.

He reached between them and began to stroke her

feminine nub with precision. Her entire body lit up and she strained toward him, needing this, needing him. He kissed her mouth again, and she felt the passion fill her whole body with hunger. She ran her hand over his arm, urging him on, feeling his strong bicep, admiring the rest of him, fit, healthy, his face sporting some whiskers, his eyes heavy-lidded, his mouth full and demanding against hers.

"I missed you," he whispered, and she tasted every word, including the regret that he hadn't been able to be with her physically since she'd left him.

"I missed you too." She gazed up at him, his expression somewhat sad now, as if he was afraid something else might take her away from him, and this—these special feelings they had for each other—would be cast aside. Again. "I'm not going back to the pack. I won't, I promise."

"We are meant for each other. I would just mate you now and—"

His fingers moved inside her and her body screamed yes. She closed her eyes and willed herself to be strong. "We need the time to get to know each other."

"Yeah."

He rested his hands on her hips and kissed each of her bare shoulders. Then he kissed her mouth and pulled her close, hugging her. He sighed deeply as if she were the most precious person to him. He was that to her.

Their lips met, slowly this time, gentle and maybe a little hesitant. But she didn't want hesitant. Didn't need gentle. She opened her mouth to him, telling him to explore her like she wanted to do with him.

She hadn't remembered just how glorious he was until now. And it all came back in a rush to her. Every delectable inch of him. And oh God, his lips. Lips that were magnificently hot and manly and perfect for kissing.

He slid his hand between her legs again and began to stroke.

His touch was slow and methodical and meant to make her beg for harder and faster. He continued to stroke her, making her wet in anticipation. "Hmm," she moaned. She could get used to this. Forget anything else.

He stroked faster, moving against her again, making her arch against his fingers, making her want harder, faster. He understood her unspoken need, speeding up his strokes on her nubbin, pressing the sensitive, swollen flesh harder. Her climax hit, crashed over her, hurtled her toward the moon and stars. She cried out, unable to stop herself.

He moved between her legs as if he wanted to thrust his arousal in her, and she wanted it, too, the ache between her legs making her want to take this all the way. It was as if her sex was calling the shots and all her previous control vanished. She didn't care. She wanted him as deep and as fully as she could take him.

But he just rubbed his cock against her mound, not entering her, teasing with every stroke, kissing her passionately again. His hand was in her hair, alternately caressing and pulling, his eyes closed as he breathed in her scent as she was breathing in his—spice, maleness, the great outdoors, the piney woods and fir trees, musk, and sex. Not to mention a whole lot of wolf.

Her legs parted wider, a dangerous business she couldn't seem to help. She pushed him back so she could stroke him next. She took hold of his erection and began to move, up and down, up and down, her lips pressed against his at first. Then she moved her mouth to his jaw, savoring the feel of his stubble, then down to his neck, shoulders, kissing his pecs and nipples. She didn't let go of his erection, continuing to work on him like he'd worked her. She took one nipple into her mouth and sucked. He groaned, and his arousal jumped in her hand. She smiled and moved her mouth to the other nipple.

She tugged on it gently with her teeth and then sucked on it and his erection jumped again, as if doing that to his nipples created the most pleasurable catalyst. Her breasts rubbed against his belly, the friction on her nipples making her feel the need to climax all over again.

As she picked up the pace on his erection, she felt his whole body tense. Loving that she could tell when she needed to change the firmness of her hand on his arousal and speed up or slow down the pace, she attributed that to their heightened sense of smell and touch, the way they could detect even the smallest changes. She licked a nipple and blew on it, then did the same with the other. He groaned again.

She smiled the smile of one who knew she held the power and would have no problem wielding it. She ran her free hand over his shoulder, moved her body over his so that her leg was inserted between his, and began to rub her clit against his leg. God, he felt good.

He lifted his leg a little to make a deeper connection, but then his face tightened, and she figured he couldn't hold on any longer. He exploded all over his stomach, the orgasm cataclysmic.

"Holy hell," he growled. "I love you."

"I love you too." She continued to rub against his leg, moving faster and faster, riding him hard and shaking the bed until her body clenched again, her second orgasm exploding in a burst of sensation. He pulled her close, their hearts beating frantically, completely in sync. Between the two of them, there was no way Sheri hadn't heard the racket they'd made. Elizabeth knew her friend would be happy for her.

"Do you want to shower together?" David asked, his voice still rough with climax.

She chuckled. "You better believe it."

Chapter 8

David didn't want to get up. He just wanted to hold on to Elizabeth forever. But he finally released her, and they got out of bed.

"Shower or tub?"

"Showering is quicker. Then we can lie down for a while, have lunch, and see the woods? Can we run in them during the day?" Elizabeth asked.

"Yeah, we sure can. And then we'll have dinner with the rest of the pack after everyone gets off work tonight."

"Do you have any cases you need to take care of?" Elizabeth watched as he turned on the hot water for the shower and they walked in together.

"I do, but nothing that needs to be taken care of right away. While I was gone, the others took care of anything that needed to be handled more quickly."

"Oh, good." She lathered up, then ran her hands over his chest and down his stomach, feeling each and every muscle along the way. "I wasn't really thinking about your job or that your partners would have to take care of your cases when you left them to come for me."

He began soaping her up too. "They will forever be

indebted to you for helping us out, so think nothing of it. This has always been in the plans."

"Okay, good." She kissed his jaw as he ran slick fingers over her breasts, kneading slowly, softly. He brought his mouth down to hers, continuing to rub in gentle circles. This brought back beautiful memories too. A hotel bathroom, sure, but him, her, making love to each other? Oh, yeah.

But not this time. This time it was just sharing the space with each other, soaping each other up, doing a whole lot of fondling and kissing in the privacy of his home, and then rinsing off and leaving the shower.

They wrapped up in fluffy towels, then raced each other to bed, dropping the towels as they dove in. That's what Elizabeth remembered about him too. Just how playful he could be. She was ready for a well-deserved nap with him.

Naked with David was especially good. She laughed at the thought of Sheri purposely leaving all her night things behind. It's like she knew just how Elizabeth and David felt about each. That's not to say Elizabeth wouldn't eventually need some, especially if she wanted to slum around the house before she dressed. But right now? No pajamas was good.

They snuggled, having fitfully slept on the plane. She wasn't sure she could get more than an hour's nap, which would probably be all she needed, then they could eat and run, and after dinner, return to more of this, but still be able to sleep tonight.

"I want to see your workplace too," Elizabeth said.

"We can go over there after we return from running, if you would like."

"Yeah, I would." Because she had an idea. For a job, actually. A job with him. Something important to help the pack out.

Elizabeth woke to the aroma of hamburger meat browning and what she thought was spicy taco seasoning. She smiled and kissed David's chest. He smiled down at her and ran his hand through her hair. "I think Sheri's making us lunch because she's hungry."

"I am too. Are you?" he asked.

"Yeah. We missed breakfast. Let's go." Elizabeth got up and opened one of her suitcases while David dressed. Sheri was right. She had grabbed everything out of the drawers and crammed them into Elizabeth's suitcases, but she was glad she didn't have to go shopping right away.

She found her underwear and T-shirts in one suitcase, among other things, and her shorts in another. She pulled on a pair of olive drab shorts and a floral peach-and-green top to match, then found her sandals and slipped those on.

David straightened up the bedsheets and then they walked down the hall to the kitchen.

"Good afternoon. I feel so much better, being able to sleep in a comfortable bed. Really sleep. I hope I didn't disturb you, but I was starving," Sheri said, looking more rested.

"My home and everything in it is yours," David said. "And lunch smells delicious. Thanks."

"Well, I found you had all the ingredients for tacos, so I made them. Though I had to look up a recipe," Sheri added.

"That works for me."

"Works for me too. We're going for a wolf run after this and then David's going to show us his office building," Elizabeth said.

"I would love to see where the guys work." Sheri filled the taco shells, adding picante sauce, lettuce, and shredded cheese to the meat mixture, and set them on plates.

"Both Sheri and I were working in dress shops as salesclerks," Elizabeth said. "I'm really not interested in doing that if I can help out with your business instead."

"Yeah, me too, if you don't think we would be too much underfoot," Sheri said.

"Do administrative work?" David brought glasses of water to the table, and they all sat down to eat.

"Right. That would work," Elizabeth said, lifting a taco. She took a big bite, breaking the shell in half.

David handed her a napkin. "I'll tell you right now, all of us would welcome the help in the office. Filing? Answering the phones? Even doing some searches would really be great." He sounded enthusiastic. "You'll see a lot of routine stuff, but sometimes we do something that can really make a lot of difference in some people's lives and in a good way."

"Good, because I think I speak for both Sheri and me in saying we're ready to do something more with our lives." She took another bite. "Sheri, these are so good. I didn't realize how hungry I was. Thanks."

Sheri smiled. "You're welcome. And I would love to do

something like that, really help someone, you know?" She tucked a scoop of loose taco filling back in the shell and crunched down. "Oh," she said, swallowing hard and grabbing her glass. "And as soon as we saw the lake, I was ready for a swim. How is the water? Is it warm enough to swim in as humans?"

"In summer, yes." David reached for his third taco.

"What about as far as anyone seeing us swimming out there as wolves?" Sheri asked.

"We own most of the property around here. We have No Trespassing signs all over," he said. "We haven't had any trouble so far." He held up his latest taco. "I think you used the same ingredients I always do but somehow yours taste better than anything I've ever made."

"Some say the food tastes better if someone else makes it." Elizabeth took another bite.

"I don't know. I always love my own cooking," Sheri said.

David and Elizabeth laughed. After they finished, David cleared the dishes before Elizabeth could help. "I'll get the dishes if you ladies want to unpack a bit. Half the drawers in the dresser are yours, Elizabeth, and the same thing with the closet. I have a ton of hangers in there for you too."

Elizabeth smiled. "I will take you up on that."

"Sorry your bags are such a mess," Sheri said, as they walked back down the hall. "I packed in a hurry."

"I'm glad you did it so I didn't have to go out shopping right away." She stopped and gave Sheri a spontaneous hug. "Thank you for everything," she whispered.

Sheri squeezed her in return and whispered back, "Guess I was right about the pajamas, eh?"

Elizabeth laughed as they headed to their respective rooms, ignoring the blush that raced up her cheeks. Apparently Sheri had heard them after all.

Sheri somehow finished before Elizabeth did and came to help her hang some clothes. David joined them.

"Hey, I've been meaning to show you the garden," he said. "You can landscape the rest of the place however you want. Or we can do it together. I can do all the hard labor. Or we can hire professional landscapers to do it. Everyone in the pack would love to help out too. They've been giving me a hard time about it because I've cleared the weeds out of the flower beds every year but never planted anything." He shrugged. "I wanted it to be your space to do as you pleased."

Elizabeth gave him a big hug. "I love you and thanks."

"I'll help too," Sheri said, not one to be left out of things.

Elizabeth smiled. "When we have time, we need to go plant shopping. But I'll have to see what works down here. It'd be different than Yellowknife." She pressed her lips together, then added, "I can plant roses in memory of Grandma." Tears unexpectedly stung her eyes, and David, then Sheri, both wrapped her up in a hug.

After a moment, he said, "Let's go have a look," and led them out to the empty garden plots. "Good dirt too," he said, toeing the ground as if he needed her to know how much work he'd put into the garden. Her garden.

She pulled him close and gave him a quick kiss. "They're perfect. I love them."

He'd raised part of the beds so she could actually sit on the stone seating and work without stooping or bending.

Owen had recommended that because sometimes he had to weed Candice's flower beds and he wanted it to be a less backbreaking task for the both of them.

"Okay. Are you ready to run as wolves?" David asked.

"Oh, yes, absolutely." Sheri raced back to the house.

David chuckled. "She seems enthusiastic."

"Yeah, we have to check out the new territory for sure. I can't wait either." Elizabeth stepped back into David's arms, loving the feeling of leaning in to him, looking out together over the land where they would make their life, feeling the press of his big body against her back. Feeling safe. "Thank you so much for the beautiful gardens. I can't wait to get started on them. When I needed some consolation, particularly when Grandma was asleep and after we had our Skype chats, or when I was waiting for the days to pass until the next Skype session, I would work on the garden—in good weather, of course."

"I'm so glad you love them. I can't wait to help you with turning it into a showcase garden." He rested his chin on top of her head, and she felt, rather than heard, his deep sigh of contentment.

Sheri woofed and raced out the door while David and Elizabeth turned and smiled at each other, then went inside to strip out of their clothes. She felt the heat filling her body, every muscle stretching until she was a blur of forms from human to wolf, so quickly that they were both wolves in the blink of an eye. Wearing their wolf fur coats, they raced each other down the hall.

David went out the wolf door first to lead the way, but it

was a hot summer's day, and the first thing Sheri did was veer off toward the lake, splash in, swim out a little way, and woof at them. David and Elizabeth woofed back, then raced out to meet her. After cooling off, they paddled back to shore, shook off, getting each other wet, shook off again, then raced into the woods, David taking the lead.

David needed to show them the way so Elizabeth and Sheri could eventually take a run or walk on their own without getting lost.

Elizabeth was thrilled to finally be there, running through the woods David had talked about so often, by his side like she'd always imagined. He was a beautiful Arctic wolf, his fur all fluffed out as if he was preening for her attention, but he didn't need to. She'd had the hots for him from the day she'd first met him. For the oddest reason, she felt like they'd never really been apart. As if the connection they shared had never had to survive any distance at all.

He was the kind of guy who was sensitive, a fighter when he needed to be, aggressively protective but only when he thought she was being threatened. He'd wanted her in a sexual way, *once* they had resolved things with her pack, and he was conscious of the issues that wolves faced—such as no consummated relations until they were sure they wanted to mate for life.

She hadn't wanted to mate him back then—not when he wasn't sure what it meant to be a *lupus garou*. But from their first Skype call, he had totally charmed her. Her grandmother too, of course. And Elizabeth had the sense, even then when things were so new between them, that he would learn to embrace his inner wolf.

She glanced around at the pristine woods and lake. Just beautiful. A red-tailed hawk flew high above, its wings stretched against the blue, blue sky. The scent of pine filled her senses and she breathed it in, looking out over the lake and listening to the breeze-stirred water lapping at the rocky shore.

They ran for about three miles, exploring, walking, trotting, running, and then returned the way they had come. They'd smelled foxes, a bear, and numerous birds and squirrels and chipmunks. And lots of wolves. Elizabeth knew Faith and Cameron's scents. And Gavin's and Owen's too. And of course David's. She recognized Amelia's and Slade's scents also. But she didn't know Candice's, suspecting it was one of the other females she'd smelled in the woods. There were two other males and a female she couldn't place. David had told her that Faith and Cameron had triplets, two boys and a girl—Corey the troublemaker, a girl, Angie, and the youngest triplet Nick. So she figured that was who the other scents belonged to.

She couldn't remember the last time she ran free like this. Had fun like this. They could run back home in the parks at night, but they had to drive and park their cars and hope they weren't seen. To be able to just leave through the back door and run, or swim, without a care in the world? It was too good to be true. She couldn't wait to go swimming in her human form too.

As soon as they were back in the house, they shifted in their respective rooms and then dressed. David threw on slacks and a dress shirt rather than jeans and a T-shirt, so she slipped into a summer dress and found that Sheri had done the same, both of them thinking so much alike it was like they were twins.

"I was thinking that after I take you over to check out the office, I might see if they need me for anything, and if you would like, you could come home and finish unpacking your things or you can just relax, look around, get comfortable," David said. "Sheri can get settled too."

"Okay, sure," Elizabeth said. "That would be lovely." She wanted to help at the office, but she figured she might as well get organized here and keep Sheri company.

It was great having her best friend staying with them, but she wondered what they would do long-term. They'd just gotten there, though, so she wouldn't worry about it right now.

"And anytime you want me to take you ladies shopping, just let me know. Both for the garden plants and supplies, but also for clothes or anything else you might need."

"That would be great," Elizabeth said, and Sheri agreed. "Oh," Elizabeth added, "I'll need to open a bank account here. I'll be closing out my checking and savings accounts in Yellowknife."

"Me too," Sheri said. "I've been anticipating this for a long time. I've pinched every penny I could, getting ready for when we were on the run." She laughed. "Guess I didn't need to after all. Here I thought we'd need to rent cars, stay in hotels, be the on lam for a while, you know? I never planned to go high class in David's own private plane."

Elizabeth laughed with her, though it was tinged with a sense of deep gratitude. So many things could have gone sideways, but they didn't. Thanks to David and the pack.

David chuckled. "Only the best for you both."

Shopping, swimming, hiking. What a life. And Elizabeth was perfectly willing to take care of things around the cabin while David was working, if he really didn't need a lot of help at the office. She didn't want to force herself on him there. Maybe if they only needed one person to help out, Sheri could, because no matter what, Elizabeth didn't want her to feel like the odd man out.

"You ready to go?" David asked, getting enthusiastic nods in reply. It turned out to be only a short walk through a wooded area to reach the building. Elizabeth remembered the scent of it from their run: a specific mix of different pack members, all blended together, that was both comforting and new.

A hand-carved wooden sign with the logo of Arctic wolves and the name WHITE WOLF INVESTIGATIVE SERVICES hung over the front door.

Elizabeth pointed at it. "Do you ever have shifters contact you to do investigations for them because they think you're shifters like them?"

"A couple of times. But we don't have that many wolves in the area. No wolf packs but ours. Still, we've had a couple of cases like that. It's interesting because they have to come in and actually see us to learn by scent if we're wolves or not.

Once, we had a red wolf shifter family drop by who were moving from North Carolina, visiting this area, and they wanted to know if we knew where any red wolf packs were located. They were thrilled we knew about the pack out of Portland, Oregon."

"Leidolf's pack," Elizabeth said. "I remember when he aided you against the werewolf hunters and my pack."

"Yeah. Once they confirmed we were who they thought we were, we met the whole family. We ended up having a feast for them before they left the area."

"Oh, how nice," Sheri said. "I doubt Kintail would have done that for a wolf family passing through. In fact, I know he wouldn't have done that."

"I agree," Elizabeth said.

"It never hurts to make friends with other wolves. You never know when it can come back to you in a good way," David said. "But we get cases from nonwolves all the time too.

"There was a man who asked us to help him locate his wolf dog that kept digging out or jumping his fence. He figured since we 'loved' wolves, as evidenced by the name of our company, we would be sympathetic to his cause. Or that we even had some wolf dogs we were raising of our own."

"And you found the dog?" Elizabeth asked.

"Yeah, easily. We took one of our 'wolf dogs' and tracked him down in the country. It's easier as a wolf to track a missing dog."

Inside he showed them around a spacious reception area surrounded by individual offices for each of the PIs. The rooms had windows looking into the reception area, but with blinds they could close for privacy. There was also a bathroom and a kitchen, a couple of supply closets, and an empty room that looked like it could be office space if someone else joined them.

It really was a nice setup.

David took some stairs leading down, talking over his shoulder. "And here's the basement. It's full size and furnished for guests who come to visit, families, and for us when we want a big indoor room for parties, especially in the winter. Most of the time in the summer, we just all meet outdoors. But it has a full bathroom, and we've even been known to come down here if we turn into our wolf halves when we least expect it."

The lights switched on, showcasing a lodge-like recreation room. The walls were white paneling, the sofas all in light blues, making the huge expanse airy and light, even though the basement had no windows. But a couple of framed paintings of views of the lake made it appear as though they were looking out at a shimmering expanse of water.

"Oh, wow," Elizabeth said. "This is beautiful."

A table for eight and a kitchen was down here, too, as well as a big-screen TV on one wall. They checked out the bathroom, which was standard-sized with a shower and tub combo, a single pedestal sink, and a toilet.

"This is a really lovely space for guests and family," Sheri said.

"We have a separate entrance through there, and a wolf door too. We also have one upstairs on the side door I forgot to show you, just in case one of us needs to come and go as a wolf," David said.

Elizabeth was thinking that if Sheri got tired of staying with her and David, she could come here, maybe, unless they wanted to keep it available for other emergencies.

On the way back up the stairs, David explained that Gavin and Owen were out on a couple of jobs but were expected back soon. Cameron was on the phone in his office, and David checked his messages. "It looks like the guys are handling everything, but with only one person in the office, I'll stay here for a bit."

"Is there anything you want us to do?" Elizabeth asked, eager to start pitching in.

David still couldn't believe Elizabeth was here with him finally, and having her and Sheri wanting to help with the office was the perfect plan. "Give yourself a minute to breathe," he said. "You just got here, no one expects you to jump right in. You can come over with me in the morning, and I can show you what you could do. But I don't want you to feel you have to do anything now. Trust me, there will be plenty of time to work."

His phone started ringing.

David wanted to go overboard to make the two women feel welcome, to choose to stay forever with his pack, to ensure that Elizabeth sought to mate him when she felt the time was right. But he didn't intend to seem too desperate or make them believe it would always be like that—always playing and just having fun when he had to work. He needed them to feel comfortable with him when things would be more routine.

"Okay, thanks, David, we will." Elizabeth kissed him, then she and Sheri headed back to the house, leaving him to it.

"This is David Davis, White Wolf Investigative Services, how may I help you?"

"My name is Jimmy Warner and I need help. My dad has gone missing."

"Tell me a little about what's going on."

"This is going to sound weird, but my father ran away or something. The police won't do anything because there's no evidence of foul play and he's an adult... You probably know the drill. The thing is, he's threatened to leave when he's had fights with my mother before, but he never did. Well, maybe for a couple of hours, but it's been three days now, and it's like he vanished into thin air. No one's seen him, no calls, texts, nothing."

"His name?"

"Mel Warner. He's a baker at Olson's Bakery. He hasn't returned to work, and his boss and coworkers are just as concerned."

"Age?" David asked.

"Seventeen. Oh, you mean my dad's. He's forty-two. I tell you, he wouldn't leave, not like this. I have a fourteen-year-old sister he adores."

"And you?"

"Yeah, we get along fine. It's just Mom he has issues with."

A lot of men left their families because they couldn't get along with their spouses and left their kids behind too. So David could get why the police weren't concerned.

"Gut feeling?" David asked. That was something the police didn't believe in, but if a family member had a gut feeling about the situation, David and his partners always listened. It wasn't something they did just because they were wolves either. They'd always paid attention to their own instincts and had better results because of it.

"I think something's happened to him. I don't think he's been kidnapped or anything because wouldn't there be a ransom asking for his return? We don't have that much money, so he couldn't have been taken to, say, open a bank safe or whatever. Or give them secrets they could sell to the Russians or something crazy like that. But something's definitely not right. I just know it."

"Did you notice any changes in his behavior leading up to his disappearance?"

"You mean was he seeing another woman? I considered it. I love my mom, but if my dad could find someone who he cared about who wasn't nagging him all the time, then maybe he would leave my mom for another woman. But his mom cheated on his dad and he never forgave her for it. So I just don't see him doing that to my mom. Besides, he wouldn't just disappear like that. He'd file for divorce. I'm sure of it."

David grabbed a pen and legal pad off his desk. "Can you give me a quick description of him? What he might have been wearing the last time anyone saw him? Your address and your dad's cell, if he had one?"

Jimmy rattled off a description, David writing as he went. "Okay. Got it."

The next topic, he already knew, would be a challenging one: payment. David was afraid money would be an issue. But they had taken cases where they cut their fees just to help someone out who couldn't afford it.

The kid answered the unasked question in his next breath: "About the money... My mom won't pay for it."

Even worse that his mother, who was the adult, hadn't been the one to contract with them to conduct the investigation. David created a mental list of to-dos in this mind. One of the first items on the list? Having a little conversation with the mom.

"But I have a job in a hardware store after school," Jimmy continued. "I'll hire your services and pay you back as soon as I can."

"We'll talk about the financial aspect later." If David could find the boy's father and put his mind at rest, he would do it, even if they didn't ever get paid. They had to be careful they didn't take on too many free cases, or word would get out and that's all they would get. But in a situation like this, he felt compelled to take the case and learn what he could.

"But I want to do this, and if I have to, I'll try to get crowd-funding for it. But I have to do it," he repeated.

David could hear the anguish in his voice. "If we find your dad and he's perfectly fine, we can have him pay for our services to locate him. How does that sound?" Not that the dad would have to pay their agency anything, because technically he hadn't contracted them to find him, but David wanted to set the son's mind at ease.

"Oh, yeah, okay, sure. That would work." Then Jimmy was quiet for a moment. "And if he's not okay?"

"Then we'll do this for free. How does that sound?"

"Uh, well, I'll still pay you for your help. If you find him, no matter what the deal is, you need to pay for expenses. So you just let me know what they are when the time comes."

"I will, Jimmy. You said he works at Olson's Bakery?"

"Yeah, on Main Street. He's worked there for years and has never been in any trouble. Everyone really likes him. In fact, he has tons of friends. It's just Mom who gets on his nerves."

Sounded like a match made in heaven. *Not.*

"I'll get right on it."

"Okay. My sister and I put up a hundred flyers, but we haven't had any response. I'll send you his photo."

"Thanks. I'll be over to talk to your mom and sister soon."

"Okay, thanks. I've got to get to work. I'll let you know if anyone gets in touch with me with any information that might help."

"Sounds good, Jimmy. Same here." David hung up the phone, then picked it right back up again.

In any missing person case, the first call was always to the hospitals. Best-case scenario, Mel Warner was laid up somewhere, already on the mend.

Worst-case scenario? A follow-up call to the county morgue.

Chapter 9

"So, give me the full scoop. How are things going between you and David?" Sheri smiled as she helped Elizabeth hang up more of her clothes.

"Good." Elizabeth couldn't help smiling.

"Seems like maybe it's better than good, eh?" Sheri raised her eyebrows a bit. "I'm so happy for you. I really couldn't imagine how you could feel that way about a man you had only seen for such a short time and then you had left behind. I suspected you'd been keeping in touch, but even then, it's not the same as truly living with the person. But when I saw you two together, I knew you had something special going on. I think it's pretty clear to everyone around you that you are meant to be together," Sheri said.

"It's still not a done deal, but I'm hoping it works out between us." She repeated the same line she'd been telling herself ever since she and David first met. "We just need time to get to know each other better first."

"Yeah, right. I mean, I see your point, but man, if some hot wolf like David was that in lust and love with me? I would mate him in a heartbeat. Then again, that's the difference between the two of us. I started dating Bentley on a lark, and now he thinks I'm his forever, when the feeling's not mutual in the least bit." Sheri hung up another of Elizabeth's shirts. "It's not the same with you and David. Oh, and I love the wolves we've met in the pack already. Everyone is so nice. It just feels so different from the way Kintail would have treated them, had he forced them to remain with the pack."

"Yeah, I tried to tell you that, but seeing is believing. I was with them back then. I saw the way they were treated. But you haven't known any packs other than ours or known any other leader besides Kintail. With *this* pack, it's more democratic since they were all turned about the same time and fumbling in the dark about how to manage their lives."

"I think we can be a real help to them, don't you?"

Elizabeth smiled at her friend. "Yeah, I do."

That evening, David, Elizabeth, and Sheri arrived at Cameron and Faith's cabin, ready to enjoy the barbecue feast their pack leaders had set out.

This was the first time they had seen the couple's three kids—Corey, Nick, and Angie—and both Elizabeth and Sheri were delighted.

"I bet you enjoy having the kids," Elizabeth said, realizing just how much she would love to have some too.

"Oh, yeah," Faith said. "It's made for some really interesting times. David has probably told you about some of our adventures."

Elizabeth smiled. "He did. But it all seems worth it, even the bad times."

Faith gazed affectionately at her offspring. "It really is."

Everyone seemed to be in good spirits, welcoming them as if they were already family. Amelia gave both Elizabeth and Sheri big hugs when she saw them, introducing them to her mate, Gavin, and wanting to hear all about their first day. "By the way," Amelia said, "Slade should be joining us soon. He got held up with some bad weather and had to circle before he could finally get back on his route." Amelia made room for a big Saint Bernard, who was checking Elizabeth and Sheri out. "This is Winston. I was taking him on a flight to drop him off with a new family, but we crashed in a lake."

"Oh, no," Elizabeth said, Sheri looking just as shocked. Especially since Amelia had helped pilot the plane here.

"Anyway, he lost out on his new home and made it with us instead, which we were glad for." She gave him a hearty belly rub. "Everyone loves him and he bounces around from one house to another, getting all kinds of loving."

The kids were hugging on him and he appeared good-natured, licking their faces and nipping at them in friendly play.

Faith handed Elizabeth and Sheri drinks. "We hope you're staying for good," she said. "Not only because we care about you for all that you did for us, but because you're fun to be with and David has been missing you horribly. And Sheri, we're so glad you're here too. We want you to be part of our pack."

"We love it here already," Elizabeth said.

"Oh, I so agree. What a difference all of you make," Sheri said.

"David tells us you'd like to help out at the agency," Cameron said. "We couldn't be happier. When we have our shifting issues, with all of us taking turns, man, we would have it covered. Right now, we're losing some business because of our erratic schedule during the full-moon phase. You wouldn't believe the number of calls we get during those few days."

Elizabeth was so glad she and Sheri could actually help them, especially with shifting problems—and really anything they might still be learning to control with their wolf halves.

"And we'll help you in any way we can to ensure you have all the credentialing you need to work as full-time PIs," Cameron said.

Elizabeth's jaw dropped. Her gaze collided with Sheri's, and her friend's entire face glowed. They wanted them to be actual PIs?

"That sounds good to me," Sheri said, her voice high and excited. "In the meantime, we want to help in the office, taking calls, whatever you need us to do."

"And we could even go with any of you that have to go on an assignment, not only to learn the ropes, but in case one of you has to shift and we can do the driving or whatever," Elizabeth added.

David smiled as if he'd been holding on to this news in order to surprise them at the perfect moment. "We'll need a couple more desks to set them all up. We have that storage room we're not using, and we can have one of the ladies at the front, fielding inquiries. They can swap off with each other whenever they want. Right now," David said to Elizabeth and

Sheri, "we juggle the calls among ourselves. But you can be dedicated to doing that for us until you have your PI licenses. And like Elizabeth said, you can go with us on cases to help get your feet wet."

"Well, this calls for even more of a celebration," Faith said. "Though I'm not sure you know what you're getting into. The guys never get around to their paper filing." She rolled her eyes playfully. "I help out there sometimes, but when the other pack members have kids of their own, I'll be setting up a day care just for our little ones."

"Uh, yeah, about that," Gavin said, squeezing Amelia's hand.

"We're going to have twins in the new year," Amelia said.

"Ohmigod, congratulations, you two," Faith said, giving both of them big hugs. "Sounds like the day care will be full in no time." The rest of the pack followed suit, and caught in the middle of all the good wishes for the parents to be, David's warm presence at her side, Elizabeth felt an overwhelming sense of being home.

Slade arrived just as the commotion settled down. Elizabeth watched his eyes pan the room, only stopping when they landed on Sheri. The smile he gave her was full of possibilities, and Elizabeth felt a thrill of hope for her best friend. Could they both be so lucky as to have found their mates here?

"What's all the cheering about?" Slade asked. "What did I miss?"

"More wolf pups on the horizon!" Faith said.

"You're pregnant?" Slade asked, looking surprised.

"We are," Gavin said, giving Amelia a hug.

Slade's eyes grew wide. "Did you tell Mom and Dad yet?"

"I only just found out," Amelia said, lightly stroking her still-flat belly. "I'll call them after we're through here."

Slade smiled. "I'm going to be an uncle!"

"We all are," David said.

Everyone laughed.

David leaned down and whispered in her ear, "And you'll be an auntie." His warm breath sent delectable shivers down her spine.

"I can't wait," Elizabeth whispered back, not exactly sure what she was referring to there.

David gave a husky laugh that shot another shiver down her spine, his eyes gleaming like he knew *exactly* what she meant.

It had been only a matter of time, David thought, before other mated couples in the pack had wolf pups of their own. Since Amelia was a royal, he'd really believed they would have had the kids sooner, but with her being a pilot, and working with her brother and parents in the business, he guessed that was why they had held off a little longer. He knew that Owen and Candice were holding off because Owen was more newly turned, and she wasn't sure about the trouble she would have with being a wolf and having kids who also would have issues. During the full moon phase, she still had little control, and when the kids were young, if she changed into her wolf, her kids would automatically too. She could just imagine being at a store shopping for clothes for them when the urge to shift hit her. Though Faith had reassured her time and again everything would all turn out. She was proof that it could work out just fine.

Everyone must have been thinking the same thing, since all eyes turned toward Owen and Candice. They smiled. "We're working on it," Candice said.

David glanced at Elizabeth. She smiled and blushed, and he had the strongest urge to take her back home, lock themselves in his room, and lose himself inside her for the next couple of hours. Hell, the next couple of days.

Yeah, he could see making babies with her, but he really wanted to enjoy the freedom of being with her as a couple long before that happened.

Faith caught their smiles and chuckled. She reached over and patted Elizabeth's hand. "Maybe you two won't be far behind."

Elizabeth said, "A mate comes first."

David squeezed Elizabeth's hand and smiled at her, trying not to let his driving need for her scare her away. She obviously still needed time.

He glanced around the room. Sheri was busy helping the kids put corn holders on their corn on the cob. One of them needed a refill on milk, and Sheri handled that, too, stepping right in to take on the role of a nanny wolf. He was happy to see her fitting in so well, though there was still the lingering worry over her family and Kintail. He'd need to find out if she'd let her family know she was safe, had left on her own terms, and was putting down roots in—Seattle.

"We thought we'd run in the woods after dinner if everyone would like to," Faith said.

"Yes," Amelia said. "I need to keep in shape before the babies come. I would love to."

"We went running with David earlier," Elizabeth said, "but I'm always up for another wolf run."

"Me too," Sheri said.

There was a resounding "Yeah!" from everyone else. That was settled, then.

They had string lights on the gazebo at Cameron and Faith's house, and lights elsewhere to help light up the party area. The wolves could see well at night, and the sun didn't set until later in the summer anyway, but even if the lights weren't entirely necessary, David loved how they looked.

When dinner was over, they all went to their own cabins and stripped and shifted so they could meet up again at Cameron and Faith's home. It was just easier that way, and once they were done with the run, they would all return to their homes, shift, dress, and have a drink before calling it a night—after the kids went to bed. It had become a tradition for them. Since the wolf pack was so new, they needed some traditions of their own. Like the dinner they'd just finished: every time a new single wolf or family joined their pack, they celebrated.

One by one, and by twos and threes, the wolves gathered. They all nuzzled each other, knowing one another by scent and learning Elizabeth's and Sheri's scents, if they hadn't already. And now they would know each other by sight too.

Having Elizabeth by his side, running with his pack, was

a dream come true for David. He nuzzled her and rubbed his body against hers in courtship, and she did the same with him. So far—and he hoped it would always be this way—she seemed happy to be here with him. It sure wasn't the same as in the beginning when they'd run as wolves from danger.

Sheri chased around the pups, who delighted in it as if she were just one of the kids. Slade joined her, jumping and pouncing, much to the delight of everyone. David could sense the general speculation from the pack as the two of them romped around.

Then they all took off, Cameron and Faith in the lead, the kids with them until they began to explore, and the rest of the wolves following, keeping an eye on the pups.

David licked Elizabeth's face and she licked his back. He could sense she was truly enjoying this—a whole pack that loved her, unlike what she'd experienced with her former pack.

Then he saw Sheri corralling Corey back onto the trail they were all trotting on, Slade nipping at their heels, and the pack sent up a racket of joyous yips and howls. Family was everything to them. Everything to David too.

He often wondered if his father had been a wolf from birth, instead of human, would he have been a better father? Or would he have been a lone wolf, not interested in raising a family, like he had been as a human?

Chapter 10

Elizabeth had had no idea how much fun the wolf pups would be while she was running with them and David through the woods. She hadn't played with little ones in forever, her own pack not having had any for a long time, most of the young ones now in their teens. These pups yipped and woofed, tackling each other and tackling the adults, Elizabeth and Sheri too. It was like she and Sheri had never been strangers; they accepted them as part of the pack right away.

Her own maternalistic instincts came to bear, and she loved watching David hide behind a tree and then jump out to scare the pups. That led to a merry chase of all three wolf pups trying to catch David's tail as they ran around and around the tree after him. He would make a good father, she thought.

Then the wolf pups were running off to tackle Owen, who good-naturedly chased them until they were tired of running. Then they licked his face, letting him know they'd had fun.

Corey was the wild pup of the bunch. She watched as he climbed to the top of some rocks and then tumbled down, while the other wolf pups, Nick and Angie, waited to pounce on him at the bottom. He popped right up, tussling with his siblings, and then was right back at it again, and Elizabeth could just imagine what he would be like when he became a teen. Wild, adventurous, getting into trouble, not with humans so much as just getting himself into hot water as a wolf because of his daredevil streak.

Corey reminded Elizabeth of a cousin of hers who had died in a plane crash in the remote area of the Northwest Territories before she met David and the others. Her cousin had been just like Corey as a kid. She still missed him. Once he'd become an adult, he hadn't tamed down even a bit. She figured he wouldn't have been happy learning she had rescued Owen and David, either. He might have been headstrong, but when it came to the pack leader, he had always done what he was told.

She loved the idea of growing with this pack, of all the new babies coming and helping to take care of them, of assisting with the older kids and the PI business. Having been isolated from her own pack and working in a dress store as a clerk, she found everything—she nuzzled David, making her thoughts on what "everything" entailed perfectly clear—way more exciting here.

After the run, they all headed back to the houses, shifted and dressed, then gathered back at the MacPhersons' home for the traditional nightcap. Elizabeth loved every moment of it.

Back at David's cabin, Sheri said, "I'm off to shower and bed."

"Night," Elizabeth and David said in unison, heading for the master bedroom.

"Night," Sheri said, then disappeared into the bathroom.

"I was so surprised that Cameron wanted us to become PIs." Elizabeth hadn't wanted to upset the order of things after they'd only just arrived. But she was thrilled they would want her to be one of them. Not just a pack member or a love interest, but an honest-to-goodness private investigator.

David laughed. "Yeah, I thought you would like that." He began to help her out of her shirt. "If the two of you, or just one of you, enjoy the administrative duties and aren't interested in becoming a PI, we won't be offended. We just want you to be happy."

"Oh, believe me, we are. What a beautiful way to end what has been a lovely day. The pups are adorable too."

He poked her hair behind her ears and sighed. "I know we should wait to consummate the relationship, but..." He made a sound, a rumbled half agony, half laughter. "I'm not going to lie. It's going to be hard."

"Hmm, we'll see how it goes. I've only been here for a day. Before, being on the run like we were, dodging bullets and bad men and a rabid pack leader, staying in hotels and riding for hours in a car, which I had to drive lots because you all were shifting like crazy"—she smiled at the memory—"that's not the same as living plain old workaday lives." Even though the sex was great between them, there was more—so much more they needed to discover about each other to make sure they would be compatible for a lifetime.

Interests, hobbies, ideology, getting along with the other pack members. Normally, parents or other family members could be a problem in couple relationships. But in this case,

David's friends were his family, so if she didn't get along with them—which she didn't believe would be a problem—that all needed to be taken into consideration.

So far, though, even she had to admit everything had been good.

Elizabeth and David showered, and after toweling each other off, she dried her hair with her hair dryer and joined him in bed, sans clothes. She'd so hoped they would be back to this kind of closeness again, and she wasn't disappointed. He wrapped his arm around her, caressing her bare skin, kissing the top of her head.

She couldn't believe she was really here with him. It had been a long flight, and after having sex and a hot, soapy shower with him, two wolf runs, the pack celebration, and getting a job, she should have been exhausted.

She wasn't. She didn't think David was either.

Letting her fingers trace swirling patterns on his chest, she asked, "So when you were in the office, did you pick up any cases to work on?"

"Yeah." He explained about Jimmy and his missing dad. "I checked with the local hospital and some farther away, vehicle accident reports, hotels he might have stayed at, but nothing."

"If you need me to help, just let me know." Wouldn't it be amazing to help reunite a boy with his dad for her first case?

She felt his smile just before he kissed her head. "I will."

Elizabeth closed her eyes and sighed. She was getting ahead of herself.

She was eager to start working on a degree to become a

full-fledged PI, but she knew there was more to it than just jumping in headfirst. There would be requirements. School. Probably a criminology degree.

The thought doused a little of her happiness. She hadn't been in school for years. What if she failed the classes? She would take them over again. Because the PIs were former police officers, they could probably help her study. The same for Sheri.

She and Sheri would get the ball rolling on that first thing in the morning.

"What are you thinking about?" David asked, his voice hushed as if he didn't want to wake her up too much if she was already drifting off to sleep.

"About enrolling in college."

He chuckled and pulled her on top of him, his arms wrapped lovingly around her. "I was thinking about this. About being with you when I've wanted this forever. To hold you close, to talk to you, and run as wolves, the whole nine yards. I didn't expect to be also working with you, but I'm glad for that too."

"Oh, I was thinking about that too." She kissed his chest, rubbing her nose across his hard pectoral muscles, just as she might have in wolf form. "But then I was thinking Sheri and I need to get registered for classes. We'll need to update the dates and things on our high school diplomas." The longevity that came with being a wolf was absolutely a blessing, but it could be a pain in the butt sometimes too.

"Right. We can do that."

"Good." She sighed. "I dreamed of this, you know. I mean,

not being a PI… That's just a bonus. But of this. You. I'm so glad we did it."

David stroked her hair. "We'd left things up in the air so much when you left us because you wanted it that way, thinking I might find someone else before you could leave Yellowknife. I worried you might find someone else too."

"You were upset with me." His hand paused on her head, just for a moment, but she felt it.

"I was." The stroking picked up again, slowly, hypnotically, almost as if he were unaware he was doing it. "I loved you," he said simply. "I understood you had to be with family, but some part of me feared you wanted to return to be with your pack and stay there. They had been your people for so many years. Not only that, but I was afraid I would bring you down."

She frowned. "Bring me down?"

"You're a royal. Your offspring would have your royal genes if you mated another royal wolf, and you wouldn't have to be concerned about them having half human genes—or the trouble with shifting, once they're old enough to do it on their own."

She lifted her head, wanting to make sure he could see the truth in her eyes. "Sure. I would be lying if I said I hadn't thought about it. We have a natural instinct to preserve our heritage, improve the line, and that's both the wolf and human thinking driving that. But we also mate for life, so there's so much more going on during the decision-making. Just meeting another wolf who is a royal is one thing. I've met them before. Single males who were looking for a mate.

I wasn't interested in them in the least bit. If I had mated one of them, we would have had full royal kids at some point, but I couldn't have been mated to any of them and kept my sanity."

David smiled, appearing pleased she felt that way.

"Anyway"—she rested her head back on his chest—"don't worry about it. Because I'm a royal, I can help the kids learn to deal with it, and I can do the same for you and the other nonroyal wolves. I can do whatever it takes to help the pack work and have fun, with the fewest setbacks possible."

Her body rose and fell with his sigh of relief. "During the new moon, you and I are going to eat out every night. Every day. We'll go to the movies and—"

She turned a little again, bringing her mouth up to his for a kiss. "We are going to enjoy each other's company to the fullest every day—new moon, full moon, whatever the moon may be."

"Okay, if you insist." He smiled that wolfy smile. "But tomorrow, you and Sheri need to find a couple of desks you would like for the office—shelves, whatever you'll need, and we'll purchase them from the pack fund. We want you to feel just as at home at the office as you feel with us after hours."

She smiled. "Thanks. Is there a dollar limit?"

"No. If we look at the setup and we think it's too much, we'll say so, but find what you want to make it work and we'll try and swing it."

"Okay, thanks."

Then she took a deep breath, thinking she needed to move off him, but he held her in place, as if he didn't want to release her no matter what. As if he felt she would vanish if she was in the bed next to him but not touching him like now.

"We're courting, too. I'm taking you canoeing, if it's something you want to do. We have an island and I can take you there," David said.

She smiled. "I'd like that."

"And the fair."

"If you win me all kinds of prizes."

He chuckled.

They lay in silence for a while, until Elizabeth realized he'd fallen asleep. She slipped off him, trying not to wake him even as she snuggled against him, her arm over his chest, a leg over one of his, claiming him for her own.

He was hers, even when they slept.

Chapter 11

David stirred, the sound of an owl hooting in a nearby tree disturbing his sleep. Elizabeth had rolled off him, but she was still snuggled against his body as if she were happy to be with him, right at home. Being with her like this was absolute bliss.

When David next awoke, Elizabeth was gone. He panicked, worried he'd only dreamed she'd been with him, like he'd done on numerous occasions since she had left him. But then he heard her talking softly to Sheri in the kitchen, smelled the coffee brewing, and realized they were just having some coffee before he got his lazy bones out of bed.

He stretched, then climbed out of bed and dressed in boxer briefs and shorts and headed for the kitchen.

"Well, good morning," Sheri said, all bright-eyed and bushy-tailed. "We made the coffee and hot tea and were trying to decide on breakfast."

David ran his hand over his stubbly chin, not quite awake. "I've got breakfast food, but I rarely eat it for breakfast—eggs, bacon—"

"And waffles and sausages in the freezer," Elizabeth said.

"Okay, I'll make it—" David said.

"No, you go shave and get ready for work. We'll get

breakfast ready." Elizabeth kissed him, and he kissed her back.

What a way to wake up: first afraid that he'd only dreamed Elizabeth had truly been with him, then this—practically having breakfast in bed.

When he rejoined them, they had scrambled eggs and sausages, tea and coffee spread out on the table. David asked Sheri, "Did you contact your family to let them know you are all right?" He kept wanting to give her the time to do it without badgering her, but he wanted to know they weren't worried about her safety.

"Yes. Sorry, I should have mentioned it already. I called my dad, since he can be more reasonable than my mom. Or, I should say, less emotional. He said he understood, and he wished me well."

Elizabeth sipped some more of her tea. She was glad David had brought the topic up and hoped Sheri had also actually talked to her mom. "And your mom?"

"She was all upset, of course. But I told them we were going to become full-fledged private investigators and finally do something important with our lives. So what could she say to that? Of course she asked if I had met someone here, and I told her there were a lot of wolves and everyone was warm and welcoming, unlike our own pack. Anyway, they said I had to live my life and they hoped I was happy. They said they loved me no matter what." Sheri's eyes were shimmering with tears, and Elizabeth hurried to hug her.

"What about Kintail?" Elizabeth asked.

"He's furious. You know him. But he hasn't made any plans to come down here, as far as they know." Sheri sipped some of her tea.

"And your brother?" David asked.

"I didn't talk to him. I'm sure he's furious with me because it puts the whole family in a bad light, at least as far as he's concerned."

"What about Bentley?" Elizabeth asked.

"He's been texting me constantly."

"Still? Why don't you just block him?" Elizabeth's brow furrowed. "You're not still interested in him, are you? I guess I should have worded that differently. Are you still interested in having a relationship with Bentley?" She hadn't meant her question to sound so derogatory. If Sheri was still entertaining the notion of mating with him, she needed to let everyone in their new pack know now. It would mean her returning to Yellowknife, to her pack, because there was no way in hell Bentley would come here. And Elizabeth didn't want him to. He would only cause trouble.

Then again, Bentley *was* controlling, and if he thought he had a chance to take over a pack whose members were so newly turned, he might just make a stab at it.

"No. I'm not interested in Bentley any longer." She *sounded* sincere about it, though Elizabeth wondered if Sheri saw Bentley again, if he might be able to convince her to take him back.

It'd certainly happened before.

"You really did end things with him, right?" Elizabeth couldn't shake the feeling things weren't quite as over as Sheri was making them out to be.

"Yeah. But you know how he is. He said I just wasn't thinking clearly about the situation and I would come around. That I just needed some time off on my own. I told him I was taking some time off, but I wasn't changing my mind about him. All he heard was I was taking some time off and then returning to him." Sheri rolled her eyes and shrugged at the same time.

Elizabeth couldn't be as blasé about it. "Did you tell your parents you broke things off?"

Sheri shook her head, albeit a bit sheepishly.

David had been listening quietly, but at her answer, he set down his fork and said, "Your parents have to know that if you have no plans to return to Yellowknife, you must have ended things with him."

"I suppose. All right." She grimaced as if she'd just been asked to swallow a bitter pill. "I'll text my parents and let them know, if they didn't figure it out already. It shouldn't be that hard, right? I mean, I already broke the really bad news to them, so..."

Still, she looked uneasy.

They finished breakfast in tense silence, then cleaned up and headed over to the office.

"You'll both need criminal justice degrees, and you'll need to 'intern' for a private investigative agency," David was explaining. "We've got you covered on that. We'll train you, and there's a great program at a college right here in Ely."

"Sounds like a plan. It will be fun for us to do it together too."

"Absolutely," Sheri said.

Elizabeth asked, "Can we get some plants for the office?"

David smiled. "Yeah, sure. That would be nice."

She pulled up an office supply website on her phone and showed him the desks she and Sheri had picked out that morning.

"Perfect." David placed the order. "Looks like they'll be in on Monday."

Cameron arrived, and David asked him if he would help him move furniture around to accommodate the new desks.

"This is going to be great." Sheri was helping move files around, and she suggested moving the file cabinet behind the receptionist desk. "It would make it easier to get to the filing and still answer the phone."

Elizabeth carried some copier paper into the room where they had the workstation printer they all used. "I can reorganize your supplies in here."

"You ladies are a godsend." Gavin came out to help. "We've been too busy managing clients to really organize things better."

"We'll take care of it." Elizabeth was glad to be able to offer any services that would lighten the guys' workload.

Owen finished a call and helped the guys move furniture around to accommodate the new desks.

"We'll need to get some more phone lines in—" Cameron said.

"I'll take care of it," Elizabeth said.

David got her the paperwork for the phone company they used.

Perfect. They could handle all the changes without the guys getting bogged down in all this, David thought. "I'll give you the password to log in to the computers and set you and Sheri up as administrators. You can field calls for the time being."

"All right." The phone rang and Elizabeth grabbed up the receiver. "White Wolf Investigative Services, Elizabeth Alpine speaking. How may I direct your call?"

David smiled. Man, they could have used her here when they first set up shop.

"Yes, David Davis is right here." She handed him the portable landline phone.

"This is David Davis. How may I help you?" He returned to his office and shut the door.

"Have you found my dad yet?"

David recognized the boy's voice. Jimmy Warner. "Not yet."

"But you're looking, aren't you?"

David tried to keep his voice even. It'd only been about twelve hours since they'd last spoken, but he understood what it meant to fear for someone you loved. "Yeah, still checking airlines, bus stations, train stations, hotels, hospitals, and police reports." He didn't usually give a detailed list of his procedures on a case, but to reassure the boy, he wanted him to know what he was doing.

"Okay, good. I just wanted to make sure you hadn't forgotten about him," Jimmy said, sounding broken up.

"I promise you, I won't forget." David had checked Mel's phone too. It wouldn't be the first time someone they were looking for purposely ignored calls from loved ones but picked up for random numbers. Unfortunately, that wasn't the case with Mel. His phone went directly to voicemail. Either the box was full or the phone was dead. Either way, it wasn't a great sign. The last location they'd had on it was only five miles from the house and then that was it.

"Okay, well, I know you gotta work and I don't want to bug you all the time, but I just wanted to check to see if you were getting anywhere with the case."

"Not yet, but we'll keep looking. You hang in there, okay?" David ended the call with Jimmy, wishing he'd had better news. But it was damn early in the case, and he knew he'd barely scraped the surface.

He went back out to the reception area to see if Elizabeth and Sheri needed him to move anything else.

"A new case?" Elizabeth asked.

David shook his head. "Jimmy's case. Pro bono."

"Do you have many of these kinds of cases? Ones you do for free, I mean?"

"Every once in a while. We try to work in the ones we know we won't get paid for if they have a legitimate case they need looking into, especially if the police suspect no foul play and won't bother to help out. Those are the ones that fall through the cracks. He sounds close to his dad, so I want to do this for him."

"You're a good man. You know that, right?"

"I try to be, but I'm not always." His brow creased, and he took her by her shoulders, pulling her gently but firmly into his office. "I don't worry about getting my hands dirty when the situation calls for it. When I have to, I can take down the worst of them."

She wrapped her arms around his neck. "That makes you well-rounded. I like that you can be both. As wolves, we can't afford to be wishy-washy or cowardly."

Then she kissed him.

Personality traits were genetic, and Elizabeth couldn't imagine having little wolf pups with a wolf who was afraid of his own shadow. They needed to live with what they were and deal with it the best they could. Which made her think of the issue of having wolf pups with David. They wouldn't have her full royal lineage. Which meant they wouldn't be able to keep their human form on demand during the full moon. Though until they were older, they would shift only when she did—the benefit of their genetic makeup that protected their offspring from shifting as babies at their own whim and creating havoc.

She could imagine the danger that would put them in if she had twin babies and one of them shifted into a wolf pup while she and the other baby were in their human forms out in public, like at the grocery store. What a disaster that would be.

She had to laugh at herself. She was already thinking of what it would be like to have babies with David, but that was an important part of who they were—wolves who cherished their offspring and cherished each other.

They were still kissing when Owen came into the office. "I need to have Candice come in to see me more often while I'm working so I can kiss her like that."

David and Elizabeth smiled at him.

Owen said, "We're so glad you're here. You should have heard all the times David talked about you. You were our heroine, Elizabeth. Candice even wrote about you in one of her books. She dedicated it to you, but we were afraid to contact you because of the issues we'd had with your pack."

"Oh, how lovely. I can't wait to read it. I have to admit I was afraid Kintail would learn where David and you were and try to force you to return to the pack."

"Now they're down two more pack members," Owen said.

"Yeah, they're probably not happy about it."

"But they were basically keeping her a prisoner there, while shunning her at the same time. That's no way for anyone to live," David said, running his hand over her back in a loving caress.

She leaned into his touch, loving how genuinely affectionate he was with her.

"You didn't deserve that. The pack leader should have realized David and the rest of our friends and I are together—a package deal. Cameron would have butted heads with Kintail all the time, if he'd forced him to join his pack too," Owen said.

"I don't think *everyone* wanted to ostracize me, but they didn't want to say so in front of the ones loyal to our pack leader. And others did see me as a traitor for doing what I did." Elizabeth smiled. "But I'm here now and that is in the past."

Owen said, "True. So did I ever tell you about how David saved my life when we were on the police force in Seattle?" Owen was clearly trying to prove how loyal and protective his friend was. Not that she didn't already know that.

"She doesn't want to hear it," David said, looking embarrassed.

Sheri stuck her head in the open door. "I want to hear it."

"Me too," Elizabeth added, laughing.

"Two to one. Sorry, David," Owen said, encouraged by their interest, though she suspected he hadn't needed the encouragement and was going to tell them regardless. He gave David a hardy clap on the shoulder. "So, long story short, this guy pushed me out of the way when an armed robber made a dash out of a jewelry store and fired a couple of rounds at me. David took the bullet and was in the hospital for three days."

"Is that why you left the police force?" Elizabeth asked, both proud of David and scared for him, even though it was years after the fact.

"No, we had been with the police force for several years. We didn't want to leave Seattle, so we formed the private investigator service."

"Well, I hope working as a PI is less dangerous than being a police officer," she said.

"Sometimes. Sometimes we've had some dangerous jobs to go on, when we didn't even realize they would be," Owen said.

Elizabeth and Sheri were looking forward to any adventure they could sign up for.

Chapter 12

Early the next morning, David stood on his back patio, steps from the woods and the lake. A fussy breeze whipped around him, but he didn't notice. The moon was still visible in the growing light of day, a near perfect circle in the softly lit sky. Elizabeth and Sheri were still fast asleep, unaware of the growing urge inside him to turn wolf. He knew he couldn't hide it from Elizabeth, but he wasn't ready to share this part of him, this lack of control, with her. Not yet.

This was going to be the hard part. Showing the women his more vulnerable side. His inability to keep his human form. He'd gone through this with Elizabeth in the beginning, much worse than it was now. But the whole situation was different back then. They weren't on the run any longer, and this was a way of life for him. He wasn't sure she could live comfortably with a mate who had shifting issues, a partner who couldn't hold his human form for at least three days during the full-moon phase and couldn't turn into a wolf to run with her during the new moon.

And their children would have the same issues. Maybe not as bad as David and his partners, and Faith and Candice, since they had been human when turned. At least their children would have one parent who was a royal wolf. But still, if

Sheri and Elizabeth found mates who were royals, too, someone like Slade even, those kids wouldn't suffer the same fate.

It was getting better, though, he thought, as he stripped out of his clothes, trying to stay quiet. He needed to get in to work, and he hoped a run in the early morning hours could knock this out of his system for the day, maybe, and then he could shift again after work tonight. In the early days, he didn't have any choice. He just shifted when the urge came on, and he couldn't stop it. And couldn't return to his human form on command either.

It wasn't like that anymore. Usually. He did have *some* control now. Just not enough.

David shifted, his body warming as he landed on all fours. His ears perked, and in the distance he heard Owen Nottingham and his mate, Candice, barge through the wolf door of their home. Candice always ran with Owen, even if she didn't need to. That's what mated wolves did for each other.

Gavin went out next. Amelia and Slade probably had flights they had to take out, so neither was with him.

David's paws padded silently across the patio, then with a leap, he dashed into the woods, dirt churning, trees going by in a blur as he tracked the scent of his pack. It was instinctive now, his ability to find his pack, his family, so he wouldn't have to be alone.

He raced to catch up to Owen and Candice, who always waited for him. He sometimes wondered if they felt bad for him because he had been the odd man out. He still might be if things didn't work out between him and Elizabeth, but he didn't let that worry him now. He veered around an ancient oak, leaped over a fallen log, and spotted Owen, who turned and barked at him to hurry up and join them. When he was finally side by side with his packmates, Candice licked him in greeting, and they started off again, sniffing the trail, identifying squirrels and birds and deer that had been through there recently.

Then they heard a woof behind him, and he gave a wolf smile. Faith and Cameron and their three wolf pups were scampering to catch up.

The pack happily took off, everyone helping to watch after the little ones who were off the trail more than on it, searching for new scents and sightings of anything that intrigued them—a butterfly, a dragonfly, a lizard that quickly scampered under a rock ledge. The world was a wide-open place of wonder and discovery for them.

And sometimes it felt that way to David too.

Elizabeth had sensed David was anxious about the full moon tugging on his wolf need to shift. They'd made love again last night, but he'd been…distracted, she thought. She wished she knew how to console him. To let him know she was there for him every step of the way. But when he left the room before daybreak, she let him go. He'd come to her when he was ready. Until then, she had to give him the space to sort it out for himself. She would be encouraging, supportive, but no matter how much she tried to tell him it didn't bother her, she knew it bothered him. And that wasn't anything she could fix.

She got up and showered, then heard Sheri showering. When they were both dressed for work, she met Sheri in the kitchen.

"Did I hear David—" Sheri peered out the window. "Scratch that. He ditched his clothes on the back patio." She sighed. "I think he doesn't want to let on how bad it is for him still."

"All the more reason it's important we're here for him and the others." Elizabeth made them some hot tea.

"I agree, but if it were me, I would go after him. Show him he doesn't have to sneak out or hide what's going on." She opened the pantry, digging around for pancake mix.

"I don't know. Maybe you're right. I was thinking he might need to do his own thing, and I might end up making him feel more uncomfortable." Elizabeth bit her lip, wondering if Sheri was right.

"You're overthinking this. He'll want to see that it doesn't bother you. I'll have my pancakes and fix some more for the two of you when you return." She nodded toward the wolf door. "Go!"

Elizabeth gave her a huge smile. "I'm going." She brought David's clothes into the living room and dumped them on the floor. Then she stripped and dumped her clothes on top of David's to say she was his and he'd better just get used to it. She gave Sheri a thumbs-up, then shifted.

"That's the spirit." Sheri smiled at her. "Go get him."

Elizabeth raced out of the house and followed David and the rest of the pack's scents.

She barked to let the others know she was coming, her heart as light as her paws flying across the ground. She wanted to run with David and then go home, and as soon as they shifted back into their human form, she wanted to make love to him. To prove to him that she loved him just like he was.

It took a moment for her to realize no one responded to her bark though.

She howled then, her wolf's voice carrying further than her bark, and got a chorus of howls in response. She'd never felt such joy as she experienced in that moment. She ran all the faster to meet up with them. Now they knew her wolf howl, and she knew theirs, just not who they all belonged to. But she'd learn that soon enough.

Then she saw David running back to her, huge and majestic, his white fur flowing in the wind. He was beautiful.

She pounced on him, partly in play and greeting and partly in annoyance that he couldn't see that she was happy for him, glad that he was what he was because if he hadn't been turned—besides the fact he would have died of a heart attack at his young age—she wouldn't have ever fallen in love with him. Not when he'd been human. Oh, maybe she would have still had the hots for him, had she met him, but she would never have felt this connected to him like she was with both parts of him—wolf and man.

He tackled her back, less aggressively, just in fun, and she knew from his scent and posture—if he'd had any doubts she would love him like this too—he was thrilled she had come after him. She still had to talk with him about this. They needed to communicate their concerns with each other. Work them out. Show how much they valued each other.

But right now, in this moment, this was all that mattered.

She pulled away from him and licked his face and he licked hers back, then rubbed up against her. This was a lovely way to start the day as wolves. Though she would have loved a kiss and a hug this morning before they went for a run. Together. They turned in unison, trotting side by side, just the way it should be. The two of them. A couple.

When they finally rendezvoused with the rest of the pack, they were greeted by a chorus of the most beautiful howls she'd ever heard. She knew they were trying to show her who belonged to which voice. After some playful romping and more chasing after the pups, the pack began to disperse, and David and Elizabeth headed back too. She suspected he'd been in his wolf coat for long enough that he could manage work for a while.

The whole scenario really brought home the pack's problem with shifting during the full moon while trying to run their office. She couldn't wait to help make that easier for all of them.

There was nothing better than feeling needed, Elizabeth thought. Other than being loved too.

Elizabeth howled as they approached David's house to let Sheri know they were on their way and she could fix breakfast for them so they could eat and get to work.

David let her go inside first. Right away, she smelled the pancakes and maple waffle syrup and sausages. Sheri was right to say she liked her own cooking. Elizabeth gave her a few appreciative yips while still in wolf form, and Sheri waved a spatula at her from the kitchen in acknowledgment.

Then Elizabeth shifted and dressed, and David ran into the bedroom to shift and pick out something appropriate for work.

He came back in, his hair damp from a quick cleanup, his smile sexy and sweet. "Thanks for coming to run with me, Elizabeth." He poured himself a cup of coffee. "And thanks for fixing us breakfast, Sheri."

"Oh, you are so welcome. I'm running to the office to try to figure out what the heck you guys did to your poor filing system. Though I use the term 'system'"—she tossed up a couple of exaggerated hand quotes—"lightly. If there's a system to that madness, I haven't figured it out yet." Sheri smiled and headed off to the office.

Elizabeth and David ate in silence for a bit, the sound of the silverware tinging against their plates unnaturally loud. Elizabeth cleared her throat. "You shouldn't have run off without me, unless you really didn't want to run with me." She tried not to sound too hurt, but wasn't sure she managed to pull it off.

"I'm sorry. I just thought—"

"That I wouldn't be sympathetic to your cause?"

"I don't want your—"

She set her fork down with a clang. "David, if we're going to do this—mate, I mean—you have to trust that I can live with it. I don't want you to feel that you have to sneak out without me so that when you return you will have your wolf under control. I love you. You love me. This shouldn't be an issue."

He let out his breath. "You don't know how I feel about this. The rest of us are used to it, but—"

"Amelia? How does she treat Gavin? Like he has a plague when he can't control his shifting? Or can't shift during the new moon?"

David shook his head, looking so lost that her annoyance began to melt away.

She took a deep breath and let it out. "Well, I wouldn't treat you like that either. We all have our frailties, our vulnerabilities. You can't know how often I worried that you would find another she-wolf to mate. It was eating me up inside from week to week, us being apart, me not knowing how long it would be for. What if some cute she-wolf came prancing up to your door and professed her undying love to you? A bird in the hand came to mind."

David chuckled.

"I'm serious. I worried about it all the time. Grandma would tell me I shouldn't borrow trouble. That I should just continue to enjoy the time I did have with you and not worry about the time I couldn't spend with you. And so I made the most of our visits—until it was time to flee Kintail's tyranny to be with you. Just you. And the pack, of course." She reached across the table and grabbed his hand, holding it tight in hers. "We can work this out, get used to the way things can be that will be the best for both of us. But we have to be honest with each other and talk about it."

"I agree. I'm sorry, Elizabeth. I was thinking I could just get this under control and join you, have breakfast, and get to work and let you sleep a little longer."

"And not take me for a wolf run too? That's just plain mean." But she was no longer upset with him, glad they had cleared the air.

David smiled and flipped his hand in hers, lacing their fingers together. "I promise to never let you sleep in again."

She loved that about him. The intimacy he always shared with her. The little things. "Okay, good."

"Good," he said. They shared a smile, then finished breakfast, cleaning everything up, and rewarding each other with a hug and kiss that left Elizabeth a little breathless. She smiled up at him. "Now this is what I wanted first thing this morning. Not an empty bed to wake to."

"I agree, by the way. About the empty bed. I would have felt the same way about you if you had done that to me." He leaned down, molding his lips to hers, sharing a maple-flavored kiss that Elizabeth never wanted to end. Her body tightened, growing warm. She slid her leg up his, wrapping it around and pulling him closer, her hips grinding into his as he walked her backward, only stopping when she bumped up against the cool steel of the refrigerator door. "And yeah," he said, pulling away and resting his forehead against hers, "this is definitely the better way to get my day going."

Unfortunately, it was also a little too late to finish what they started.

She pulled away with a rueful grin and straightened her clothes, her eyes promising to come back to this later. "Okay," she said, trying unsuccessfully to brush his hair out of his eyes. "Are you ready to go?"

"No." He smiled. "But I think we'll be missed if we don't."

When they arrived at the office, Sheri was on the phone and no one else was in their offices. She put her hand over the receiver and said, "This one's for you. A callback on the Mel Warner case. Gavin had a call out, Cameron's not here yet, and Owen is running down a lead."

"Okay, I've got it." David took the call in his office.

"How did things go between the two of you? You looked happy enough when you returned from the run," Sheri said, back to filing. Elizabeth pulled up a chair beside her and started to help.

"Good. He's not going to slip out to run without me anymore."

"That's good, or I would have had to give him a talking-to."

Elizabeth smiled. Sheri would have, too. "How have things been?" Elizabeth pulled out a stack of papers piled up in Owen's to-be-filed box. "Geez. We really need to get these guys to start filing stuff online. This is ridiculous."

"Agreed," Sheri said. "Though so much of this is handwritten notes, papers they've accumulated for receipts, and other important documents on cases. Aside from this paper disaster, things are good. I was answering phone calls, Owen and Gavin took the cases and were off, leaving me to run the whole place. And then you and David showed up. That's been it."

"We'll need some protocols now that we're working here on how to handle walk-ins and phone calls if the guys are out on jobs or can't handle them because of shifting issues." Elizabeth went into Gavin's office to get his to-be-filed papers.

"Hey, I'm just getting Owen's papers-to-be-filed nearly caught up. Don't bring me any more," Sheri teased.

Elizabeth smiled. She was going to love working with Sheri in the office.

A couple of minutes later, David popped his head out of his office. "Faith said everyone's swimming tonight at the lake if we want to join them. That's the joy of living right on the lake. It's light out late in the summer, and we can play to our hearts' content after work."

"Now that sounds just perfect," Elizabeth said.

"I'm all for it," Sheri said. " I sure love Seattle."

After work, they headed home to change into swimsuits. No wolf swimming tonight. Sheri was in and out of the house in record time. "See you there!" she called.

Elizabeth rushed to get in her one-piece blue swimsuit to follow her. David kissed her shoulder, debating whether they could let themselves get sidetracked for a moment. It was tempting, no doubt, but then he pulled on his board shorts. There would be time for that later.

Elizabeth ran out of the bedroom and dashed through the house. "Race you there," she yelled.

"You got it."

Elizabeth was already out the door by the time he grabbed some beach towels and bottled water and headed outside.

She was slipping off a pair of sandals next to a lounge chair. "I beat you."

He laughed. "Not yet," he said, nodding toward Sheri already heading back to shore from the swimming platform in the middle of the lake.

She smiled mischievously. "Wanna bet?" And she took

off again, running to the water's edge and plunging in, swimming strong strokes out to the platform.

David put the towels and water bottles on their lounge chairs, glad he had four of his own for when a couple of others dropped by in the summer to enjoy a visit, though if they needed more chairs, they could bring some more over.

Sheri walked out of the lake, smiling. He handed her a towel.

"Thanks."

"No problem." He nodded out toward Elizabeth, who'd reached the platform and was sunning herself on the wooden planks. "I'm glad she loves to swim."

"Yeah, for being from such a northern territory, we both love it," Sheri said. "I hurried up, thinking I would give you two some privacy."

Smiling, he shook his head. "Elizabeth wanted to swim. First."

"Yeah, I figured it would take you guys longer than that." She winked. "She's so happy here with you. She worried so much about just seeing you again, I know, even though she wouldn't let on." She held a hand up, shielding her eyes as she peered out over the lake toward the platform. "I'm happy she's so happy."

"Thanks, Sheri." David figured if anyone really knew how Elizabeth was feeling about everything, it would be Sheri. "I'm really glad you're here too. Even though she knew most of us, you've known her forever. It makes a difference, having you here. For all of us."

"I feel the same way." Sheri patted him on the bare chest. "Just keep up the good work."

He smiled. "I fully intend to. Anytime you and Elizabeth need some together time alone, you just let me know. I know how important friendships can be."

"Well, truthfully, we'll need to pick up a few more things at the store. I brought what I thought we would need, but you know how that goes. If we weren't staying here long-term, that would have been one thing."

"Of course."

Sheri smiled and gave him a hug, which he hadn't expected. "Thanks for taking me with you."

"We're really glad to have you here." He stared out at his own little slice of paradise, appreciating the moment, the view, his happiness, the vision of Elizabeth as she stood up and did a running leap off the platform, slicing into the water with a clean dive.

The rest of his pack began showing up, breaking the spell—or maybe adding to it, he wasn't quite sure.

"What are you doing standing around? Let's go!" Cameron said, joining David and slapping him on the back before dashing into the water. Sheri dropped the towel and ran after him, ready for another go-round.

David raced in too, diving into the water and swimming as fast as he could to beat his friend.

The race was on with everyone cheering—Owen telling David he could never make it in time to catch up, Gavin telling Cameron he should have gotten more of a head start to win, Sheri swimming along gamely, trying not to suck in a bunch of lake water while laughing. It was hilarious to hear them cheering each of them on, and David had to concentrate on beating his friend and not laughing and swallowing a bunch of water. Even the kids were in high spirits, yelling in their loud, high-pitched voices to hurry, hurry.

"Uncle David, you can win! Daddy, you can win! Go, Sheri, go! Beat 'em!" He knew they had the concept down that the one who reached the finish line first won, but they didn't seem to want any of them to lose. Family was family, after all.

David had nearly caught up to Cameron, either because he'd slowed down a bit for having a head start, or because David really had rallied enough to catch up, and at the last moment, they both reached the platform at the same time. They laughed and everyone cheered, then cheered again when Sheri slapped her hands on the edge next to them.

They climbed out, laughing, and congratulated each other.

The kids were already heading out to join them, and Elizabeth, who'd been paddling around watching the race, swam over, gliding next to them until they all reached the platform, the rest of the pack splashing and calling out to one another. David pulled Elizabeth up, tucking her between his legs as they sat close, their wet bodies sun-warmed and slick. She leaned against him, secure in his arms amid his family, his land, his life.

David tilted his face up to the sky and closed his eyes.

Paradise, indeed.

Elizabeth loved it here. The area was beautiful, the lake an added playground, and the cabins were all within sight of each other but far enough away to have privacy too. What a great place to raise a family. She hoped if Slade and Sheri weren't interested in mating each other, another male wolf would show up and Sheri and the new male would fall in love. But Cameron and the others might not want another male wolf encroaching on their territory. What if the new wolf was an alpha and a royal and wanted to take over the pack?

Then again, she didn't think any of these wolves would bow down to another male wolf, since the men had grown up together in Seattle and had been best of friends all this time. They were a tight group, and being turned made them even closer. They would stick together.

Sheri was smiling, looking happy to be here even if she didn't have anyone to date. Elizabeth was glad she was here, and in that moment, in David's arms, she made a decision.

She didn't want to drag out getting to know him all over again. He was eager, and so was she. What they needed was time together, just the two of them. She didn't want Sheri to feel left out, and she hoped she would understand, but she really did need some time alone with David.

Chapter 13

The next morning, David was having shifting issues again just as he planned to make breakfast, and he was trying not to be annoyed about it. He had made love to Elizabeth early this morning instead of going for a wolf run, and he faulted himself for not doing what he knew had to be done during this phase of the moon. But she'd been in such a loving mood, he had soon forgotten all about the moon and only thought of pleasuring her.

He'd planned to make breakfast for them after, but his body warmed and he was feeling the pull to shift. "Go ahead and make whatever you want." He knew he sounded irritated, but he couldn't help it. Instead of inflicting his bad attitude on Elizabeth and Sheri, he stalked back to the bedroom, nearly growling in frustration. He hated that about the full moon, that he couldn't do his usual routine, and that meant checking messages at the office and being the first one in there in case they had any walk-in clients. Plus he wanted to get to work again on the Mel Warner case and now that would have to wait too.

"We've got it," Sheri called.

"Yeah, you made us administrators," Elizabeth said, raising her voice so he'd hear. Neither of them moved from the kitchen to check on him, and he appreciated the space. He felt like a lousy mate prospect, but he would have felt worse if she tried to come in and baby him. She'd said she was fine with it; he just hadn't come to terms with that yet.

"We'll make breakfast and see you over there," Elizabeth added.

He barely heard her, the pull so strong now that he really had to fight it. He ditched his clothes and shifted in a flash.

"I'm calling Cameron to let him know we're going in to the office," Elizabeth said. "Do you need anything?"

David ran into the living room as a wolf and bumped Elizabeth's hand, letting her know he hadn't meant to be all growly. She smiled down at him, leaned over, kissed his cheek, and ran her hand over his head. "We can do this. That's what we're here for. And for more." She smiled at him.

"The more is what I want," Sheri said, getting ready to leave the house and acting like David having to shift was no big deal.

"We'll find you someone." Elizabeth had the phone to her ear and said, "Hi, Cameron, this is—" She glanced at Sheri. "I got an answering machine."

"This is *really* why we're here," Sheri said. "Just think, during the full moon, we can take over the pack."

David smiled. He knew Sheri was joking, but he loved that she could make light of what he felt was a dark situation.

He licked Elizabeth's hand, and she laughed. "Yeah, but they'll all be back to their human forms and we'll be in trouble."

"We'll open up the shop, talk to clients, and tell them you all will get back to them as soon as you can. Maybe one of the other guys hasn't shifted," Elizabeth said, hopeful that someone could come in and soon.

Sheri pointed out the window with her free hand. "Well, Cameron and Faith and their pups are all out for a run."

That discounted them.

Elizabeth called Gavin, and Amelia answered the phone instead. "He's a wolf right now. I can take a message for him. I'll be leaving to take a flight out in a few minutes."

"Sheri and I are headed to the office. We'll do what we can until one of the guys can show up," Elizabeth said.

"Okay, thanks. I'm glad you all are here. My brother and I are taking some flights out and can't hang around, with the summer tourism in full swing. We get a lot of seaplane sightseeing tours over the lakes, and we're taking a lot of canoeists into the BWCAW this time of year. Um, that stands for the Boundary Waters Canoe Area Wilderness. Welcome to the pack!" Amelia said.

Elizabeth smiled. "We're glad to be here."

She gave David a big hug. "We'll see you when we see you." She hoped he wasn't stuck as a wolf for a really long time. Not that it would bother her, but she knew it would bother him.

Then she and Sheri walked over to the office. All the homes were privately screened from the office, making it look like it was sitting in a park. They were really off the beaten path out here, so most people called in their requests for services, or emailed them, or filled out a secure form online, but some still came in to speak with the investigators in person, probably wanting to see their setup and make sure they were getting what they were paying for.

The building itself was made of logs, but more modern rustic than old-cabin-in-the-woods. They had a good-sized parking lot and a large sign out front so passersby could see the phone number, website, and name of the business.

Inside, the place was immaculate—no trash accumulated on the investigators' desks, no used coffee mugs, and no one smoked. It looked like the place was newly opened, the men's degree completions and awards they'd earned while on the police force in Seattle and their PI licenses all beautifully framed in each of the offices.

"You know, the place looks a bit too clean," Sheri said, checking messages.

"What do you mean?" Elizabeth asked as she turned on a computer at the receptionist's desk and logged on.

"It's too new looking, like they just opened for business."

Elizabeth liked clean and neat. "We still need to get plants."

Sheri smiled.

"Plants add to any decor."

"You know how I kill potted plants. Stick it in the ground, and it does fine for me. Plant it in a pot, and I'm in trouble," Sheri said.

"I'll water them." Elizabeth loved plants, indoors and out.

"Okay, sounds good. I can't believe they've been

managing this on their own for so long. I think seeing them all shift like that put it in perspective for me."

"Yeah, me too. And not just one or two wolves in the pack have trouble with it, but almost the whole pack." Elizabeth looked at some canvas prints they could hang on the wall of forests, lakes, Arctic wolves. "I know how it was in the beginning. I was there. I guess I just thought it would get better with time. I know it has to have, but I guess I thought it would be much better than this."

Sheri had begun filing documents, a seemingly endless task. " I really didn't have a clue. It's one thing when we have one or two wolves in a large pack who have issues, but when practically the whole pack does? I really feel for them."

"You're not afraid how that might affect you?" Elizabeth asked.

"That one of them will get caught, and we'll all be outed? No. It just makes me more determined to stay and help out. I can't imagine working here all this time without more royal wolves to be here for them. And Amelia and Slade can't be because of having to fly so much."

"Right." Elizabeth was glad her friend would feel that way too.

They worked in silence for a while, then Sheri said, "I hope that I won't be too big of a nuisance staying with you two."

"No, you're not." Elizabeth wondered if Sheri somehow sensed how anxious she was to have time alone with David. Another thought had just occurred to her though: Maybe it was Sheri who wanted the alone time.

"We haven't been too…um, noisy, have we?"

"No." Sheri blushed. "It's just that you're getting to really know David, and here I am in the middle of it. Maybe I should stay with one of the other families. In fact, I might hop from one to the other so I can get to know them better."

Elizabeth didn't think Sheri would really be happy with doing that. "Only if you really want to and you're not just saying that for my sake or something. You're my friend, and we did this together."

"No, I forced this on you." Sheri sighed. "You two need the time alone to get to know each other. I just don't want to come between you. The two of you need to be mated." Sheri held up her finger as she began listening to voice messages, and Elizabeth took the opportunity to empty Cameron's office of to-be-filed paperwork.

"So what did the messages say?" she asked when she came out.

Sheri said, "We had some requests for investigations on new hires at one of the hospitals. I'll log them in on the computer and send a note telling them we're on it. I wonder how long it will be before—"

The door to the agency opened, and Elizabeth hoped it was one of the guys, finally getting control of his shifting, but instead a woman walked in, and they suspected she was a potential client. *Great.* They hadn't had any training in how to handle a client who walked in the door when no PIs were available.

"Hi, I'm Elizabeth Alpine, an administrative officer for the agency. How may I help you?"

"I need to hire an investigator to look into my business partner's finances. I'm certain he has been stealing money from the firm, but I need evidence before I can get the police involved. I'm Mitzi Moore, and the firm was my husband's. When he died, his partner tried to buy me out. I've been suspicious of him for a while. My husband knew him as a childhood friend and trusted him completely, so I couldn't do anything about it back then, but now I have to make sure he has not been robbing the firm blind. We're a printing company and print documents, books, flyers, whatever needs to be printed all over the country. My grandfather actually started the business, and my father ran it until I married my husband, and he took it over. Then he brought in this friend, who became his partner. Anyway, the shares were split between the two of them, well, until my husband died. Now I own half the company. I would buy him out, but I want to know if he has swindled the company first. His name is Edgar Cooper. Can you take the case?"

Elizabeth blinked. That was...a lot of information all at once. She wasn't even sure Ms. Moore took a breath. She cleared her throat and said, "All of our investigators are out on jobs right now, but as soon as one of them gets in, we'll tell him about your situation, and he'll call you and let you know what he needs."

"You can't call one now and just let him know? I need to either have you check into it or go to another PI office."

Sheri spoke up. "Let me text them." Her fingers were already flying over her phone. "One of them will let you know soon."

"I'll wait." Ms. Moore took a seat on the chair in the reception area.

Great. Elizabeth and Sheri exchanged glances with each other as the woman took out her phone and began texting someone.

Then the door opened again. Elizabeth and Sheri turned as one to see if it was one of the PIs, but it was another potential client. Sheri smiled at the man and took him into an office, explaining as she went who she was and that the investigators were all out on jobs. "So, how may I help you?"

A few minutes later, after a conversation too low for Elizabeth—and more importantly, Ms. Moore—to hear, the man nodded, took the business card Sheri offered to him, and said he looked forward to hearing from an investigator soon.

Just as he was about to leave the office building, Elizabeth heard Owen and Gavin talking to each other as they came inside.

The man stepped up, interrupting them. "Your administrative officer, Sheri, said one of you would call me about this job, but if you're here now and I can talk to you about it..."

Owen shook his hand. "Come into my office, and thanks, Sheri."

Then Gavin said, "You must be Ms. Moore?" and gestured to her to follow him to his office. Guess he'd gotten Sheri's text.

Sheri joined Elizabeth and said, "Man, I wish I was already a PI and could work the cases for them."

"I was thinking the same thing. At least we're enrolled in the classes now so we can get a start on it."

Chapter 14

Back in Yellowknife, when Bentley and Hans went to see Kintail at his home, he knew the news wasn't good. Though he knew what it was already. Elizabeth had managed to leave the pack, and no one had stopped her.

"Where the hell is Sheri?" Kintail asked. "You were supposed to bring her here."

Bentley looked at Hans as if he were the one who was supposed to know because Hans was Sheri's brother. But the thing of it was, Bentley was Sheri's boyfriend, so he ought to damn well know where she was!

"She's not home," Hans said, sounding irritated.

Kintail narrowed his eyes. "Where is she, then?"

"I don't know. Mom and Dad don't know. We used lock-picks to get into Elizabeth and her grandmother's house. Her suitcases are gone, all her clothes are gone, the fridge was empty, her grandmother's clothes were gone. There was no indication where she went. Oh, and her car was in the garage."

"And Sheri's car?" Kintail asked.

"No idea," Hans said.

"No?" Now that surprised Kintail. He thought they would find her car there along with Elizabeth's, while the women, presumably, took off in the car of the mystery woman from dinner.

Hans shrugged.

Kintail frowned. "Did you check Sheri's room to see if her things were at your parents' home?"

"Uh"—Hans glanced at Bentley—"no."

"Go now, and call me with what you learn." *Incompetents.*

"We'll do that." Hans turned to leave, with Bentley following behind him, arguing like children.

"You should have thought of that first," Bentley said to Hans.

"Why didn't you think of it? You're supposed to be her boyfriend, so you say," Hans said.

"You're her brother."

"And I'm not my sister's keeper."

The door closed behind them, mercifully, and Kintail shook his head. He called Hans and Sheri's dad, even though he knew they'd just left on a vacation to Cancun. He doubted they had any idea Sheri or Elizabeth were even gone.

Still, he had to try. They wouldn't get away with this. Not while he was pack leader.

"Hey, it's Kintail. Did Sheri say anything at all about taking a trip anywhere, like to Seattle?"

Stuck at home while Elizabeth and Sheri were in the office, David felt worry start seeping in again. He was afraid that no matter what she'd said, if Elizabeth had any doubts about being with him—and she must have, since she hadn't decided to be his mate yet—this might have tipped the scale in favoring a quick retreat for her. Sheri too.

He finally managed to shift. He threw on clothes and walked to the office.

Two cars were sitting there, and he hoped things hadn't been too busy for them.

But when he walked in, he found Elizabeth and Sheri huddled over a computer together, pointing at the monitor and agreeing or disagreeing about something, while Gavin was taking care of one client and Owen the other.

"Oh," Elizabeth said, jumping from the desk chair. "We got some inquiries for background investigations." She handed David the requests.

"Come into my office." He took Sheri and Elizabeth there and shut the door. "This is your first official training." He showed them how to do thorough background investigations on potential new hires for a business, using the multiple databases they had at their disposal.

"Oh, wow, how cool is this?" Sheri asked, wide-eyed.

"It is." Elizabeth read over some of the information on the monitor.

David motioned to the screen. "We get a lot of these, and we want to be thorough so that hiring the wrong person doesn't come back to bite us, but we also want to get the results back as soon as possible so that the business—the client—can hire or reject the application without too much delay."

"Right," Sheri said, as he showed them how he went through the various sources to investigate the cases.

"Now, we don't tell them who to hire, but we'll give them the details of what the individual applicant's criminal records look like. In other words, it's on the businesses to do what's right for their employees and customers."

"Good," Elizabeth said.

"These five potential hires are clean, no records. This one has five parking violations and four moving violations—all outstanding. Now, if it were me hiring the person, I would say no because he just doesn't seem to want to obey the laws and he hasn't taken care of his violations. What if he was the same with working in an office? Ignoring the rules and regulations?"

"I agree," Elizabeth said.

"Do you both want to work on these, then?"

"Oh, yeah," Elizabeth said. "Filing papers and answering the phone is important, but actually handling cases? I'm in."

Sheri was eager to do them too.

David had a high-priority mission of his own this morning. Make the ladies legitimate U.S. citizens. That would mean making sure they had all the papers they needed, including birth records, social security numbers, all that. Every pack had to play around with that because the pack members aged so slowly. He could imagine someone whose passport said they were born forty years earlier than they looked in human years. Or driver's licenses, any ID like that.

It was just something they had to do from time to time—not as much for David and the other newly turned wolves, since they hadn't lived that long as wolves, but royals who had lived a long time already definitely had to hide their true age.

Elizabeth and Sheri worked on cross-verifying information

on the applicants, and then after David looked them over, he had them share the information with the businesses.

"We can do these from now on," Sheri said, the pleasure at having done a good job evident in her joyful expression.

"What's next?" Elizabeth asked.

"I'll see what else we have that you can work on. Anything that takes some research in our databases should work. We'll need to work out salaries too."

"Looking forward to earning our keep," Elizabeth said.

He smiled and kissed her. "Believe me, you'll earn it. We've needed some administrative help, but when we have shifting issues, we'll need you for investigations too. Thanks for being here for us."

"Yeah," Gavin said, coming to join them after his client and Owen's had left. "You managed to get us a couple of cases we would no doubt have lost because all of us were having shifting issues this morning. It's the worst at the peak of the full moon. So now the worst of it will be over."

"Oh, that's good. Ms. Moore seemed…eager to meet with you," Sheri said.

"She was happy we're getting right on it. Speaking of which, Sheri, I need to take a trip to start the investigation. If you don't mind, you can go with me, and if I have trouble with shifting again, though usually we're good for several hours, you can help me out," Gavin said.

Sheri handed Elizabeth the papers she had in hand to file and smiled at her. "I'll help you with this when I return, if you're not done by then."

The phone rang and Elizabeth hurried to answer it. "This

is Elizabeth Alpine at White Wolf Investigative Services, how may I help you?" She glanced at David. "Just a moment, I'll see if one of our investigators is free to take your call." She put the call on hold. "She's looking for her birth mother. Is that something we do?"

He nodded. "I'll take the call." Once Elizabeth had transferred the call to his office, David said, "This is David Davis, how may I help you?"

"My name is Lisa Lamont. I have a medical condition that means I need to locate my birth mother as soon as I can. Is there any way that I can solicit your services to locate her?"

"Yes, we'll take the case. I need to get some more information from you."

"My mother gave me up for adoption when I was a baby. I never knew the reason. My parents only just told me that they weren't my birth parents. I'm still shocked over the news. I never suspected they weren't my biological parents. According to them, my mother said my dad had died in a car accident and she couldn't take care of me any longer." She gave David the names of her adoptive parents. "They said they were eager to talk to you, but that I had to initiate the request. They'll pay for your services, whatever they entail."

A few minutes later, Cameron walked into the office and said, "Hey, Elizabeth." He frowned. "Where's Sheri?"

"She's gone with Gavin to help him on a case, and David's on a call."

"Oh, good."

The phone rang and she answered it. "Yes, let me check and see if one of the investigators is free to talk with you." Elizabeth put the call on hold. "A case of a missing champion-sired standard poodle?"

"I'll take it," Cameron said. "Good work."

She smiled. Then the phone rang again, and she answered it.

David worked on the details of the contract with Ms. Lamont, then refocused on the Mel Warner case.

Elizabeth stood in his doorway. "I have a call for you," she said. "Jimmy, the teen looking for his father."

"Okay, perfect. I was just about to dig back into that. Could you check with the hospitals in the area for me again? I checked twice, but he wasn't there. But you can confirm it for me again. While you're at it, you can check with the hospital about Ms. Lamont's birth records." He slid his notes on the case across the desk. "Here's her information."

"I can do that." Elizabeth grabbed the paper off the desk, then nodded to his phone. "Jimmy's on hold for you."

David picked it up. "David Davis, how may I help you?"

"It's me, Jimmy. I...uh, I need to come in and talk to you."

The tone of voice, the slight undercurrent of guilt... Every one of David's police instincts—not to mention canine instincts—told him Jimmy knew more about the situation with his father than he had first let on. "Yeah, come on in. My schedule is open right now."

"Thanks, I'll be right there."

"Jimmy's coming in to see me," David called out to Elizabeth. "Send him in as soon as he gets here." And David hoped he would still be fine, no shifting difficulties.

Elizabeth came back to his doorway. "Will do. I checked the local hospital. No one by the name of Mel Warner has been admitted."

"That was fast. Thanks."

A few minutes later, Jimmy showed up. He either lived in the woods on the property or had already been on the way there, as quickly as he had arrived. And the pack would have known if he lived in the woods.

Elizabeth directed him to David's office.

Jimmy shook his hand, his palm damp with sweat. David surreptitiously wiped his against his jeans.

"Hi, I, uh, guess I need to tell you something else."

Jimmy sounded like he knew he was in trouble. Smelled like it too—worry and anxiety coming off him in waves, his hands clutched together and then shoved in his pockets, his brow furrowed, and he just stood there like he wasn't even supposed to take a seat. But worse, he smelled of wolf.

Not that him being a wolf was a bad thing, it just meant David had to handle the case in a different way. As a wolf, the dad wouldn't have willingly abandoned the family. At least, David didn't think so.

David had the teen take a seat and closed the door. "Yeah, what else is going on?"

Jimmy breathed in deep, his nostrils flaring, then let the

breath out. "You're one too." He finally took a seat. "But you're not a gray like me."

"We're Arctic wolves."

"Right. The sign. I knew that's why you used that for the name of your PI office. At least I hoped so."

"So what's the problem?" David was worried the teen had done something to his dad, and maybe he had come to confess to him.

"Okay, the deal is, uh..." Jimmy looked down at his lap, then up at David, appearing a little panicked.

"Just spit it out. If whatever you tell me will help us to find your dad"—and David damn well hoped it meant that they would find him alive and well—"then we need all the help you can give us."

"Okay." Jimmy took another deep breath. "The thing is, my dad..." Tears filled the boy's eyes, and he looked out the window. "He's not a wolf."

David just stared at him in disbelief for a moment. "He's not a wolf?" That changed everything. *Lupus garou* mated for life, unless one died, and even then some never looked for another mate. But if Jimmy's father wasn't even a wolf, that meant Mel and his wife would not have the same commitment to each other they would have had as wolves.

It was also extremely hard for a wolf to impregnate a human. It happened, but most times they couldn't conceive that way.

David frowned. "Is he really your biological father?"

Jimmy let out his breath in a huff. "Okay, look, he's my dad. I love him. He doesn't have to be a wolf for me to care about him. Mom would never turn him because she didn't want him having issues with shifting. My biological dad died a long time ago in a boating accident. I don't even remember him. My mom married Mel soon after. He has really been the only dad I've ever known."

Which David totally understood.

"But I think in the back of her mind, she always felt she could divorce him if she wanted to—because he's human—and I think that's where this is headed, but—"

Tears filled Jimmy's eyes again.

"Mom was still working her shift at the hospital as an RN. I'd made up my mind that I didn't want to lose my dad, so I shifted into my wolf and went to meet him when he came home from work. I mean, I hesitated because I really didn't want to scare him or...or hurt him, but at that point I knew I'd gone too far anyway. He'd seen me as a wolf, even if he hadn't known it was me. Some part of me reasoned he *did* know, and I had to turn him now because it was dangerous for us, for him, if I didn't. He had to be one of us." His eyes pleaded with David to understand. "He was just standing there looking horrified, like he was a statue and couldn't move. And I couldn't either, realizing I just couldn't attack him. I couldn't." He wiped away tears with his arm, looking every inch the kid he was.

"I finally got my courage up and I raced up to him. He tried to run, to get away, but I bit his arm. He cried out, then shouted to my sister and me to stay in our rooms and lock our bedroom doors—"

As if a wolf, or even a dog, if that's what Mel assumed it was, could open a door, David thought.

"My sister was at a friend's house, which was why I did it then. I heard him running to his bedroom, and I knew he was getting his gun that he keeps in the top drawer of his bedside table. I ran back to my bedroom, shifted, and pulled on my shorts."

David felt his pain. He'd never been close to his father growing up, but Jimmy seemed really close to his—except for the rather big secret he'd had to keep from him.

"Anyway, he ran down the hall to my bedroom and tried the doorknob, but I'd locked it. He asked if I was okay..."

Jimmy clenched his teeth and appeared to be fighting tears again. "I–I didn't really think through all the consequences. That he wouldn't be able to work his day job. That he would have trouble with the shifting during the full moon. My mom and sister and I are all royals. I just didn't think about all that. Not until *after* I had bitten him, and he left and disappeared. I kept thinking he would return, and I would explain what I was. What Mom and my sister were. That he was one of us now. But he didn't come back."

David leaned back, thoughtful. "This puts the situation in a whole different light. We need to locate him and tell him what's going on." David never told clients he was a wolf—not that he usually had to with other shifters—or how he became one, but in this case, he thought it might help.

"I was turned a few years back against my will. I didn't know *lupus garous* existed. So I know what your dad's going through. Several of us were turned, and none of us had a clue what we were doing or how to deal with it. We need to teach your dad that he's not going crazy, that you and your mother and sister are also wolves. He's going to want to stay away from you to protect you, thinking somehow the wild dog or wolf in the house had turned him and it had nothing to do with you."

"I hadn't thought of that. I kept thinking he would come home and I could explain everything to him. Shift and prove I was the wolf and he was just like me now." His expression was remorseful. He'd created this nightmare and had to find a way to make things right. "My mom's going to kill me."

"Okay, look, as *lupus garous* we mate for life. But since your mom didn't turn your dad, she's not responsible for him, so that's another issue."

"I'm responsible for him. I know that. I'll take care of him and teach him how cool it is to be a wolf." Then Jimmy frowned. "Wait, you mean she could still divorce him?" Jimmy sounded disheartened that his plans could blow up in his face.

"Yeah, she could, and no one would fault her for it. But maybe she will see something different in him now that he's a wolf. Your dad has been there for you from the beginning, right?"

"He has."

"Then maybe that will help her see that he's the right wolf for her. But we can't plan on it. We just need to find him before he causes havoc as a wolf someplace." David didn't want to mention that someone could shoot him. The boy was devastated enough as it was.

"He loves Mom. I had hoped that if he were one of us, she would change her mind about him. But now... I really screwed up, didn't I?"

"We'll just have to find him first and see where it all goes. But you need to let your mom know, too, and your sister, if she doesn't already know. Your mother might even know where he might have gone."

"Oh, I never thought of that. She's on duty right now, but I'll text her."

David knew the boy had done this because he loved his dad, but man. What a mess.

"Call your mom and then put it on speakerphone so I can speak with her too."

Jimmy sighed heavily. "All right." He touched his screen a couple of times, then said, "Hey, Mom? I'm putting this on speakerphone so that a private investigator can talk to you."

"You're not supposed to call me at work unless it's an emergency, Jimmy, and I told you not to see a PI," his mother said, sounding highly irritated.

"I turned Dad. At least I think I did."

His mother was dead silent.

"I'm a wolf shifter," David said right up front. He wanted to be clear with her right way before she had a heart attack, thinking her son was talking to a PI about being a wolf shifter. "David Davis. Everyone at my agency also is a *lupus garou*. Your son bit your husband, and no doubt he's probably confused. He might be shifting out of control during the full moon, who knows where. We need to find him right away. Whether you keep him for your mate or not is up to you, but your son wants to continue to see him, and we might have to find a pack he can belong to that will help him out."

"Jimmy!" his mother said, irate.

"I didn't want you to divorce Dad. He loves you and we love him. You shouldn't have married him if you didn't want to mate him for life like we're supposed to, like you've drummed into Cass and me."

"Maybe he has gone to his grandfather's old hunting cabin," Jimmy's mom said. "We'll talk about this later. If I think of any other place he could be, I'll call you." Then she hung up on them.

"Do you know where his grandfather's hunting cabin is?" David asked, annoyed with the woman for not telling him directly. Time was of the essence. What if the dad was out running as a wolf and was shot by a hunter? If he was killed, he would turn into his human form. That would be devastating for his family and could be disastrous for their wolf kind if anyone saw him shift from wolf to human.

"I know where it is. It's out in the woods so I don't know the actual address, but I can take you there," Jimmy said.

Elizabeth popped into the office. "I can come with you."

"You lead the way, Jimmy, and we'll follow behind."

David told Cameron what they were doing and then he and Jimmy and Elizabeth headed out to the parking lot. "Wait here for us, Jimmy. I have to get my Jeep and I'll meet you over here."

"Yeah, listen, I'm really sorry about all this."

"It'll work out somehow." It might not work out the way Jimmy wanted, but David would do everything he could to help, even if that meant moving Mel to a wolf pack in another location.

Should he still be alive, that was.

"Would you take him in your pack?" Elizabeth asked as they climbed into his Jeep at his house.

"If his wife keeps the family intact and they all pull together to help him out, it could work. You and Leidolf were there for us when we needed the help, so I would like to think we would be there for him too."

"Okay, that's understandable. But if the wife doesn't want to be there for him, where could he go?"

"There's a pack in Montana and three in Colorado, and Leidolf's pack is in Oregon. They're not really close, but if Jimmy feels strongly enough about being with his dad, he could join him there and help his dad acclimate to the changes in his life."

David honked as he pulled into the agency parking lot to let Jimmy know they were ready to go. David followed the teen's car, hoping they would find his dad before it was too late.

Chapter 15

"What do you think the mom will want to do?" Elizabeth asked. They'd turned off onto a dirt road a ways back; the Jeep bumped along behind Jimmy's car.

"You know it had to have been a shock to her to hear that her son had turned her husband. She needs to process the information. Maybe they'll work it out as a family, maybe not. The thing I worry about is that she might have met a wolf and wants to be with him, and she has been pushing her human husband into wanting a divorce so that she can mate the wolf."

"Why not just divorce him first?" Elizabeth asked.

"Because whatever made her care about him in the first place, and the fact he had helped her raise her kids all these years, probably influenced her not to just divorce him."

"It's so sad."

"Yeah. I guess she wasn't interested enough in him to turn him. Or maybe she felt it would be too much of a disservice to him and she truly does love him." David glanced at Elizabeth. "You and Sheri are just what we needed in our lives, by the way."

She laughed. "Nice segue."

It took them a good hour to reach the cabin in the woods.

The one-story home featured a lovely wraparound deck with big rocking chairs and small round tables that overlooked a pristine lake. David was thinking it was a really nice place to be a wolf, so at least the dad had that.

They saw a red Dodge Neon sitting next to the cabin. Jimmy called David on his phone and said, "That's Dad's car."

"Good." David hoped Mel was in human form and wouldn't run away from them as a wolf. He watched for any movement at the house or surrounding area but didn't see any.

"Look," Elizabeth said. "The door to the cabin is wide open. I don't see a doggy door. He would have had to leave the door open as a wolf."

They left their vehicle and Jimmy rushed into the cabin, calling, "Dad! Dad, it's me, Jimmy!"

"Hold on." David glanced down at a flannel shirt and jeans lying on the wooden floor. "Are these his? Looks like he's out running."

"Yeah, they're his." Jimmy began stripping, dropping his shirt right next to the pile of clothes David had just pointed out.

"No, you need to stay in your human form so you can reason with him. He won't know it's you, otherwise. His sense of smell might not be developed enough yet to recognize your scent. Elizabeth and I will run as wolves to try and track him down. We'll howl when we find him, so you'll know he's safe."

"All right." Jimmy pulled his T-shirt back over his head.

Elizabeth and David stripped and shifted. After using the

clothes to get his scent, they shot out the door and started tracking him. Mel had marked the area with his scent, whether he meant to or not. His paws left a scent, and he'd peed in a couple of locations, the instinctive urge to mark his territory coming into play.

They kept running, noses to the ground, then up in the air, twitching, recalibrating, losing him, then finding him again. Finally, they spied the wolf standing next to the lake about two miles east of the cabin. He hadn't seen them yet, but David knew it was him. He was a gray wolf, his fur all blacks and grays and tans. Though the Arctic wolf was a subspecies of gray wolf, their coloring was nothing alike.

David shifted. "Mr. Warner, your son, Jimmy, is here. We're all wolf shifters, here to help you through this." Then David shifted back into his wolf form.

Mel just stared at them, not moving an inch in any direction, not that David blamed him. The whole business could be such a shock to the system that he could understand the dad's reluctance to go with them.

David shifted again so he could speak with him further. "Mel, we need you to come to the cabin with us. Your son is waiting for us to tell him we found you. He's worried about you. We'll explain more there." Then he shifted back to his wolf. Elizabeth shifted next to him, then back again, to show Mel that David was telling the truth.

They waited. They weren't returning without him. David howled then, calling for Jimmy, hoping he could convince his dad to return with them. It would take a while for his son to reach them, but like earlier in the day with the car, Jimmy had already been on his way. He raced into the clearing, skidding on his hind paws as he spotted them.

So much for listening when David told him to stay put. Not that he blamed the teen.

He woofed at his dad as if Mel would understand him, and then, after the barest of hesitations, Jimmy shifted into his human form. He walked toward his father, who took a step back.

It was one thing to realize his son was a wolf, another to accept the reality. And to accept his son was the one who had done this to him.

"I want you to come home. I'm sorry I bit you. I didn't want Mom to divorce you. You've been the best thing for me, keeping me in line, just like a wolf father would have done, had I known my own. But I realize now how wrong I was to do this, to turn you without giving you a choice. I told Mom. She's furious with me, understandably. Please come back with us to the cabin so we can talk." Jimmy shifted again, the blur between forms so fast that even his father, who hadn't once looked away, would have difficulty believing what he had seen.

Jimmy approached his father slowly and rubbed against him, nuzzling his face when he didn't back away. Then, he gave him a quick lick. His dad looked like he was either shocked by the wolf affection or just didn't know what to do about it. David felt for him, recalling just how hard it had been for him and his friends when they had first been turned.

Then Jimmy moved away, and his dad still stood there as if he couldn't decide if he wanted their help or wanted to be by himself to figure this out. But David knew that with friends and family, he would adjust much better than being a lone wolf on his own. Candice could attest to that.

Mr. Warner finally began to follow Jimmy, his tail down, looking like a beta wolf. Jimmy's tail was straight out, confident, glad his dad was coming with them.

David and Elizabeth brought up the rear. When they finally reached the cabin, they waited for Jimmy and his dad to enter the house. Elizabeth and David followed.

Jimmy shifted and began getting dressed. Elizabeth and David shifted, too, so they could talk to Mel. He probably didn't have any ability to shift back at will right now. He was lucky he hadn't shifted while he was driving the car to the cabin.

"Sorry, Dad," Jimmy said, giving him a hug and burying his face in his dad's neck. "I just wanted to stay with you."

His dad licked Jimmy's hand and rubbed up against him. The quiet sound of muffled tears filled the cabin. Mel stood still, letting his son cry against him. Finally, Jimmy let go. His voice raw, he said, "I hired a private investigator to find you, worried you would get yourself hurt or killed. They're wolves like we are, so they were the only ones who could help me find you."

David and Elizabeth finished dressing. David stepped forward. "I'm David Davis, a private investigator with White Wolf Investigative Services. This is Elizabeth Alpine, my associate. She's a royal like your son, daughter, and wife, which means they have very few human roots mixed up in their genes. I'm more like you, bitten against my will, though it saved me when I was having a heart attack."

David sat down on the couch with Elizabeth, and Jimmy took a seat on a chair. Mel lay down on the floor, listening to David speak. He explained about the phases of the moon. He told Mel all about how he had been turned and about the difficulties he and his fellow PIs had had with their business because of it. "Not only did we have the shifting issues, but when we returned to Seattle, we learned a gray wolf pack lived there. They didn't want Arctic wolves living in their territory. And they didn't like that we were newly turned—dangerous to their kind. We had our established PI practice there, so we had to move to another location where we could manage the agency and still hide what we were. You probably won't be able to function in a job where you have to go to work on a regular basis. Online jobs are the way to go."

"We know it's a lot to take in," Elizabeth said. "All the changes, learning how to communicate with each other, learning about the good things—the increased longevity and faster healing abilities, better hearing and sight—but the shifting can be a real issue. Eventually, you'll have some control over it like David does. It just takes time. But you'll have Jimmy to help. And us."

Mel let out his breath, and David wished he knew what the man was thinking. But at least he had people to talk to who were knowledgeable about wolf shifter business. When David and his friends had been turned, they were all totally clueless.

Jimmy got a call on his cell phone. "It's Mom. Yeah, Mom, we found Dad." He glanced down at his dad. "He's a wolf and he hasn't been able to shift back. He's all right though, not hurt or anything... Yeah, at Granddad's cabin. We're staying here. Cass is at her friend's house. Okay, I'll tell him. We'll see you in an hour, then. We'll be right here. Love you, Mom." He ended the call. "She's coming here to help. You should know, she didn't have anything to do with this. If you're going to be mad at someone, it should be me."

"We mate for life as wolf shifters," David said, glad the wife was coming. He hoped the situation between the wife and husband would be resolved to everyone's satisfaction. "In other words, no divorce. The problem is she married you before you were a wolf. We have no unwritten rules about that. We're supposed to be with others of our kind to continue our species. Not only does that mean you don't have to remain with her since you were human when you married her, but you can try to find a wolf who would be interested in mating you too. It means for life, and we live very long lives."

Mel raised his wolf brows.

"Yeah, Dad. So if you and Mom can't get along, there's no sense in you staying with her. I never thought I would say that, but it's not fair to either of you. Maybe she's interested in seeing some other wolf. You might be happier with someone else too. I hate to say it, but it's true."

"Are you with a pack?" David asked Jimmy.

"No, not around here."

Then David told Mel where he knew of packs that were located elsewhere. "We'll help you find one that's suitable for you to join. They'll want you to be able to do some kind of work, something that won't be an issue when you shift, and you'll have to follow their rules to protect yourself and for them to protect themselves. But it'll be a good life. You can still have a good life."

Mel finally shifted, grabbed up his clothes, and headed for a bedroom.

When he returned, he ran his hands through his blond hair. He opened and closed his mouth three times before he settled on: "I–I don't believe any of this. Does anyone want any water?"

David thought Mel needed to be doing something, anything, while he tried to come to terms with this.

"Sure," Elizabeth said, David asking for some too.

Mel came back empty-handed, as if he'd completely forgotten what he went into the kitchen for. Knowing he had changed but unable to comprehend the extent of what had happened to him. "You're saying you've always been a wolf?" he asked Jimmy.

"Yeah, Dad. From birth. Whenever you were away on business trips, we would run to our hearts' content as wolves. One time you came home earlier than expected, and we were scrambling to shift and dress before you saw us."

"I remember that. Cass wasn't back and everyone was being kind of cagey about it."

"Yeah, she was hiding in the tree house until I could sneak her clothes out to her. I–I was hoping if you were one of us, you couldn't leave. That Mom couldn't divorce you. I never knew a wolf who married a human, so I didn't realize you both would have to decide if you would stay together. I thought it was a given."

"Your heart was in the right place." Mel rubbed the top of

Jimmy's head, and the tension David had been holding eased out of him. At least this part of Jimmy's case would have a happy ending.

"We can leave when your wife gets here or wait and see how things work out. She might want to just see you for a while as a wolf and maybe things will improve between the two of you," David said.

"I hope so. I love her and that hasn't changed. And I love my kids. They're like my own flesh and blood. This"—he gestured helplessly at himself—"doesn't change that either. It's just…a lot to wrap my head around," Mel said.

"That's understandable. Another thing you should know: if you are injured as a wolf, your blood will show you're a wolf, and as a human, fully human. But if you're killed as a wolf, you'll shift back into your human form," David said.

"Naked," Mel said.

"Correct. Also, we try not to ever get into criminal trouble that will land us in jail. For those who can control their shifting, it's bad enough to face confinement and not shift if someone's hassling you on the inside. But as a newly turned wolf, it'd be disastrous." He had an idea. "One of the packs that would be the best for a new wolf is the one in Silver Town. They run their own town. They take care of their own. You would be safer there."

"Not with your pack here?" Mel asked.

"As a lone new wolf, you might not find our pack to be the best fit right now. Almost all of us are newly turned, too, and wouldn't be able to look out for you the way you'll need it. But if you stick together as a family, and your wife and the kids are there to watch out for you, then sure, we could manage it. If others hadn't been there for us, I don't know what we would have done," David said.

"Which is why my friend and I have joined them. Neither of us have trouble shifting," Elizabeth said, taking hold of David's hand and squeezing. "We can run things while the other wolves are…wolves."

"Okay, so I need to quit my job."

"Yeah, probably. Accidentally shifting in the middle of a bakery might cause some comment," David said, trying to lighten the mood. "Plus driving can be a problem. You should have seen us trying to get from Maine to Seattle, and then learning we couldn't stay there either. The new moon is our friend, no shifting then. Though once you're used to being a wolf, you miss not being able to shift and run as a wolf then."

They all went out to sit on the porch and enjoy the view of the lake, the breeze blowing the fir tree branches, the geese flying overhead, the waves lapping gently at the shore. David hoped Mel could find some peace in all the beauty around them.

Mel finally broke the silence: "I have to tell you, when I was bitten, I thought Jimmy was a wild, rabid dog. Once it seemed like it was gone, I wrapped a towel around my arm and left to get a tetanus shot or whatever. But halfway to the hospital, my arm started tingling like crazy, and then I began to feel like I was burning up and I needed to strip off my clothes. I thought I was losing my mind." He laughed, but there wasn't much humor in it.

"I pulled off on a side road, yanked off my clothes, having no control over my actions, and the bandage came off. No wound at all." He took a deep breath, closing his eyes briefly. "And then I was a dog, or later I realized I was a wolf. I started to worry that maybe the wolf wasn't really gone from the house when I left. What if it went after Jimmy? Or jumped out at Cass or my wife when they got home? If a wolf could do this to me, then it could do the same thing to them. I've been going mad, thinking about it." He reached out, squeezing Jimmy's arm. "I'm glad you're safe."

"I'm so sorry, Dad," Jimmy said. "So sorry. I wasn't thinking, and I've messed it all up so bad. You could have had an accident or been shot, and it would have been all my fault."

"It's okay, Jimmy. I'm okay."

A car drove up on the gravel drive, and Jimmy raced down the steps to greet his mom. Mel stayed put. David thought he was afraid to speak with his wife about all this.

David wanted to give them their privacy, but he had to know if Jimmy's mother was going to take care of her husband or if they needed to contact the Silver Town wolf pack and see if they could take him in.

"Mel," she said, coming up on the porch with Jimmy. "I'm so sorry we didn't tell you about what we are, but we couldn't. And I didn't want to turn you, knowing this is what would happen. It wouldn't have been fair to you." She hugged him fiercely. "I'm so sorry."

"What now?" Mel asked, looking at her with tears in his eyes.

"We'll work things out somehow."

"If things don't work out, we'll find a pack for him to

join." David didn't want to leave this hanging, and he wanted her to know there were other options if she really didn't want to stay with her husband.

"Thank you. I guess Jimmy's got your number," she said to David.

"I do," Jimmy said.

"How much do we owe you?"

"Nothing. Call it a wolf favor. And if you ever need our assistance with another matter, be sure and give us a call." David handed her his business card. "I hope it all works out for you. All of you."

He and Elizabeth got into his vehicle, and she brushed away tears. "What's wrong?" he asked.

"Nothing. It was just touching to see Mel's relationship with his son, and I don't know, maybe even the mother will come around."

"It might take some work, but maybe it will turn out okay. Maybe she'd been distancing herself from him because he *wasn't* a wolf. Think of it. She would have had to watch him die. And explain why the hell she wasn't aging like he was. Could be she thought she was protecting him, and now she doesn't have to anymore."

"That could be, yeah."

"So maybe it will work out."

"I loved how you said he could join your pack if his family looks out for him. He looked so relieved. I didn't know your cases could be this... Well, I don't know. Real, I guess. Real people. Not like when doing background investigations for employment applications."

"Yes. We have some really great stories, where everyone's happy. But we also have not so great stories. It's really a mixed bag, and we never know which ones will turn out all right and which ones won't. Otherwise, I would give you and Sheri all the feel-good stories."

"But then you'd get all the tough cases. I would never want to do that to you."

He smiled at her. "But I'd have you to lift my spirits."

"Do you ever feel like you were meant to do something bigger? I felt like where I was I wasn't doing anything for anyone. I wasn't needed. Some of that was because I was on the outs with the community, with the wolf pack. But I kept feeling like I was needed to do something more important with my life once my grandmother was gone. She was what was important to me at the time. Her, and seeing you again."

"Helping us out *is* a big thing, Elizabeth."

"I'm glad we can do that for you, for our kind, especially since our own pack members turned you. Do you ever regret having to leave your own home to live here? It's so different from Seattle, I imagine."

"No. We've made a new home here. It's so much safer here for us than Seattle. Not only because of our shifting issues, but because we're white wolves. We don't blend in. All it would take was one picture of us running around the forest reserves in Washington and people from all over would be wanting to see us and trying to capture the white wolves on video. Not only that, but I could imagine scientists trying to capture and tag us."

"That happened once to Kintail. No one dared laugh to

his face, but there was a lot of laughing—good-naturedly—behind his back. Man, was he pissed."

David chuckled darkly. "I bet."

"Of course, we destroyed the tracker, and I'm sure the scientists wondered what had happened when he just disappeared off the radar. But then we worried the same thing could happen to any one of us, and it wasn't so funny."

The road underneath the Jeep turned from dirt to asphalt, the hum filling the air as they left the woods behind them.

"Hey," David said. "While we're out, why don't I run you by the bank and you can open a new account. And if you'd like, we could go shopping for a car for you. It's my treat. We'll take care of Sheri too. Then you can get around whenever you need to, without having to rely on me or another packmate. Think of it as being your signing bonus."

"Are you serious?"

"Yeah, I am."

"David, it's too much."

"No. You both need to feel free to do whatever you like. We want you to have that freedom."

"Thank you, David. You are the best."

"It wasn't just me. Everyone agreed. We always have pack funds for extra purchases, and Candice has a big inheritance. She was the one who suggested it first, actually. And I have a large trust fund I received when I was twenty-one and invested wisely. My mother had married a wealthy landowner in Australia, and she moved there to join him."

"Oh, you never told me that. But are you sure about buying cars for two of us?"

He smiled. "Believe me, she's happy that you are both taking over the job she and Faith would come in to do. Gives her more writing time."

"Okay, then I'll take you up on it."

They went to the bank first and Elizabeth opened an account with her new ID, thrilled David had taken care of all that. Then once she had her account established, she wrote a check off her Yellowknife account, not closing it yet because she had an employment check still being direct deposited into the account and some bills that were on autopay. She realized she also needed to talk with a real estate agent and start the process of selling her grandma's house. And she had to arrange for someone to sell her car.

Afterward, they went to a car dealership and she bought a blue Honda Odyssey, the pack's treat.

"So what's next?" she asked.

"Back to work. We're going to try and run down Ms. Lamont's biological mother." His stomach growled audibly, and he laughed. "But after lunch. Is fast food okay?"

"Yeah, sure, whatever you like. I like about anything."

"You love cheeseburgers," he said.

"You remembered."

"It's hard not to. It didn't matter where we wanted to stop, you had a craving for a cheeseburger."

She laughed. "No lies detected."

"I know just the place. You can follow me there."

She did, and once they arrived at the burger place, she parked her car next to his and joined him in his so they could go through the drive-through together.

Once they had their burgers, his bacon and hers cheese, they ate them in the car, the windows rolled down. "Sorry that we can't go in and eat inside," David said, "but at least this restaurant has trees shading the parking area."

"No problem. When the new moon is here, you can take me anywhere."

"That's a deal." And David realized that, ever so slowly, his fear over whether she would want to be with him after she saw his lack of control had vanished. She'd experienced it all firsthand and was still there, right next to him—and maybe she would be forever.

"You're right," Elizabeth said, breaking into his thoughts. "This is great." She took another bite of her burger.

"Yeah." He had to look away for a second. "It is."

A light squeeze on his thigh let him know she understood he was talking about more than burgers.

Just then, Gavin pulled through the drive-through. He smiled. "As you can see, we are all big fans of this place."

After Gavin got his order, he pulled his car around, parked next to them, and climbed into the back seat. "So what's going on with you?"

"We found Jimmy Warner's father. Jimmy had turned him, and we talked him down, made sure he understood what it all meant, what to expect." David filled Gavin in on the family's background. "Verdict's out on whether the family stays together or not."

"I've never heard of anything like it. What a mess."

"Yeah."

Gavin smiled at Elizabeth. "A cheeseburger, I see. Glad some things don't change."

She laughed. "Wow, I must have eaten a lot of cheeseburgers last time I saw all of you."

"We didn't think you ate anything else," Gavin said.

They ate in companionable silence for a bit.

"How's your case with Ms. Moore going?" David asked.

"I think her instincts are dead on. The business partner has a shady background, including money-laundering charges. Who knows what else. I'm still digging."

"Oh man," David said.

Elizabeth wiped her lips with her napkin. "Makes one wonder if Mr. Moore didn't die of natural causes."

"Sure does, doesn't it?" David agreed, crumpling up his wrapper. "Something else we're going to have to check into." He turned around to face Gavin. "Are you feeling all right?"

"Yeah, it's there, the urge to shift, but I'm handling it. I've got one more lead to check out, then I'm heading back into the office—just in case. The full moon pull eases off in the next day or so, but I hate taking chances," Gavin said.

David agreed with Gavin; he couldn't wait for the full moon phase to pass. Usually he just lived with it, but because he wanted to be with Elizabeth without constantly thinking about it, he was more anxious than ever to get past it.

"What are you up to after lunch?" Gavin asked.

"Heading back to the office too," David said.

"Maybe I should drop off my car at the house and then ride with Gavin," Elizabeth said.

"Sounds good to me," Gavin said, crumpling up his own wrapper and tossing it into the bag beside David. "Elizabeth can be my designated driver."

David smiled. "I think each of us needs one." He leaned over and kissed Elizabeth, and she kissed him back. "Okay, see you there in a bit."

Elizabeth and Gavin both got into their cars and left.

David rolled his shoulders, realizing again that the tension he typically felt this time of month, the worry for his packmates, wasn't as strong as it normally would be. Elizabeth had his back—had all of their backs—and man, did it feel good.

Chapter 16

Kintail seethed. Hans had reported back that Sheri's bags were gone from her apartment and some of her clothes had been cleaned out. That meant she had gone with Elizabeth and the others to the United States, he was certain. Then Bentley showed up, bad news written all over his face.

So what else was new?

Kintail said, "What is it?"

Even though Kintail's people could send him text messages or call him, the pack knew he wanted updates face-to-face. It was a way for him to see facial expressions and gauge whether they were being truthful with him.

What made him the angriest was that if Bentley had just mated Sheri, none of this would have been an issue. They needed some new blood in the pack—wolf pups—to continue their line. Kintail and his mate hadn't had any success so far, but maybe Bentley and Sheri could have.

Bentley said, "So, we checked Seattle and their PI agency, but they're not there. And haven't been for a while."

Damn it! Kintail prowled from one end of the living room to the other, his mind churning. Where? Where could they have gone?

"I was thinking we need to hire a private investigator to search for them." Bentley's voice was hesitant, as if he knew the reaction he would get from that suggestion wouldn't be favorable.

As much as Kintail hated the notion of hiring a PI because Cameron and his friends were all PIs and it just irked him, he figured that might be their best bet right now. His pack didn't have the resources or the training to find the runaway wolves. He had two police officers who had worked for him back in Maine, where some of Kintail's pack members had guided wilderness tours in the winter, but they wouldn't do him any good in Seattle—or wherever Cameron's pack had ended up.

"I could find one here in Yellowknife—" Bentley said.

"No. We start in Seattle, where we know they were." Kintail had done his own research, scouring David's Facebook page, taking particular notice of the lake in the pictures. But David was still showing his home as Seattle, and he never once mentioned the name of the lake. Kintail tried an image search, but there wasn't enough of the lake to go on.

He'd always doubted that story—that David had actually mated someone—and now Kintail was certain he hadn't. That it had all been a ruse to pretend that Elizabeth would have no reason to leave her pack and join him. Fake mate. Fake pictures. All to fool him.

Kintail growled, punching out at the wall in anger. Behind him, Bentley jumped.

"Okay, I'll get right—" Bentley said.

"Wait, the last contact they had with wolves was Leidolf and his red wolf pack in Portland, right?"

Bentley scratched his head. "You don't think Leidolf would have taken them in, do you?"

Kintail thought the red pack leader would be smarter than that. It would be difficult to keep the human population from knowing that a group of newly turned Arctic wolves were living in the Portland area. "I wouldn't think so. He's a sly wolf. But maybe they spent some time down there. It's the only lead I can think of, beyond them still being in the Seattle area. And truly, they probably couldn't hold their wolf forms well enough to manage their PI operations in Seattle. Maybe they are still in the area but are keeping themselves separate. Working remotely or something."

"Oh, sure, I didn't think of that."

Which is why Kintail was the pack leader. "You know if you and Sheri had just mated, we wouldn't be having this issue."

"I know. I've tried to convince her, but she just kept putting me off."

"She could be with another wolf right now." Kintail mentioned it to light a fire under Bentley if he needed one. "Or if not right now, she could soon mate another. So it behooves you to find her now."

"Okay, I'll hire a PI out of Seattle and tell him what we know about the men so far. And the reason we're trying to track them down?" Bentley looked a little flustered. No wolf liked to think the she-wolf they wanted to mate might throw them over for another wolf.

In the pack, Sheri hadn't shown any interest in the other wolves, though Kintail knew of one who was trying to get to know her better, if Bentley would just give her up.

"Do we need to give him a reason? No. Just do it."

"Yes, sir." Bentley left, and Kintail was feeling even more irritable.

Sheri was the type of she-wolf who would go along with just about anything. Whoever was more alpha could convince her to do what Kintail wanted her to do. Now she was being influenced by Elizabeth and Cameron and his people, and he wasn't going to stand for it without a fight.

Though if Cameron and his people were with Leidolf and his red wolf pack, that would cause more issues. Kintail knew Leidolf would go to bat for his own people and not cave to Kintail's demands. He didn't know how strong Leidolf's pack was, how many fighting wolves he had, so that could be a real problem. Whereas with Cameron and his men, they were few in number and they didn't stand a chance against Kintail's pack if they were on their own. Being newly turned, Cameron and his friends wouldn't fight as well either, not against royal wolves who had been born that way and had fought other wolf packs for ages.

So Kintail hoped Cameron and his pack were on their own. They just had to find them before Sheri ended up mating one of them! Elizabeth might be a lost cause—he could end David just for mating her—but he figured some of his pack members wouldn't approve.

But Sheri, she was another story. She should still be available, and he had to make sure she still was by the time they found her and brought her home.

While Elizabeth was out helping Gavin with his case, David decided to hold off on Ms. Lamont's case and instead took

Sheri over to the dealership. He also took her to the bank so she could set up her own banking accounts.

"I can't believe how wonderful it is being with your pack. Kintail would never have done anything like this for us," Sheri said. "Do you want me to park my new car at the office or somewhere else?"

"You can park at my house."

She gave him a hug and then followed him home in her new car.

With that taken care of, David started back in on the birth-mother case. Elizabeth and Gavin returned shortly thereafter. Gavin went into his office, and Elizabeth checked in with David to see if he needed anything.

"Yeah, let me bounce some stuff off you." Sheri was back at her desk, and he motioned for her to come in too. When she did, David continued. "Lisa Lamont was born on May 2, 2003, in Ely, at the local hospital," David said.

"So she's eighteen now and suddenly has a medical condition related to her parents?" Elizabeth asked.

"That's what she says. We have no reason not to believe her, but we need to keep in mind adopted kids, or adults, can be curious about who their real parents are, why they gave them up for adoption, and what they look like. We find very few actually want to meet with their biological parents when we locate them. They just had to know something about them. Others have met their parents, but they don't really feel any kinship with them. They weren't raised by them, don't have any real shared memories, and often have a different social and economic status. Sometimes, they form a bond with the birth parents, but in our experience, that's rare."

"Okay, so what you're thinking is that she's just curious about them and doesn't have any health issue?" Sheri asked.

"It's a possibility, that's all. Just something to keep in mind. Either way, we'll certainly try to find them as quickly as we can. There's nothing in the laws that says we can't locate the biological parents, even if they hadn't intended for the adopted child to learn who they are."

Sheri said, "Instagram! We need to check that, Twitter, Facebook, anywhere that the birth parents might have been on to see if we can locate them that way."

He nodded, then gave them the basics on how to track down possible information about the birth parents through the databases they were tapped into, though Sheri was right. These days, social media was the easiest way to get started.

They got right to work, and David did too. While David was doing research on the biological parents' case, Elizabeth and Sheri moved over to another computer and were looking into other databases to try to dig up something they could learn about the parents. He was glad they were really getting into the super-sleuthing business with him and his partners.

"Oh, here, what do you think?" Elizabeth asked. "A Reese Riley gave birth to a baby girl on that date. There were three baby girls born at the same time, but Reese didn't list a father."

"Yeah, that's a good possibility," Sheri said. "Let me write that one down."

Their eagerness made David happy. He left his desk to see what else they had learned.

"What do you think?" Elizabeth asked him. She showed him a post.

"Is that Reese Riley?" he asked.

"Yup. And check out the one daughter there."

He peered closely at the picture of a girl, younger than their client, but a spitting image of the picture Lisa Lemont had sent them of herself. He looked at the woman with her, clearly her mother. The resemblance seemed to be more than a coincidence.

"Yeah, that could be her mother. Looks like she goes by Reese Matthews now." He returned to his desk and began checking in his databases again, using the information Elizabeth had found on Facebook. Location: Denver, Colorado. Loved skiing and mountain climbing. Had three girls and sold online cosmetics. Her husband was a lawyer.

They seemed to be well off, so he wondered why the parents, if they were the client's parents, had given her up for adoption. There was no mention of any health conditions either the husband or wife had; as often as she posted, he figured she would have mentioned it.

No mention of giving a baby up for adoption, but he wouldn't have expected that. If this was her, she'd have been a teenager when she'd gotten pregnant. She looked young for being the mother of an eighteen-year-old.

Sheri had been busy looking at her own screen, and jumped up. "I have it! This woman, Reese, uh, Matthews now, left high school early. Before her junior year," Sheri said.

"Homeschooled?" Elizabeth asked.

"No, she posted about a private school," Sheri said.

David rubbed his chin. "What if she was forced to give up the baby? Parents, the school, people around her could have convinced her she didn't want to keep the baby because of her age. Especially if she didn't have support. It happened all the time. Still happens."

Sheri piped up again. "Okay, looks like she has a brother."

They looked up the brother on Facebook. Elizabeth said, "I wonder if she had a falling-out with her family." She pointed at the brother's profile. "He has pictures of himself with his parents several times for different occasions, birthdays, Christmas, Thanksgiving." She pointed at Reese's screen next. "While she only features pictures of her own family during all the holidays and for birthdays. They all live in Denver, so it's not like it's too far to visit."

"Okay, so that could be a good clue," David said. "Are the parents online? Do the parents say anything about family?"

"Hang on," Sheri said, tapping away on her keyboard. Her mouth pursed in concentration as her eyes moved across the screen. "Okay. The mom has a page. She doesn't post much, but seems like they..." Her eyes moved again. "Yeah, she only posts about the son and his family and about themselves. Nothing about the daughter and her family. Nothing about their three granddaughters."

"I want to call her adoptive parents and see what they can tell us about her parents—if they know anything. I'll check with our client first to make sure it's okay, even though she said I could contact them. She might have changed her mind," David said.

He went back to his office and placed the call. "We might

have found your birth mother, but we need to do some more digging to make sure. I want to speak to your adoptive parents to see if they might remember anything that would give us another clue about it."

Their client was silent for so long, David suspected she hadn't told them.

"If that's okay with you," he said.

She finally said, "Can't you just give me the name of the woman you found?"

"I'm sorry, no. We haven't verified anything definitively yet. But I know time is critical, since you need information for medical reasons."

Another long pause.

He sighed. "If this isn't for medical reasons, and you just want to learn about your mother, I understand."

Her heard a sniff on the other end of the line. "I only recently found out, you know?" she said. "That I was even adopted. I mean, I've wondered. For a long time, actually. My brother once said I don't look like anyone else in the family. His comment stayed with me for years. When I finally confronted my mom about it, she seemed shocked, but...yeah. She told me I was." There was another long pause, and David let her have the time. "I got angry. I felt lied to, and I felt... I don't know. We didn't talk, my parents and I, for a while. And things aren't too good now either, but I have to know. I just need to. That's all. For me. And for my baby."

David hesitated, then finally said, "You're pregnant?"

"Yeah. And when my mom found out, she said 'like mother, like daughter,' so I know my birth mom was young, maybe even younger than me. I want to know if my baby will have any medical complications or if my birth mother had any with me. And..." She sighed, then repeated, "I just need to know why."

"Listen, the most important thing to remember is your mom wanted you to have a good life with a family who could take care of you, maybe in ways she wasn't able to at that time. Hold on to that." He rubbed his eyes, tired, and his heart was breaking for this girl. "And if your adoptive mom knows your birth mom was young, there's more she might know, too."

"Okay," she said. "I think you should call them."

"Thanks, Lisa. Now, if I do verify the identity of your birth mother, I have to warn you that she might not want to see you. It's not that she didn't love you before she gave you away, but that she most likely hasn't told the rest of the family. *If* she has one," he quickly said, not wanting Lisa to get the impression he knew who her birth mother was for sure.

"I know," she said, but he wondered if she really did. Too many times he'd seen hopeful children hurt in situations like these. "Sorry for not being upfront with you about all this."

"No worries. We just want the best outcome for you—for you to feel some closure, whether you get together with your birth mother or not. And maybe have some peace of mind where your baby is concerned."

"Okay, thanks."

"I'll keep you posted." They hung up, and David took a deep breath. Jimmy had a happy ending; could he go two for two?

He told Elizabeth and Sheri what he'd learned about the case.

"I see what you mean when you say no telling how these cases are going to turn out," Elizabeth said.

"Yeah, and also: everybody lies," Sheri said.

David smiled, heading back to make the call to Lisa Lamont's adoptive mother.

He'd barely introduced himself when she said, "You're trying to find Lisa's birth parents, aren't you?"

David raised his brows. "Uh, yeah, she said it was okay to call you to ask some questions."

"Listen. Reese Riley is Lisa's birth mother. She was sixteen and wild. Reese and I were friends in high school. She would never tell me who got her pregnant. She might not have known who it was herself. My parents took in Lisa when she was just a baby, raising her as their own after Reese's parents disowned her. But they began to both have health issues, so when I was nineteen and married, I formally adopted Lisa from them. She was three years old at the time."

"You were young yourself," David said.

"I was. But I'd been told I couldn't have kids, which, newsflash, turns out I could, but I already loved Lisa, who'd always felt more like my daughter than my little sister. Besides, Reese's parents shipped Reese off right after Lisa was born, even though I know it crushed Reese, and it was clear they wanted nothing to do with Lisa, so it just made sense for her to be with me." She sighed. "I totally lost track of Reese after that. I don't know what her married name is now, or if she's even married. She could be dead for all I know.

"I feel terrible about what I said to Lisa when I found out she was pregnant. I said it in a moment of anger, and as soon as the words were out of my mouth, I realized how much I must have sounded like Reese's parents. I never want her to feel unloved like Reese must have. I want to be there for her and the baby."

"Well, Lisa wants to learn about her birth mother and wants to know if she's going to have any medical difficulties with having the baby. I can tell her what you've told me, or you can. Which would you prefer?" David asked.

"I'm afraid things might not go well between us if it's just the two of us. Can we meet in your office and discuss this? You could be the mediator."

"Yeah, sure. Do you want to call Lisa and ask her when she would like to come in? I'm free all afternoon," David said.

"I'll call her and talk to her about meeting with her at your office. I'll let you know what she says," Ms. Lamont said.

David hung up, hoping Lisa and her mom—her adoptive mom—could work it out. There was clearly a lot of love there.

He told Sheri and Elizabeth what he had learned.

"Okay, so if she had just asked her adoptive mother in the first place, she wouldn't have incurred any investigative charges," Sheri said. "Do we still get paid?"

David smiled. "Yeah. She signed a contract. But beyond that, if the woman on Facebook is the mother, the two of you did locate her. We'll have the discussion in my office to wrap up matters. After that, it's up to Lisa to reach out to her birth mother or not. We don't have to take any part in that."

"So is Reese the same woman we found on Facebook?" Sheri asked.

"I would say so, but when Mrs. Lamont comes in, I'll get a confirmation." David's phone rang.

"We'll come at two, if that works fine for you," Mrs. Lamont said.

"It does. Thanks. And I'll send a picture of Reese Matthews to you to see if you can identify her as your friend," David said. "Hold on."

It was quiet for a minute while David sent a link to the Facebook profile, and Mrs. Lamont got it. "Yeah, that's her... Oh wow, she even has a couple of pictures on there with me when we were kids at the beach and on a hike, about a year before she got pregnant."

"Maybe your friendship isn't really over."

Mrs. Lamont agreed. "Okay, we'll see you in a little while."

"Okay, see you then."

David gave a satisfied sigh, glancing at a wall calendar to check the day. Everything had been so crazy lately, he'd kind of lost track of things. It was a Friday. If he could wrap up the Lamont case, he would be free to do something special with Elizabeth. Maybe even all weekend long. In any event, he planned to do as much as he could with her, to show her the area, to spend some downtime with her, and just enjoy being with her.

The guys all covered for each other if they had something special they wanted to do with their significant others, or even if a couple of the guys wanted to do something, so he was certain they would take any cases that needed immediate attention over the weekend.

He glanced out the window of his office at her, watching as she and Sheri chatted while tackling yet more of their paperwork. He reminded himself he didn't want to overwhelm her with doing too much. He didn't need to cram it all into one three-day weekend.

David had started poking around in a case of a man allegedly cheating on his wife when Mrs. Lamont and Lisa arrived to speak with him, early. He didn't mind early, though, especially when he saw both women looked like they had been crying. But they smiled at him and it seemed that maybe things between them had somewhat been resolved.

They sat in the chairs beyond his desk and he said, "Lisa, your mom has stated that Reese Matthews, formerly Reese Riley, is your birth mother."

Mrs. Lamont reached over and squeezed Lisa's hand, then told Lisa everything she knew. From their tearful expressions, he had thought they might have already discussed it.

"I'm so sorry, Mom," Lisa said. "I should have just talked to you."

Mrs. Lamont scoffed. "I don't blame you, after what I said. I think we really needed this intervention." She brought out her checkbook. "I'll pay whatever costs you've incurred over this."

"Thanks, Mom. How do you feel about me getting in contact with Reese?" Lisa asked.

"It's up to you, but after you meet with her, I would like to get in touch with her too."

"Do you think you'll ever be friends again?" Lisa asked.

"I don't know. But it's worth a try."

Lisa sighed. "Well, when I get in touch with her, I want you to be there with me."

Her mom smiled and gave her a hug. "I will be, whatever you need. For you and the baby. I can take care of him or her while you're getting a degree—because I still want you to do that. You'll live at home with us, like you'd planned before. It's all good." They shook David's hand and left the building, arms around each other.

Elizabeth smiled at them as they walked out and gave David a hug. He could get used to this.

"They don't all turn out that way," he said.

"But it sure is nice when they do," Elizabeth said.

"It's possible that Reese won't want to have anything to do with either her daughter or her friend from so long ago, but you never know. She might, and her birth mother might even be there for her grandchild too."

"That would be good." Elizabeth leaned back in his arms, her smile contagious. "By the way, thank you for taking Sheri to open a bank account and helping her to buy a car. She said you got a good deal for her too."

"You're welcome. I didn't want her to feel left out. About tonight... We've had such a whirlwind of activity that I didn't even realize it was Friday night. I should have mentioned it before, but I was thinking we could get a bite to eat at home for dinner and then paddle out to the island in the middle of the lake, then figure out how we want to spend the weekend."

Gavin spoke up from his office. "We'll handle anything that comes up so that the two of you can have some fun. As much as you have covered for us so that the rest of us can spend time with our mates or families, it's well deserved. We all agreed to this. Plus we already stole Sheri for the night. Amelia and I invited her over for dinner."

"Oh, yeah, I need to visit more with Amelia—and Gavin—after our wild escape mission. I have to thank her for saving us from Kintail and the rest of his thugs," Sheri said.

Elizabeth gave her a hug. "You'll have a good time."

"I will, and so will you. The two of you need this time together." Sheri went back to—what else—filing.

"Thanks, Gavin." David hadn't wanted to assume anything, not knowing exactly what their caseload looked like. He was down to the one case for now, the cheating husband case, and that could wait until Monday, but that didn't mean his partners had the same leeway.

"Thank you, Gavin," Elizabeth added.

"See you later," Gavin said, and Owen and Cameron chimed in, too, from their respective offices.

Sheri gave Elizabeth another hug and then went back to work, looking completely at ease among her new packmates.

The sun was still bright overhead as David and Elizabeth headed outside. Normally, he left late in the day, tying up any and every loose end before heading home...because he didn't have anyone to go home to. Or else he'd have dinner with one of the families, lingering with his friends for the same reason. But now? Now he had Elizabeth to spend time with. And Elizabeth to go home with. It could just be the two of them. Not always, of course. He wasn't selfish that way. They'd both do their own things, spend time with others. He was happy to share her with the family.

But as he slipped his hand in hers as they walked back to his cabin, talking about what they could make for dinner, he thought sometimes it was nice not sharing too.

Chapter 17

Once they arrived back at the house, David and Elizabeth both headed for the bedroom to change to go boating. Though every time she began stripping off clothes, unless it was to shift into her wolf—well, even then—David had to fight getting sidetracked.

"So what do I need to wear?" Elizabeth stood in front of her closet, hands on hips.

Smiling, he pulled off his dress shoes, shirt, and trousers and gave her a suggestive glance.

She chuckled. "I know. For you, nothing at all." She motioned to his boxer briefs. "I feel the same way about you. But for canoeing and the island, what's best to wear?"

He grabbed a pair of board shorts out of his drawer. "Swimsuit, shorts, shirt, light jacket for tonight if you think you'll feel chilly. I'll gather the rest of the stuff together, but I thought we could roast marshmallows on a campfire, swim, and hike as wolves on the island."

She decided on a bikini while he pulled on his board shorts, then grabbed a bag to carry the rest.

"Hiking shoes too," he added, "though we'll be exploring the woods as wolves, most likely, but just in case we make a trek in our human forms, they're the best to wear."

"Okay, sounds great."

David couldn't wait to take advantage of it being summer and the days being so much longer. More time to show Elizabeth the things he liked to do in summer. Even though they could see well at dusk and dawn, he still wanted to show her what it would be like during the daylight hours. "Have you ever paddled before?"

"No," she said. "But I love boating and being on the water, so I'm looking forward to doing this with you."

"I'll show you the ropes. It's easy. Before we were turned, the guys and I did a little of everything. Whitewater rafting, mountain climbing, hiking, canoeing. The only difference now is we can do the hiking as wolves too. So when we reach the island—that will take us an hour or so—we can strip and shift and run as wolves all over it."

"That sounds like fun. This truly is the perfect place to be wolves."

"It is. We have rock climbing nearby too."

After they had a dinner of stir-fried rice and beef and bell peppers, they cleaned up the dishes. David packed up some gear: food, water, beach towels, the first aid kit, a sleeping bag, a small tent—just in case they stayed overnight—and a tarp. He also grabbed a couple of life jackets. They carried all the stuff out to the boat shed. They hauled out the canoe and paddles, threw the backpacks and other gear over their shoulders, then brought it all down to the shore.

"Sure is easier doing this with two people than one," David said as they set the canoe on the shoreline. "I think that's it unless there's anything else you want to take with you."

"I'm good."

"I'll be the stern paddler," he said, "since I'm heavier and know how to do this. You are the bow paddler."

They loaded the gear into the boat and pushed the boat farther into the water, the stern just touching the bank.

Before they got in, they slipped on their bright-orange life jackets.

David steadied the boat by holding the stern between his legs. "Now, just step in, keeping to the middle, and sit on the bow seat there. Hold onto the gunwales, the top edge of the hull of the boat, while you're moving around so you don't fall overboard."

"Okay, I think I've got this."

Once she was seated, David held onto the gunwales and placed one foot into the boat. Then he pushed away from the shore with the other foot and climbed aboard.

They heard a loon on the lake some distance from where they were as they paddled silently, the breeze-stirred waters bumping at the blue canoe, Elizabeth's light-brown hair tousled and caught in the breeze. She was as beautiful as he had remembered. Gone was the fear of Kintail and his minions. She was happy, and he couldn't have asked for anything more.

"This is so peaceful," she said. "So nice to relax like this after dealing with the cases you have to handle."

"It is. We all love to come out here. Eventually we'll teach the kids how to paddle, but it's great for romantic interludes too."

She raised her brows at him.

"Not that I've had any."

Elizabeth laughed. "Okay." They drifted for a moment, letting the breeze push them along. "Does the lake freeze over in winter?" she asked.

"Yeah. So that means ice-skating."

"Now, that I can do."

He smiled. "Good. That was something we all had to learn to do. The kids are learning too."

"You said you go whitewater rafting?" she asked.

"Oh yeah, we have a couple of places we go. Have you done that?"

"Nope, but I would love to try. The kids are too little, aren't they?"

"Yeah. We go when our shifting isn't an issue, and we take turns watching the kids."

She smiled. "I can see you are good with the kids."

"We always volunteered to work with the kids at special events when we were on the police force in Seattle. I think a lot has to do with being shifters, sure, but some of it has to do with parent issues growing up. At least for me."

Elizabeth didn't say anything to that, but he could see the thoughts churning. Instead of following that line of conversation, though, she said, "So you go whitewater rafting with your friends?"

"Yes. It's more fun with all of us there, and we all have a good time with the kids too." He smiled, remembering the last time they went. "Corey gets into more trouble because he's not afraid of anything. Or he likes to pretend he isn't. I've seen him jump straight in the air when he was a wolf and a butterfly landed on his nose. And then he quickly looked around to see if anyone saw him being so un-alpha-like."

She laughed. "I can just see it. Do the three kids ever flip the alpha role among themselves?"

"Oh, sure. When Corey was lost, Angie was all alpha until he returned home. She had taken on the role and bossed Nick around as soon as Corey had disappeared. Someone had to be the boss. When Corey returned to the pack, it took him a while to resume his position as top wolf among the siblings. We've never witnessed that before, so it has been a real learning experience for all of us."

"I bet. Especially for Corey."

"Yeah, he was reluctant to stray from home for too long after that. Now he's back to his indomitable self."

She laughed.

They enjoyed the peaceful solitude again. He'd paddled out here countless times, even with a couple of kids in the boat, or with one of his buddies. But being with Elizabeth made it extra special.

When they were closing in on the island, they steered straight to the shore, head on.

"Okay, what we need to do is everything in reverse to get out. Stay low and slide your hands along the gunwales, or 'gunnels' some call them, for support. Take a step at a time, keeping your feet placed on the center line of the canoe. Then you can stabilize the boat for me, and I'll walk the entire length of the canoe to get out."

"Whoa," Elizabeth said as she stood up, wobbling a bit and pinwheeling her arms for balance. "Okay, I got this." She leaped out, hands raised above her head like a champion boxer when she found her footing. Her excited laugh was contagious.

David followed, and they carried all their gear up to the campsite. Then they carried the canoe up to a spot under the trees since they were going to spend several hours there, though he had thought of staying overnight if Elizabeth liked the idea. He figured even if they didn't, they could use the tent for extracurricular activities, if the mood struck. And man, did he ever hope the mood struck.

He pulled the Arctic wolf towels out of one of the backpacks and set them on the bench he and Owen had handcarved before Candice had come into his life. Cameron, Faith, and Gavin had made the other.

"This is so neat," Elizabeth said. "It's like your own private getaway, minus the cabin."

"Yeah, we had fun doing it. Did you want to run as wolves first? Then swim?"

"Then make love?" She motioned to the sleeping bag and tent.

He smiled. "Great minds..."

"That sounds good to me." She moved into the woods to strip off her clothes and shift into her wolf.

Even though they hadn't heard any sounds of anyone out here, that didn't mean they didn't have to be careful. Anyone could pull up in a canoe of their own at any time. But this particular evening, he heard no one talking, didn't smell any smoke from anyone's fire, and there was nothing to indicate anyone else was here.

Still. He joined her in the woods, quickly jerking off his sandals and shorts, boxer briefs and T-shirt, only to see her shift and stand there watching him hungrily as a wolf. He smiled and shifted. They greeted each other as wolves do, as if they hadn't been together all this time. It was just an innate thing and he loved it.

He took off running, Elizabeth at his heels, as he showed her the rest of the island. They explored all the nooks and crannies along the shoreline first. When they came to an area full of stacked rocks, she ran back in the woods and shifted, then hurried back to the shore so she could stack her own rocks. At first unsure as to what she was up to, he quickly shifted, joined her, and helped add more rocks—seven in all. Once they had made their own creation, they shifted back into their wolves.

They raced around the whole island, chasing each other back and forth. Sometimes they had to swim along the shore where the trees were growing down to the water's edge. And then he took her for a slower inspection of the interior of the island. A few trails had been made—wolf trails, all of them carrying the pack members' scents. But he smelled a bear too, a black bear's recent scent, and David paused, Elizabeth stopping right beside him as they both sampled the air, their tails held out still, their ears twitching back and forth as they listened for any sign that the bear was still there.

Two wolves could chase off a bear, but if it was a sow with her cubs, that was a different story. Still, he hadn't smelled but one bear's scent and it was male. David doubted a mother bear would swim all the way out here with cubs.

David started to walk again, searching for the most recent scent trail the bear had left behind and still not smelling any other bears.

Elizabeth was right behind him, and he knew she would back him up if he got into a confrontation, but he hoped it wouldn't come to that.

He always brought an emergency first aid kit with him in case anyone was injured, a flare gun, too, that he could use to warn off the bear. Not to injure it, because they deserved to live in the area as much as the wolves did. But to scare it off so neither of them—the wolves or bears—had to fight. Nonetheless, David's instinct was to search for the bear, and that kept him moving forward. He found evidence of where the bear had torn red berries off some sarsaparilla vines, his black and brown fur snagged on the heavily spined plant and on a dense thorny thicket of raspberries nearby.

David finally reached the shore, Elizabeth coming up beside him, and both of them saw the big black bear swimming back to the mainland, far away from them and their gear.

They lay side by side on the rocky shore, tails waving, watching the majestic animal paddle away.

David nudged Elizabeth's face and she licked his nose. He smiled at her, stood up, and waited for her to follow him. But she didn't move, her gaze locked on the bear, as if she just couldn't look away, should he return.

David gave her a little woof. She let her breath out, stood, stretched, and joined him. Then they raced back on one of the trails to their camp.

As soon as they arrived, Elizabeth darted past David and splashed into the water. He watched as she shifted in the lake, her silky brown hair floating all around her.

He smiled and raced in after her, splashing her before he shifted and pulled her into his arms. The kiss they shared was soft, wet, and glorious.

"Wow, I never imagined running into a bear here. You didn't tell me you had bears on the island." She peppered kisses along his jaw, his neck, his collarbone, her arms wrapped around his waist as they treaded water.

"We've smelled them on the island before, but we've never actually seen one. And we've made dozens of trips here."

"What else haven't you told me about?" She raised her brows, but she was smiling, appearing more interested than worried.

"A cougar, on occasion. Moose. We spied a fox once and chased off a couple of coyotes. They were not claiming rights in our territory. The moose can be dangerous, so that was an interesting situation. All of the critters were on the mainland though, not on the island."

"No alligators or crocodiles, right?"

He chuckled. "No."

"Okay, good. I can handle about anything else, but the idea a predator might come after us in the water—that's another story. I didn't smell any other recent signs of bears, just the one, but I still wanted to make sure he didn't return to the island."

"Yeah, I was afraid you were going to want to stay there all night if you had to."

"No, just long enough to make sure he was far enough away so that we could do this and not worry about him changing his mind and swimming back."

"He won't." David kissed her cheek. "Did you know they say that to be attracted to your mate, you have to think of your mate in an attractive way? In other words, sure, the physical stuff is nice, but it's your inner beauty that caught my full attention. When I first saw you, when Owen and I were locked up in your pack's lodge, you had this look about you that said you hated what Kintail was doing with us, that you wanted to help us in the worst way. But you were afraid to help us in the beginning."

"I wasn't sure whether to free you or not. It was a dangerous proposition, and not just for me. I had to worry about my grandma, how she would be treated if I was found out. And I could have been putting the rest of wolfkind in danger by letting the two of you loose on the world. But...there was just something about you." A droplet of water caught on her eyelashes, and he was mesmerized by it. By her. "I knew it was crazy to have such strong feelings for you when I barely knew you, but I did consider that if you ended up in my world in Yellowknife, we could...date."

She blinked, and David kissed the corner of her eye, catching the droplet before it vanished. "I would have, if it had only been me and I hadn't had buddies I was worried about."

"Yeah, I know. And that's why I love you."

He hugged her close. "If it had been you and Sheri—"

"Oh, yeah, I thought of her too. That if she had been locked up, I would have done anything to free her."

"And if you had been caged, she would have done the same for you."

Tears filled Elizabeth's eyes. "She did. By helping me to escape Kintail and the pack this time."

He kissed her again, her mouth against his pressuring him to allow her entrance.

And he parted his lips for her, taking in her tongue, stroking it, tasting her essence as she was tasting his. Her legs wrapped around his hips and she had to feel what she was doing to him, his erection already steel-hard. He ached to sink himself into her, to mate, to make it forever. But until she was ready for that, he would continue to make love to her like this. To enjoy her on any terms until the time was right. Everything he did with her, he hoped, would convince her that he was the only one for her.

He moved his hand to her breast and massaged, the warm water surrounding them, the breeze stirring it, causing little waves to caress them. He moved to her other breast and massaged. She practically purred.

He had to keep his legs moving, though, to keep them from drifting too far from the shore or the campsite. He could envision getting so lost in kissing her that they would drift off and then have to make a long swim back as either humans or wolves. That wasn't part of his plan for seduction.

She reached down and cupped his buttocks and gave him a squeeze. He kissed her jawline and her neck down to where the water touched it. He was so ready for her, to bring them both to climax. He should have set up the tent first!

"Ready to go in?" he asked, his words rough with need.

"Hmm, and continue this other 'discussion' inside the tent?" She smiled at him. "Only if we're going to do more of this."

"I love it when we're both thinking along the same lines." He kissed her and then released her. "I'll get the tent set up for a little bit of privacy just in case some boaters happen by."

"That sounds like a good idea. I would hate to be caught on camera."

Then they swam in to shore, and once they were standing on their feet, he swept her up in his arms and carried her to the bench and their beach towels.

"Such a romantic," she said, kissing the drips of water clinging to his chin. "I love it."

"Only for you." He wrapped her in a towel, hating to cover her up but noticing goose bumps from the lake breeze. "I'll start a fire after we're done and before we paddle in for the night." They dried off and spread out their towels on the bench to dry. She helped him with the tent, and it went up in record time. Once inside, he grabbed the sleeping bag, rolled it out, and opened it up. She zipped the tent closed behind them and then they were on the sleeping bag, and without a single word between them, they came together.

He ran his hand over her breasts, his thumb and forefinger rolling a nipple between them, the sweet buds already peaked. He would never tire of this, of her. He slid his hand down her back and then her buttock as they faced each other, resting on their sides on the double sleeping bag.

He bent his head and tasted and teased her nipples with

his mouth and tongue. She combed her fingers through his hair and moaned softly as he lavished attention on them.

He swept a hand down her side until he was at her hip, then slipped his hand between her legs. He kissed her as she moved her leg aside for him so he could pleasure her like he'd done before, only this time on an island in the middle of the lake with the loons calling out to each other as the sun began its slow descent into the woods beyond. The water lapped at the shore and the breeze whispered soft caresses against their skin through the screened windows.

He heard the honking of a flock of geese flying high overhead, but the only sound he cared about was the soft gasp Elizabeth made any time he touched her just…like…

That.

Elizabeth's breath caught, and it was the most beautiful sound in the world.

Chapter 18

David absolutely bewitched Elizabeth. She couldn't think of another term that better described the way she felt about him. She had never had much of a sexual appetite for male companionship, and she had figured it was just her. But with David, that was the farthest thing from the truth. She didn't feel that way about anyone else, only him. A heated gaze, a sexy wink, a smoldering smile, and he had her hooked. And it was good. Oh so good. She deserved this, deserved him.

He began to slide his remarkable fingers over her clit and stroked with precision and finesse, working her up to a climax. It was amazing having this experience with him away from civilization, out in the wild, away from the rest of the pack; it couldn't have been any more perfect than this.

He claimed her mouth again as he continued to stroke her, and she wanted in the worst way to just say screw it and let's mate. She kept holding back. Why?

Her mind went blank; what he was doing was taking her to another plane of existence. One filled with exquisite pleasure.

She ran her hand over his hip, feeling his buttock, and he worked on her faster, harder, stroking her to completion.

She cried out, the sound echoing across the lake. It made her feel wild, untamed, and every bit an animal in human form—and she loved it.

Then she was straddling him, stroking him as he ran his hands over her thighs, his fingers squeezing in rhythm with her movement, his face tight with need.

She began to stroke him faster, with just the right pressure, enjoying this as much as she enjoyed coming, the way the fading light fell across his face through the tent's screen door, the way the sun's golden rays cast oranges and reds and purples across the rippling lake water.

The loons' intriguing calls were fading, but she heard the sound of an owl hooting from far away and another answering its call.

Being out here like this was a real joy; bringing David to orgasm, the same. She moved off him, still holding on to his flagpole-stiff erection and continued to stroke him. But she needed to kiss him too. And she did, sliding her tongue in his mouth, and he was sucking on hers, caressing her tongue with his.

"Yes," David gritted out against her mouth, and then he exploded. He pulled her on top of him and just held her close, cuddling with her within his powerful embrace, and for some time they just lay there, listening to each other's rapid heartbeats and the sounds of the cicadas singing in the tall grasses in the woods getting more raucous.

"God, this couldn't have been any more perfect," David said. "Being here with you."

"Just beautiful." She kissed his cheek.

"Are you ready for me to build a fire? Do you want to roast marshmallows?" he asked.

"Yeah." She wanted to stay like this forever, just glued to him in an embrace, but she knew they needed to paddle back home. Unless they just stayed out here for the night. "But first, a dip in the lake."

Then she moved off him, unzipped the tent, shifted into her wolf, and ran off to take a dip in the water to wash off. He shifted in the privacy of the tent, too, and joined her.

When they returned to dry off, they grabbed their towels in their mouths and went into the woods. Two well-trained white dogs, if anyone were watching from a distance. Then they shifted back into their human forms and dried off.

"Did you want to stay the night? Out here?" she asked. Away from the pack. Just the two of them. She hoped he would.

"I was hoping you might like to. I brought some oatmeal and brown-sugar oatmeal bars for breakfast, just in case. Bottles of water, no coffee or tea, but we can get that when we paddle the canoe back in tomorrow." David thought she might like to, but he hadn't wanted to ask her until she had a chance to see the island for herself first. He remembered taking a girlfriend camping—when he was still human—and she'd abhorred the whole camping experience. The smoke from the fire. No mattress to pad the earth. It had been a bit buggy, hot during the day, rainy, and then cold at night, and she'd only brought a silky nightie. She'd immediately wanted to go to a hotel. So he wasn't taking it for granted with Elizabeth that she would love the great outdoors, even though she was part wolf.

She smiled, took a deep breath, and let it out. "This is why I like you so much. You and I truly do think along the same lines."

"We do. We can set up the tarp to cover the tent in case it rains. It's not supposed to, but we can set it up anyway."

"Sure, that will protect us from the wind too. I noticed the place you set the tent up was incredibly smooth, not rocky, no twigs, soft even. I was expecting some lumps and bumps like when I normally would go camping in the parks around Yellowknife."

David was so glad she was used to camping. "Yeah, we have several 'bedding' areas that we made so we can sleep out here without bringing air mattresses or anything. I didn't want to let on how we like to have the comfiest spot while sleeping out in the wilderness. It's not wolf-like at all."

She chuckled. "Even wolves like to get comfortable." Then she glanced out at the lake. "You don't think the bear will come back tonight, do you?"

"I doubt it. They're usually out at dawn and dusk. But I'll hang the food in a tree anyway, so we don't have to worry while we're sleeping."

They dressed inside the tent, then started to collect some kindling to build the fire. They piled it on top of the log in the firepit, and David got it going with a lighter.

He pulled out the bag of marshmallows and the extendable forks, and they sat down next to each other to roast marshmallows.

"Do you do this often with the others?" she asked.

"Sure. A few times during the summer. But we also give each other the space to do this on our own. Even Faith and Cameron come here without the kids, just to get away and have time to themselves. We are all happy to babysit."

Elizabeth's face turned thoughtful, almost sad, and he wondered if she was thinking of him out here by himself, when everyone else would have their mates with them.

Whatever she was thinking, she shook it off. "Have the kids been here, though? I thought I smelled a faint scent of them."

"Yeah, we've brought them a few times. We have to pack more for the trip, and we take all the canoes, and then it's a fight about which kid gets to go with which adult or adults."

She chuckled. "The kids fight over the adults or the adults fight over the kids?"

"Oh, it's a back-and-forth thing. The kids love it. But we plan to bring them out some more this summer since they're getting older."

They poked their marshmallows into the fire; hers caught fire, and she quickly blew it out, laughing. "It's still good that way, nice and melted on the inside."

He agreed.

They ate about three apiece and shared a bottle of water between them. Before it got too late, he called Cameron. "Hey, we're safely at the island, but we're staying the night."

Elizabeth washed their forks and packed them away in the backpack when she was done.

"Okay, let us know if you get into any trouble. Did you take anything with you for breakfast?"

"A little bit. We'll be fine."

"Well, we can remedy that in the morning if you would both like."

David smiled. "You guys are the best. And thanks. Oh, and we spotted a male black bear on the island. He swam off earlier, but just to let you know."

"No chance of it returning tonight?" Cameron asked, sounding concerned.

"I doubt it." David appreciated his friend's concern. "But if he does, we'll shift and chase him off. Night, Cameron."

"That sounds like a good idea. Night, David."

Even though the early night sky was clear, he and Elizabeth set up the tarp over the tent just in case. Then he hoisted the backpack high into a tree nearby to keep the bear, if it should return, from getting it.

The camp secure for the night, they crawled into the sleeping bag together, and with the tent flap open so they could see out through the screen door, they watched the sun set, the sky darkening, the stars appearing.

"This is magical," she said, his arm behind her neck, and his other hand behind his head like a pillow.

"With you here, it truly is." And though he'd had a lot of memorable experiences with his buddies camping over the years, this one topped them all.

A shooting star raced across the midnight-blue sky, and Elizabeth made a wish. That she and David would be mated wolves before long and they would be together for a very long time. "Did you make a wish?" she asked, her voice soft. She didn't want to chase away the magic or wake him if he had chanced to fall asleep before she did. This was just too nice, and she didn't want to close her eyes and sleep for anything.

"Yeah. You?" His voice was dreamy.

"Absolutely." She had texted Sheri earlier to tell her that they were staying on the island tonight, and of course her friend told her just to mate already, which had made Elizabeth smile.

For a long time, they just lay there watching the beauty of the sparkling lights, their fire slowly dying. The water lapping against the shore, swimming, hiking, canoeing, and being out in the sunshine during the day and making love, of course, had made Elizabeth sleepy. Though she wanted to live in this moment forever and watch the twinkling stars all night long, she finally curled up next to David and fell asleep.

The next morning, David heard the paddling of canoes headed in their direction and laughter from the kids, Angie saying "There they are! Right there!"

David smiled and glanced over at the other half of the sleeping bag where Elizabeth had been when she'd gotten a little too hot snuggled up next to him. She was gone! Suddenly, he thought of the bear dragging her away and he jumped up from the bedding, even though he smelled no sign of the bear in the tent. "Elizabeth!" He was throwing on a pair of boxer briefs in a hurry and leaving the tent.

"I'll be right there. I was just getting some business out of the way on the other side of the island," she called out, and he heard her moving in his direction, but still out of view. "Don't worry. I didn't return to Yellowknife."

He sighed with relief, his heart returning to a normal beat. "You didn't take the canoe. I was more worried about the bear coming back."

She came into view and she was as lovely as ever, even though she looked like they'd made love all night long last night, her pretty hair tousled. She began braiding it, as if she knew just how she looked.

"You would have heard a lot of racket if that had happened. Wolf growling, biting." She smiled at him and he gave her a hug and a kiss.

"Yeah, and I would have been there with you to chase him off. Did you have a good night's sleep?" He slipped back into the tent and finished getting dressed.

"Yeah, the best. And you?"

"I did. Listening to the water lapping at the beach, snuggled with you, it was the best. I can't believe you slipped away without disturbing me though."

"We were all tangled up together, but I was very careful to untangle myself, one limb at a time, without waking you. I think you were dead tired though."

"Oh, I thought you had gotten hot and moved away from me."

"No. I just had to go to the bathroom."

"Have you been up for very long?" He still couldn't believe he slept through her leaving him.

"Yeah, for a while. I left my clothes in the woods, shifted, and ran along the trail to check for any more bear signs. I didn't want any surprise attacks. Then did my business."

He nodded out toward the lake. "The crew is coming. I'm going to find where you went and—"

"Scent mark over my spot. I know how possessive you males are."

He laughed. Yeah, they were, and when it came to Elizabeth, he definitely was. He headed into the woods.

When he returned to the campsite, he found that Elizabeth had rolled up their sleeping bag and set it outside. She had started the fire too. She was the perfect camping mate. He helped her take down the tent and secure it; then they went in search of more kindling and firewood for when the others arrived.

"I saw everyone coming, the kids excited to see us. Do you always do things like this?" She was picking up more twigs.

"It's kind of a ritual, I guess. I hadn't thought of it, but in the past, after we had our homes built and during the summer, Cameron and Faith came to spend the night at the island. We asked if they would like breakfast, and they thought it was a lovely idea. They were already mated way before then, of course. Then when Owen and Candice were together, they wanted to wait until summer and then they paddled out and stayed overnight. When we asked them if they wanted us to bring them breakfast, they said no way!" He grabbed up some fallen branches.

Elizabeth laughed.

"They told us to wait until lunchtime, so that's what we did. By then it was a tradition, and Gavin and Amelia expected it of us. Of course with you, this time is different because we're not mated. But they still want to show us a good time."

"And maybe hope we mated during the night?" She arched a brow.

He smiled. "I'm sure there is that."

"Well, if things keep going the way they are, I'm guessing that won't be long. We can do this again, and they can bring breakfast, or lunch, to a newly mated couple."

"Hot damn, yes!"

She chuckled.

The canoes arrived at the shoreline, everyone yelling greetings, the kids not bothering to wait to jump out, getting their feet wet and not caring one bit.

David was glad to see Slade and Sheri in one of the canoes.

"No flight this morning?" David asked.

"One of our standby pilots took over for me since I said we had a really special event planned." Slade glanced at Sheri as if to say she was the reason he wanted to do this, more than anything else.

"The other standby pilot took over for me," Amelia said. "This is important."

Elizabeth smiled. "Well, this is super fun."

"We want to see where the bear was," Corey said.

"We'll take you for a run on the island after we fix breakfast," Faith said, everyone helping to carry food and cooking gear out of the canoes. They'd brought everything. Bread to make toast, eggs already scrambled and ready to cook, sausage links and bacon.

"So no more bear signs?" Sheri asked.

"No, I checked it out this morning," Elizabeth said.

"I did too. Once he left last night, that was the last we saw of him. Though once we start cooking, he might return to see if we left anything behind," David said.

Before long, they were eating around the campfire, drinking coffee and hot tea, and telling campfire tales.

"You should have seen the time Owen and I were chased up a tree," David said. "It was as if the bear had known we had hunted bears—unsuccessfully, I might add. Payback, you know."

"I agree. I thought we were goners," Owen said. "He was on us before we could even blink, no time to get out of our clothes to shift so we had to run for it. Now, we're talking a grizzly, too, not a black bear. They're known to be more unpredictable. I swear he was like some furry monster from a horror show where the critter is bigger than life, stronger, more determined to kill the poor screaming humans trying to escape him."

The kids were listening in fascination, though they'd heard the story before. Sheri and Elizabeth hadn't.

"Were you screaming?" Corey asked.

"No way," David said, winking at Elizabeth. "That's what happens in the movies. We were just trying to make it to the closest climbable tree and get up it before he got either of us. I swear I don't think I've ever climbed a tree that fast in my life."

"Yeah, me either. Though grizzlies can climb too, if they

are determined, so even there we weren't safe. He did make it up a little way, but he lost momentum or decided he wasn't that interested in us and slid back down to the ground." Owen took another bite of sausage.

"We were out of breath, hearts pounding, smelling of fear," David said. "The bear wasn't done with us though. He circled the tree, pawed at it, even pushed at it with his paws as if he could shake us out of the tree. He stretched up to reach us, but we were high enough he couldn't get to us. He was grunting and snorting, irritated, aggressive. We sat in that tree for an hour before he finally sauntered away. Our cell phones weren't picking up any reception either so we couldn't warn the others to stay away."

"We still didn't leave after that. Even though he didn't come back to the tree, we could hear him snuffling and making noise in the underbrush some distance away. We figured he was scouting for grubs or berries, and we didn't want to risk it," Owen said.

"Where was this?" Elizabeth asked.

"Montana," Owen said.

"I was with them," Faith said. "We had no idea the trouble Owen and David had gotten themselves into. We didn't even think about it until they didn't return for lunch. At that point, we went into search mode."

"Oh, no," Sheri said.

"Yeah, well, we had bear spray and a rifle with us—not to shoot a bear, if that was the trouble—but to be prepared, just in case. We never expected to find Owen and David in a tree." Cameron smiled, having never let them live it down.

"That would have been you, too, if you had been with us." Owen poured himself some more coffee and refilled everyone else's mugs.

"I'm glad you were all okay. What about you, Faith?" Elizabeth asked.

"Oh, I thought I was the smart one. I stayed at the cabin. So while the guys were following David and Owen's scent trail and discovering that a grizzly had been after them, the grizzly had left their area and come to the cabin where we were staying. Darn cell phones weren't working at all," Faith said.

"Oh, no," Sheri said again.

"Yeah, well, it worked out in the end. The guys came back, scared it off, and we ended up reporting it to the park rangers. We didn't want anyone to hurt it, knowing what it's like to be wolves that people want to hunt, but we didn't want innocent campers to be hurt or killed either. That bear was hungry. At some point, it was going to hurt someone."

"Okay, then, that decides it," Sheri said, slapping her hands on her thighs. "No going to Montana."

"I'm flying out there in a couple of weeks and thought you might come with me, Sheri," Slade said.

She smiled brightly. "Hmm. If I'm flying high above the danger, I suppose I can make an exception."

He chuckled. "We'll have to land, but not in bear territory."

Chapter 19

Once the pack members finished eating and cleaning up, they walked around the whole island looking for any other bear signs, a science lesson for the little ones. Angie found the bear's scat. Nick discovered bear fur caught on a couple of brambles. Corey located the bear's paw prints in the sand.

The kids loved exploring and learning how to track and be wolves, even when they were in human form. Still, while they were on the island, all three kids and Faith and Sheri ditched their clothes, shifted, and raced around the island as wolves—until they heard paddlers on the water talking to each other. Corey swore he heard one man say, "Damn, did you see the Arctic wolf on the island?"

"No, let's head that way," the other man said.

The pack members wearing their wolf coats hurried back into the woods, shifted, and dressed; then they all met at the shore where the pack members' canoes were. They loaded up their canoes and got ready to paddle back to the mainland and their homes, done with their fun outing.

They were already on the water when one of the men shouted out to them, "Hey, did you see the white wolves on the island?"

"No wolves!" David shouted back. "But we saw a black bear. He swam back to the mainland, though, or we wouldn't have hung around." Unfortunately, like the bear had left fur, and footprints, the wolves did too. Most people would chalk them up as dog prints though. Hopefully, that would be the case with these guys too.

But it did worry them—how could it not?—that these men might say they saw the wolves, and wolf biologists or others would descend on the area to see if wolves had returned to the mainland. Which gave David an idea.

All the canoes were paddling toward the mainland in a unified force, and David said, "Hey, Amelia, since you have sources for rehoming dogs, can you find us a couple of big white dogs that look similar to Arctic wolves that we can take in?"

Everyone smiled at David, and the kids shouted, "Yay!"

"Good idea. We should have done that a while ago. I'll begin a search right away," Amelia said, dipping her paddle in the water.

Maybe no one would come to check out the men's claims, especially if they hadn't actually taken photos of the wolves. And if they got a couple of big, white wolf-looking dogs, if anyone chanced to see a wolf and came to investigate, they would just show the dogs to them. End of speculation.

"We can help her find just the right dogs," Elizabeth said.

"It will be a fun project for all of us," Faith said.

"We want to help," the kids said.

And that was their weekend mission. To locate at least two white dogs that would be companions to their beloved

Saint Bernard. And to help keep them out of trouble if anyone came sniffing around, so to speak.

"Puppies or full grown?" Candice asked.

"Full grown," most everyone agreed.

"Puppies," the kids said.

"How do we explain about the wolf pups the men might have seen?" Sheri asked.

"How about we find a pup we can raise and a young adult dog too?" Amelia asked.

"We need them to be comfortable with wolves," David said. "If they smell us—especially an older dog—they need to be content with what we are. The dogs might not realize we're wolves, never having been around them, but they would still smell our canine scent, and we need to be a good fit," David said.

"I agree," Amelia said.

Once home, Sheri announced she was going to Faith and Cameron's house to do dog searches with the family. Elizabeth didn't know if it was to give her and David more alone time, or if she really wanted to start right in looking for potential dogs. Maybe a little of both. Either way, Elizabeth sent her a grateful smile.

As soon as Elizabeth and David were inside, Elizabeth said, "I need a shower. Do you want to join me?" She stripped down and tossed her clothes into the washing machine on the way to the bathroom. She might have swayed her hips a little more than she normally would have, then looked over her shoulder, her eyebrows raised in question.

He hurried to join her. "Yeah. I do."

She laughed and raced for the bathroom; David joined her just as she got the water in the shower hot enough. He slid his arms around her waist and growled into her neck, lightly nipping the skin there. She laughed again and wrapped her legs around him. "You are so much fun. I adore you," she said, and kissed his mouth.

He held her against the tile wall and kissed her back. "You are a dream come true."

An hour later, washed, dressed, and entirely satisfied, David made some more coffee, and Elizabeth had a cup of tea.

"I never thought of having dogs to raise because they could serve as camouflage for us as wolves, but it's a great idea," Elizabeth said as she opened a laptop and started a search.

"Yeah. I don't know why none of us ever thought of it. Probably because we haven't had any trouble with sightseers. We've been pretty isolated up till now. But before it can become an issue, we need to do something about it."

Instead of looking for dogs, David was on his phone doing searches for white wolves spotted at the island.

"Oh, that's a good idea," she said.

"Yeah, I figured it would be good to know if anyone has ever reported anything."

Elizabeth switched her focus, too, and started doing white wolf searches. But after a while, when she couldn't find anything about wolves, she started doing dog searches again. If the pack could get a dog soon, that would alleviate some of the concern they were all feeling, having been so close to being caught.

David glanced at her screen. "Do you see any that might work?"

"Yeah, I'm marking the pages. And I found an article about wolves who rescued some snowmobilers in North Dakota. Apparently people thought they were Samoyeds or white German shepherds or something."

"That was actually Owen and Candice."

"You're kidding," Elizabeth said, her eyes going wide.

"Nope."

"I'm looking forward to hearing that story some day. But anyway, Samoyeds really do look similar to an Arctic wolf."

"I agree. Alaskan malamute would be good too."

"Did you find anything about the men in that canoe reporting that they'd seen wolves in this area?"

"Not yet. It's early still, though. But I did find an old reference to Arctic wolves being here from two years ago."

Elizabeth's brow furrowed as she read, but then she smiled. "Did you see the comments? Doesn't seem like anyone believed him."

"It only takes one though."

"That's true. We have issues in the Canadian Arctic sometimes, but it's different up there. People are more used to seeing Arctic wolves there than they would be seeing them here," Elizabeth said.

"True. Even gray wolves create a lot of interest." David

leaned back, rolling his shoulders and sighing. "You ever wonder what it would be like if we could just be ourselves? Let everyone know who and what we are?"

"Yeah, but you know how that would go. Can you imagine the fear? We'd be a scary oddity at best, captured and experimented on at worst. No thanks. I would rather we have our anonymity and pretend we're like everyone else. Maybe in some future world they would be more open to us, but I won't hold my breath," she said.

"I agree. Hey, would you like to go to a drive-in movie tonight after dinner?"

Elizabeth smiled. "I would love to go."

"Okay. I think they are showing *Jurassic Park,* lots of cool dinosaurs, people screaming, running away, dinosaurs eating people. Some good, wholesome fun."

She laughed. "Sounds good to me."

That afternoon, they got with the rest of the pack members to have lunch together. They didn't always do this, but when they had urgent business to attend to and wanted to let new pack members know they were all in this as a team, they did. It was like having a celebration of families together, and it just felt right.

Candice showed Elizabeth some dogs she had found. "These are the breed of dogs I said dug out the avalanche victims when Owen was with me. They seemed to be perfect for the role."

"I found that article on you both. That was amazing," Elizabeth said. She showed her phone to the others. "I found a couple of places where they're looking to rehome their pups. These are white Alaskan malamutes."

"I have to say"—Candice pointed a pup out to Corey—"that pup looks a lot like you when you were around that age and bit me."

Corey smiled. "Nah. I looked like a wolf." He puffed out his chest, and Elizabeth smothered a smile. "This one looks like a dog."

"Sure, but I'd never seen a wolf pup before, so you were just a cute little puppy as far as I knew. I never once imagined a *wolf* would approach me at the campfire," Candice said.

"I was hungry," Corey said as if that explained everything.

Candice laughed. "Well, this pup is located only about an hour away, so since none of us are having shifting issues now, maybe we can go check it out."

"Yeah, let's go for it," David said.

The kids wanted to go with Candice, and Sheri said she would go with her, too, to help with the kids. David suspected they would be coming home with the puppy no matter what. That meant housebreaking, leash training, and everything else that went along with teaching the puppy who was in charge. They needed to get this done, but they didn't want to end up with a dog that was a problem for the pack rather than a solution.

Candice said on the phone, "Yes, we would like a female."

David raised a brow.

Candice smiled at him. "We're on our way!" She, Owen,

and Sheri loaded up the kids and headed out. The rest of the pack continued their search, hoping to find one nearby who needed to be rehomed.

Finally, Elizabeth said, "Here! A couple is divorcing, and he's going to Alaska and she's moving back home to Florida. Neither wants the responsibility of the dog. She's a white German shepherd, about an hour and a half from here."

David had thought he and Elizabeth would just chill this afternoon after lunch, but she appeared excited to go check the dog out.

"I'll go." David didn't want anyone to think he was clinging to Elizabeth, but if she wasn't going to be home with him, he wanted to see the dog too and help them make a decision. He just hoped Winston would be good with a couple of new dogs in the pack. Though as good-natured as he was, David figured he would be.

Elizabeth took hold of David's hand and kissed him. "I know you had other plans for us today."

"Are you kidding? We're going to see a dog. Doesn't get much better than that." Well, maybe keeping her in bed the rest of the afternoon until they had their dinner and went to the drive-in would have been better, but dogs were a close second.

Amelia and Gavin joined them and it didn't take long before David and the others arrived at a home that was up for sale an hour and a half away. As soon as they pulled into the driveway, they heard a dog barking.

"I just can't take care of her," the owner said after they all introduced themselves. "I'll be living at home with my parents for a while, and my dad is allergic to dogs. He never came to visit me because of it. I hate to give Velvet up. She's a lovely dog, but with my husband and me splitting up, I just don't have a choice."

Amelia was already looking over the dog, and Elizabeth was talking to her and calling her to come.

"She's housebroken and doesn't chew on anything she shouldn't. Well, she steals socks, and tissues from the wastepaper baskets, but she doesn't chew on them. She's a collector and just takes them to her bed."

Gavin laughed.

The woman frowned. "So who is actually planning to give her a home?"

"That would be us," Gavin said, gesturing to Amelia. It was too complicated to try to explain anything else. "Elizabeth and David live nearby, though, and will watch her if we ever need a sitter."

"Oh, well, good. She loves people and she hates to be left alone. Both my husband and I worked, so she would get lonely."

"She won't be lonely at all," Gavin said. "How is she with children?"

"When I take her to the park, she loves meeting them. They'll come over and hug on her and pet her. She's really a great family dog."

"Okay, good, because we're both planning families," Gavin said.

Elizabeth and David shared a smile, and his heart soared. He hoped they would be mated wolves sooner rather than later.

Chapter 20

David crouched down and talked to Velvet. Running his hand over her soft white fur, he looked so cute. Just like when he was playing with the kids.

Elizabeth got the rest of the details from the woman about diet and health and shots and anything else she could think of. Velvet seemed to like all of them. A nice friendly dog that should get along with them, Elizabeth hoped.

The woman's cell phone rang. "Excuse me, I need to get that."

"So, what do you think?" Elizabeth asked.

"I'm all for taking her," David said. "She'll get furrier as she gets older. She's got a fair amount of fur now. And she seems nice and friendly with all of us."

"I agree. She seems perfect, sweet-tempered. A little bigger than her breed normally."

"Do you think she's old enough to—" Amelia stopped talking when the dog owner came back into the room.

"I have another couple coming to check on her. I just need to tell them if you're undecided or not," the woman said.

"We'll take her," Amelia said, smiling.

They packed up the car with everything the dog would need and thanked the woman, promising to give Velvet a wonderful home.

"It was a good thing four of us came to check her out." Elizabeth carried a sack of dog toys and a big box of treats. "She seems good with all of us."

"And she looks like she loves to go for a car ride," Amelia said when Velvet jumped right up into the back of the hatchback and looked at them like she was wondering why they hadn't left yet. "I had a dog once that was terrified of riding in a car, and he would get motion sickness too."

David got a call from Candice and put it on speakerphone. "Hey, did you get the puppy?"

"Ha, as if you didn't already know the answer to that question. There was no way we were coming home without the pup—not if the kids had any say in it. Not that any of us adults objected to it either. Her name is Pearl. How about you? Cameron said you were checking out another dog."

"Yeah, we're on our way home with her. She seems like a real good match. Velvet's her name."

"Okay, good. Then we're all set. Who gets to housebreak the puppy?" Candice asked, a smile in her voice.

"I suggest Winston and Velvet. They can show the new pup the ropes," David said.

"Sounds good. We'll see you soon," Candice said.

They finally arrived home and the whole pack gathered to meet the new dogs. The dogs were eager to meet each other and the *lupus garous*; it appeared everyone would get along just fine. The puppy was already plaguing Winston, biting at him and play-bowing. Gavin fetched the tug-of-war rubber toy out of the stuff they unloaded from the car, and Winston grabbed it, lying with one end in his mouth while the puppy tugged ferociously on the other.

"Now hopefully our ploy will work if anyone witnesses us running as wolves," Faith said. "And if nobody's too put out by it, we'll keep the puppy at our house for the time being because I'm home, though Candice could too—"

"But the kids want the puppy at your house." Candice smiled. "And Winston will stay with you to help housebreak Pearl. Since I'm home all the time, I can take care of Velvet until she gets used to the area."

They were all in agreement. David would have loved having one of the dogs at his place, too, but he figured he and Elizabeth could use the time to work on their *own* relationship—though housebreaking or taking care of a dog could be a first step in pre-child-rearing.

As a group, they took Winston and Velvet for a walk through the woods while Gavin worked on leash training with Pearl. Sheri was going home with Slade afterward to have dinner, and David heard they were going to the drive-in theater too.

"Hey," Gavin said, struggling to get Pearl to listen to commands as he tried to teach her to walk on the leash, "we are going too."

"Uh, so are we." David heard the very slightest bit of annoyance in his voice.

Gavin heard it too. He laughed. "Sorry, old man. They finally are showing something that both Amelia and I want to see. So the two of you are going?"

"Yeah, that was the plan for tonight."

Gavin smiled. "We'll try to park far away from you."

Really loving the pack dynamics, Elizabeth chuckled, just as glad that a bunch of them were going. "Don't worry about it. We're a pack, right? We ought to take up a whole row of the parking area with just our pack members."

"I agree," Amelia said.

"Well, you can count us out at least," Faith said. "*Jurassic Park* is way too scary for the kids at this age."

"Can't we see it?" Corey asked.

"No. You would have nightmares, and all three of you would end up in bed with us," Faith said.

"Amelia and I need to do all this stuff before the kids are born," Gavin said.

Everyone laughed.

"Sorry, buddy," Owen said, slapping David on the back good-naturedly. "We're going too. Candice loves her dinosaurs."

"So everyone is going but the MacPherson family?" David asked.

Faith smiled. "Yes, we'll take all the dogs for the night."

"Yay!" the kids said.

After a while of starting and stopping as the new dogs marked their territory, Elizabeth and David ended up way ahead, strolling by themselves. Elizabeth enjoyed the pack, but it was nice to have the solitude too.

She was just about to say as much to David when she

heard a noise, something large moving toward them through the bush. He apparently heard it, too, because both of them stopped abruptly, heads cocked so much like their wolf selves.

In her mind, she pictured the black bear they'd seen on the island, hungry and focused. "Do you think it's the bear?" she asked loudly, hoping to scare it off. It was important to not startle an unaware bear, but to make noise and hope it would go away.

David started talking loudly too. "It could be a bear! Keep making noise!" He was shouting it out in warning to the others.

Candice yelled back, "I'm coming!"

Owen yelled, "Me too! Kids and dogs are being taken home! Hang on!"

Elizabeth was glad the kids and dogs were going home. Dogs could really rile a bear and they wanted to keep the kids safe. "We're heading your way!" Elizabeth shouted.

That's when they saw the bear. A dark and hulking shape peered out at them through a break in the trees. It was very still, curious. David took Elizabeth's hand, clutching hard. They didn't run, both of them standing tall as they yelled in its direction.

"Go home! This is wolf territory!" Elizabeth said.

"Well, it's their territory too—" David started, but Elizabeth cut him off.

"Work with me here," she said.

He smiled. A moment later, they smelled Candice and Owen, and a moment after that, they ran up behind them.

"Is it the same one that you saw on the island?" Owen asked.

Candice took her phone out and tried to snap some pictures of it. Within seconds, though, the bear gave them one last look, sniffing the air, then turned and ambled off.

"Yeah, it's the same one," David said. "I can smell it."

"We're going to have to scare it off for good. It's too close to the cabins," Owen said.

They waited a little longer, and when they felt reasonably assured the bear wasn't going to follow them anywhere, they all headed back home.

"How are you going to scare him off?" Elizabeth asked.

"We might have to get the wildlife service to relocate him. We're not feeding him, but if he's attracted to our homes, our kids and dogs, we could all be at risk. If he would just stay on the other side of the lake, we would be fine. But once they think they can get free food, even if we're not offering, he could return," David said. "Though it's possible we could chase him off as a pack of wolves and he would stay away."

"We try not to run as wolves too much during the day, but it might be worth it to get rid of him," Owen said.

"Why not now?" Elizabeth asked. "Do you think four wolves would be enough of a deterrent?"

"How about eight of us?" Slade hollered out.

Elizabeth turned to see Sheri, Gavin, and Cameron racing past Slade as wolves.

In unspoken agreement, the rest of them stripped and shifted, and as a wolf pack, they headed out after the bear. She could see how well the pack worked. Not to kill the bear, but to corral him like a ranch dog would do in herding cows or sheep.

They chased him for miles, toward the other side of the

lake. At times, they let him pause and growl at them. Even charge them. But they were too fast, sometimes running in bursts of forty miles an hour. Finally, once he was about ten miles from their homes, they eased up, watching him continue to lumber away until he was out of sight.

They still waited, making sure he didn't come back, Elizabeth nuzzling David's face, Owen and Candice rubbing against each other, the others just panting and watching for the bear. Then they made a detour to the lake, drank some of the water, and loped all the way back to where they'd left their clothes.

Elizabeth hoped the bear wouldn't ever return, but if they couldn't keep him away as wolves, they could always reach out to the rangers. But even then she knew bears could still return.

She loved how unified the pack had been. How they all worked together, first taking care of the little ones and the dogs, then coming to David and Elizabeth's aid should they have still needed it.

She was both tired and amped up, ready to return home to make love to her wolf and take a nap. Their nice little walk with the pack members and the dogs had turned into a wild adventure, and she couldn't be prouder of the pack or of belonging to it.

When they finally reached their clothes, they hurried to dress and headed back to the houses. Elizabeth and David led the pack, hand in hand.

"That was one big bear," Slade said.

"Yeah, if I'd still been hunting," Owen said, "it would have made a great prize. But I'm glad we let them live in peace with us now. Or relative peace, as long as they're not hassling us on our side of the lake."

David wholeheartedly agreed. "If it hadn't been for me having a heart attack and being turned into a wolf, Owen and I would still be searching for bears to hunt in season. Not that we ever had much luck."

Owen laughed. "Yeah, we were the worst bear hunters in the world. Now we're no longer hunting them, and instead we have to deal with them as wolves—karma, I swear."

"You know, you were talking about the one that treed you. The grizzly?" Elizabeth said. "Well, I was looking up about tree-climbing black bears, and they can climb a hundred feet in thirty seconds. So I'm glad we didn't try to climb a tree to avoid this bear. They look like huge teddy bears and you would never think they were that agile."

"And you never run away from them as a human because they can run over two miles at twenty-five miles per hour," David said. "If they'd been chasing us? Bad news for us."

Candice laughed. "I'm definitely going to write a bear encounter into my new book." She gave David and Owen a laughing glance. "And don't be surprised if you recognize a few details."

A caravan of cars headed to the drive-in theater after dinner. They arrived early enough for the pack members' vehicles to take up several parking spaces in a row. If they hadn't been a bunch of newly mated or nearly mated wolves, they would have doubled up in some of the vehicles. But this was like date night for all of them.

The stars were out, the moon waning, and it was just beautiful, especially because Elizabeth was cuddled next to David on the bench seat in back.

"This is amazing," Elizabeth said.

"Yeah," David said, casually rubbing her shoulder. They weren't teens groping in a vehicle, but he did love being able to snuggle with Elizabeth at the drive-in, something he had done as a teen with a girl in Seattle. But as a wolf, and with a woman he truly cared about, this was so much better.

Even though he'd seen the movie plenty of times before, when the T. rex charged the Jeep, David felt the urge to hit the gas and get out of there.

"Jump!" Elizabeth said later, talking to the movie characters. "Grant will catch you!" She turned toward David. "He should have gotten down. He made it all that way up, climbed over, and then suddenly froze? This reminds me of a couple having a long kiss or speech where the aliens are attacking all around them. I'm like, can you please just get a move on? Save the kissing for when your lives are not in peril."

He smiled and kissed her. "Maybe it's because they might not live through whatever it is, and they need to have that last farewell kiss before they die."

"Well, they *are* going to die if they don't get a move on."

When the movie ended, Elizabeth lifted her head to David's and pressed a soft kiss to his lips. "Thanks for this. I really had fun."

"I agree. I haven't been to a drive-in theater since I was a teen and was still human."

"Well, we're going to have to put this on our list of fun things to do." She was already looking up the drive-in's next feature. "The movie *Ghost* starts next Friday."

"It's a date. What do you think about going to the fair Sunday night?" David asked.

"Oh, yeah, but if we go, we should take the kids."

"They're going already. But I thought we could go on our own. Just us."

She laughed. "Sorry. I think of fairs and kids, but yeah, that would make for a fun date. When did you want to go?"

"We'll go early in the evening and have dinner, when everything is all lit up. We can ride the rides, play the games—"

"You'll win a stuffed toy for me?"

"I thought you could win one for me."

Elizabeth laughed. "Happy to."

David started the car. "Maybe if Slade isn't taking a group of tourists out in his seaplane, he can take Sheri. He loves stuff like that—so he tells us," David said. "He hasn't really had the time since he joined our pack."

"Okay, I guess if he isn't able to go, she would be thrilled to ride the rides with the kids."

"Right." He was really trying to carve out some good quality time with Elizabeth, so he hoped that was true.

They were nearing home when Elizabeth got a text. "Ooh. Sheri is staying overnight with Slade. She said not to make anything of it, but she wanted to give us more of the weekend off to be together, and he has two spare bedrooms."

David smiled. "That's still good news for them. And for us."

Maybe tonight would be the night. With Sheri gone and everything going so well, maybe Elizabeth would be ready.

David didn't think he'd ever been so nervous about proposing a question to anyone than the one he was dying to ask Elizabeth:

Will you mate me, Elizabeth?

Chapter 21

As soon as they walked into the house and he locked the door, Elizabeth was ready to throw herself at him and make love all the way. She knew he was the one for her—from his every word, every deed, every action. She hoped it wasn't too soon to pop the question to him. She worried he still was somewhat at odds over his shifting abilities and was afraid to tie her down to his world as a newly turned wolf, and offspring that wouldn't be royal wolves either.

But none of that mattered to her. And it didn't matter if he said no to a mating right away either. She would give him the time he needed. But she was determined to make him hers. If not now, then soon.

She wrapped her arms around his neck and pressed her body against his. He settled his hands around her waist and smiled down at her.

"Do you want to—" they both said at the same time.

She paused. He paused. Each waiting for the other to say what they had to say.

Then she and he both started up again. "Do you want to—" And this time they laughed.

"Mate!" she said.

"Oh hell yeah. You took the word right out of my mouth."

This was it. The real deal. David couldn't be happier. He reached down and pulled off Elizabeth's sandals and kicked off his flip-flops. She was yanking up his T-shirt while he was trying to remove hers. They ended up laughing at each other before he released her shirt, and she pulled his shirt up over his head. Then his hands were on her shirt again, pulling it up and off. She reached down to unfasten his belt, and he was undoing the button and zipper on her white shorts.

It felt frantic and hurried and hot and, God, he had to have her now.

Then she unbuttoned his denim shorts and pulled down the zipper. Together, they slid down each other's shorts and began kissing again, him in his boxer briefs and her in her bikini panties and bra.

He cupped her breasts and began to kiss her throat while she tilted her head back and purred.

She slid her hands over his pecs, her thumbs rubbing his nipples in a gentle caress, making his cock jump. And when she leaned down and licked his nipples, he had to pause and take in the erotic sensation, loving the feel of her, of her mouth on his heated flesh, her lips soft and moist and her tongue teasing.

Then he ran his hands over her breasts and pulled the bra cups down so they were framing her breasts. She was beautiful. Every inch of her. He kissed one breast with reverence, and then the other. Then, like she'd done with his nipples, he ran his thumbs over them, the nubs peaking already. He licked one, though he took it a step further and suckled it. Then he did the same with the other, licked it and pulled on it with his mouth until she arched her back and he smelled their pheromones raging, the musky scent of their sex enveloping everything.

Their hearts were beating hard and their blood was rushing through their veins. Then he was massaging her breasts again and kissing her mouth. She was the stuff of dreams. Yet she was his dream come true now.

She kissed him back, her tongue slipping into his mouth, deepening the kiss, the eroticism building. She rubbed her body against his, her breasts against his pecs, her mound against his erection stirring for release. She raised her leg and rubbed against his leg, parting her legs for him, enticing him to take this further.

He slid his hand down to rub her between her legs, her panties slipping between the folds, wet, ready for him. He reached down and slid them down her legs, and she kicked them off the rest of the way. She pulled his boxer briefs down, and he hurried to dispense with them. Then he swept her up in his arms and carried her to the master bedroom where, before she had arrived, he'd only fantasized about taking her as his mate.

Now it was really happening.

He dumped her on the bed in a tangle of arms and legs, and she laughed and scooted over to make room for him.

He climbed in, his mouth on hers again, both of them on their sides, his hand sweeping down her back, finding her bra still in the way and hastily removing it. He moved on to her hip before he pulled her leg over his, spreading her to him.

Oh God, she was so wet. He stroked between her legs, feeling her readiness on his fingers, the heat of their bodies, and the sound of their thumping heartbeats filling his ears.

"Oh, yes," she whispered against his mouth, sounding seduced by his touch, just like she was seducing him with her scent and touch and whispered breath. "You are wonderful," she said. "I love you." And then she grew quiet as he slipped a finger into her slick channel.

"I love you, Elizabeth, with all my heart."

What a joy it was to be with her now—and to know this was forever for them.

Elizabeth was overjoyed David had wanted to be her mate. She'd known in her heart what she had wanted, but she was also a royal wolf and he was not. So she'd had to let him decide how far he wanted to take this. Although it wasn't like she would have let him go. She would have stood by his side forever. Her first love. And she'd wanted him to be the only one for her.

He made her feel renewed and excited about everything in life, whereas before she had just been getting by. He did that for her. Made her love every moment of her existence.

Now, he was stroking her to climax, the feeling of impending release dragging her upward toward the moon, and she needed this, craved it, but not from anyone else. Just David.

He slipped his fingers out of her and she wanted to protest, but then he was stroking her feminine nub again, and she was flying toward the sun and the moon as if they could coexist until the moment when they collided in one beautiful explosion of happiness. She cried out with joy. "David!"

He gave her a wickedly lustful smile, kissed her mouth, and then moved her onto her back, kneeing her leg aside. His penis pressed between her feminine lips all the way to the goal. She wrapped her legs around his hips, wanting him to go deeper, to hold him tight, to never let go.

He seemed to want the same and thrust inside her, slowly at first, then gaining momentum and thrusting harder, faster.

This was so good, the union between wolves, the way they said "I do" forever and ever.

"Love you," he said, his breath unsteady as he continued to surge into her.

"Love you back," she said, her voice just as ragged, the need just as great.

He continued to thrust into her, and she could see not only the tension in his face but the rigidness of his body, the way he was holding back for a moment, the way he pushed in all the way to her womb right at the end. The climax. He breathed out words, a prayer maybe, but she was lost in her own slice of heaven. He pumped into her a few more times and then he stayed inside her, kissing her face, her forehead, cheeks, jawline. Her mouth, and the kiss lingered there. "You are the only one for me."

She wrapped her arms around him, her legs still holding his hips tight to hers. Her wolf. Forever now.

"I couldn't love you more."

That night, Elizabeth slept better than she ever had. It was morning when she glanced over at David, who she thought was asleep, but he was watching her and smiling.

She moved closer, and he wrapped his arms around her in a good-morning hug. "How long have you been awake?" she asked, kissing his bare chest.

"Just a few minutes. I didn't want to disturb your sleep."

Then they heard the kids calling to each other outside.

"Just play chase!" Faith yelled. "No hide-and-seek."

"They sure keep Faith on her toes," Elizabeth said. She planned to get up and make herself some tea, but this was just too nice, snuggling with her mate, listening to the sounds of children's laughter. And David didn't seem to be in any hurry either.

She was half drifting off to sleep when she smelled bacon and sausage cooking outside. "Faith and Cameron are having breakfast outside?"

"Smells like it. Come on, let's get dressed and grab some coffee and tea." He kissed her nose.

She wanted to just lie there and enjoy this lazy time with David, but he was already leaving the bed and heading to the bathroom. She sighed, but when she heard the shower turn on, she happily got up to join him.

"I'm not sure," he said, soaping her down, "but the breakfast might be for us."

She frowned at him. "For us?"

"Well, the guys and I did that for Cameron and Faith,

even though they were mated by then, once we had settled in our homes. And after that, we did the same for Owen and Candice and Amelia and Gavin once they were mated."

"Oh." Elizabeth panicked and hurried to finish up.

"It's fine. No rush." He gently lowered her head into the water. "Your hair still has shampoo in it." He kissed her cheek and lovingly rinsed the shampoo out. She closed her eyes and enjoyed the sensation of his hands caressing her head, his fingers massaging her scalp like a pro.

"Thanks, mate of mine." When there wasn't a sud to be seen, he turned off the water and grabbed a towel for her.

She kissed him again. "You are my hero."

"That's what I always want to be for you."

She hurried to dry her hair, and then she left the bathroom to grab some clothes and dress. "What if we hadn't joined them outside for breakfast?"

"They would have done it another day and another, until they celebrated the big event with us."

"But what if it's just a coincidence and breakfast really is just for them?"

David peered out the window while wearing only his fresh boxer briefs. "I would say we are invited to breakfast."

"You mean they know we mated? How would they know?"

"This pack just always seems to know. It was bound to happen. I think that's the reason they wanted to make sure that Sheri had a place to go for the weekend."

Elizabeth pulled on her T-shirt and looked out the window. "Well, we might have not done it yet."

"Then an early celebration, telling us to get on with it."

She shook her head, but a smile teased the corners of her mouth. "Well, we'd better not keep them waiting."

He finished dressing as she pulled on her sandals.

"One thing you should know about me, though. I don't like making grand entrances." She seized his hand and pulled him through the house.

He chuckled. "I already knew that about you. But you've been making grand entrances in my life since the first time I met you. And I love it."

They headed outside and everyone paused to watch them and then cheered. "Congratulations!"

Even the kids stopped chasing each other around and joined in the cheer.

A blush stained Elizabeth's cheeks. "Thank you," she said, while David beamed beside her.

Then he pulled her into his embrace and dramatically swept her back, kissing her until she was breathless, and everyone cheered again. Well, except the kids. She heard one "eww" coming from Corey; Angie and Nick were quiet, smiling. They would all have their day when they were older, Elizabeth thought, if they were lucky.

Sheri came up and took both her friend's hands in hers, turning Elizabeth this way and that.

"It agrees with you," she finally said, pulling her in for a tight squeeze. "I'm so happy for you," she whispered against her ear, and Elizabeth had to blink away tears.

"Sorry for disturbing you, but in case David didn't tell you, this has just become a tradition," Faith said.

David's ears tinged a bit red. "I have to admit my mind was on other things."

Everyone laughed.

"We don't plan to keep you all day, but after breakfast we have a pack wolf run, just to celebrate having a new mated pair in the pack," Faith said.

Slade offered Sheri a cup of tea.

At least Sheri was learning the traditions if she ended up mating Slade, Elizabeth thought.

And from the looks between the two, Elizabeth wondered if the pack would be serving breakfast again before they knew it.

Chapter 22

Sunday night, Elizabeth and David went to the fairgrounds, and so did the others. They went every year with the kids, but this time, for the first time, David wasn't alone. They all went their own ways, but David and Elizabeth ended up in line at some of the same rides with them.

At the Ferris wheel they got on and saw Sheri setting two of the kids on a seat while Cameron and Faith took the other. Then Owen and Candice climbed aboard, and right after them, Gavin and Amelia. The whole pack was together in all things, it seemed.

David smiled and kissed Elizabeth.

"I love how your pack sticks together. It's like half of the fair is made up of wolves," Elizabeth said. "I feel on top of the world with you."

Once they were done with their ride, they all gathered at the base.

"What's next?" Cameron asked.

Owen said, "We have to try for prizes at the shooting gallery and the strongman game."

"The strongman game first," Gavin said. "I can beat all three of you."

Amelia's brother came up to join them. Slade smiled at Sheri. "Sorry I'm late. Flight was delayed."

"You're just in time to prove to these guys you can hit the hardest," Sheri said, smiling at him.

"No way," Gavin said. "I'm winning this one."

They had always been competitive with each other in that way. They were used to it and the women in their lives were amused by it, glad they always did it in good humor.

Gavin went first and struck the lever with such force, the puck soared to the top and rang the bell. Amelia chose Winnie the Pooh as her prize.

Then Owen went next and also won. Candice picked a wolf. "Because it looks like you, Corey." She ruffled his hair and he ducked away, but he couldn't stop a pleased grin from sneaking across his face.

Cameron had to hit it several times to win for all the kids *and* his mate.

The guy in charge of the game was just shaking his head as Cameron swung the hammer, then swung again, and again, and once more, the bell ringing gaily each time. The kids ended up with a wolf, a tiger, a leopard, and a jaguar. Faith picked out a lion, and Cameron ended up looking a tiny bit sweaty, not that he would ever admit it.

It came down to David and Slade. David let Slade go first.

Slade stepped up to the plate. He had a lot to win for—pack acceptance, playing with the guys when he had never been in competition with them before, and proving to Sheri, even if they didn't end up being together, that he could win her a prize too. Which he did. All the pack and other fairgoers around them were watching how well the men had done and cheered for Slade too.

"You must eat your Wheaties," David said, taking hold of the hammer.

"Oatmeal. It gives me strength." Slade winked at Sheri, who was cuddling her new stuffed jaguar.

With everyone else winning a prize, David couldn't fail. How would that look to Elizabeth? With all his might, he slammed the hammer down on the lever, sending the puck flying. The bell pealed and the crowd set up another roar of approval.

Elizabeth picked out a giant stuffed Winnie the Pooh, saying, "I always wanted one of these." And he felt like a hero.

Then it was off to the shooting gallery. Law-enforcement training and wolf eyesight gave them an edge and they weren't afraid to use it.

Another round of prizes for all filled the pack's arms to overflowing.

They ate turkey legs and caramelized popcorn and went through the house of mirrors. Corey had a blast the whole way through. Angie and Nick weren't as adventurous.

Toward the end of the night, the kids began dragging, and David was ready to take Elizabeth home.

"Is everyone about ready to pack it up?" Cameron asked.

There was a resounding yes, and they headed to their vehicles in the parking lot. Sheri was going home with Faith and Cameron to get some tired kids ready for bed. David wondered if Slade had offered his place and she turned him down, or if she just wanted to help out with the kids. He hoped everything was okay there.

The cars made a parade home. Then they piled out in twos and threes, waving a sleepy good-night all around.

David and Elizabeth entered their house and turned on some lights. "Nightcap or…" David said, already anticipating her answer.

"Or," she said with a wicked grin and raced him to the bedroom.

The next morning, David knew he had to get out of bed and get in to work, but this was so nice, cuddling with Elizabeth. She finally stirred, as if she realized he was awake, and smiled at him.

"We have to get in to the office. Our furniture is being delivered today!" Elizabeth sounded like a little kid on Christmas morning.

"All right, honey." He smiled at her and kissed her. "I can't believe we are mated."

"Me either, and it was high time." She tossed the covers aside and began getting ready to go to work.

He watched her for a few minutes, then finally dragged himself out of bed, thinking if it were a slow day, maybe they could slip back over to the house for a few minutes.

She hurried off to the kitchen. "I'll fix breakfast."

He still wasn't ready to roll out of bed, but he smiled, glad she was at least awake and with it.

"And I'll put some coffee on for you," she called.

He finally joined her, had a cup of coffee, and she served up waffles and bacon.

"Easy and quick." She sat down to eat her breakfast with a cup of lavender tea.

"If it's a slow day," he said, "we could slip away back to the house."

"To have lunch?" She smiled knowingly at him.

He smiled. "Yeah. Lunch." He picked up a piece of bacon and bit off a chunk, chewing slowly.

She kissed him on the cheek but was all business after that, rushing through her waffle, cleaning up before he was barely though, then tugging him out the door to get going.

"Are you always going to be this excited about going to work?" he asked, letting her pull him wherever she wanted to go.

"Hopefully, but today the furniture is arriving."

He chuckled and let her excitement wash over him. When they got to the office, Sheri was already working on more new-hire background investigations, and everyone else was getting coffee and sorting through their cases.

The office furniture came in right after they arrived, and Elizabeth and Sheri got to work setting everything up just the way they wanted. He hoped they could make it their own and feel like a real part of the agency.

Sheri had to have a stash of chocolate—candy bars, cookies, whatever—in her desk. Not that she ate chocolate all day long, but she said she just liked having it for a quick pick-me-up later in the day. And she also had a picture of her with her family in a brass frame sitting on her desk. Add her new wolf mouse pad and calendar, and she was all set to go.

Elizabeth was still getting her desk set up when more furniture arrived from another company. This was comfortable seating for adults waiting for one of the investigators to speak with them.

Then David came over to see if he could help either of them with anything, but they had a plan. A more comfortable waiting area was taking shape under their direction, with a couple of puzzle games and books for kids and magazines for adults.

"We want to get a large aquarium, and Sheri and I promise to take care of it," Elizabeth said. "It will make working in the office even more pleasurable. And when Faith has to bring the kids over here for one reason or another, they can see the fish or help feed them, and read the books or play with the puzzles."

"Okay, sure," David said. "And I'm sure the rest of us will be happy to help with the fish, once we learn what we're supposed to do." After the ladies had set things up, he realized that the office really was much nicer and less austere. He guessed he and his partners had been so busy with work that they hadn't really considered doing anything like this—just for themselves and for their mates for when they dropped by.

"David, do you think you can do without Sheri and me for a little bit?" Elizabeth grabbed her purse.

"Yeah, sure."

"Okay, we're going to a nursery to pick up some plants for the office. And then I'll look at some for the garden, but I'll take you with me when we pick those out. Maybe tonight after work?"

"Yeah, we can do that." He suggested Friday night so they could have the weekend to plant them, and she agreed, waving on her way out the door. He thought of all the time he'd spent weeding those garden beds, envisioning his nights with her, planning and digging and planting, and a deep sense of contentment stole over him.

Cameron came out of his office and smiled. "Wow, what a difference," he said, admiring the new layout. "This looks so much better."

Gavin and Owen popped their heads out to see the final product.

"They could be professional interior decorators," Owen said.

"Yeah, but maybe don't tell them that," David joked. "We don't want to lose them."

In Yellowknife, Bentley arrived at Kintail's house, finally looking like he had good news, and Kintail was ready for it. "What did you learn?"

"They're living in a place south of Ely, Minnesota. I mentioned to the PI who was trying to track down their agency that they were fond of white wolves, just thinking maybe that would help him narrow his focus. And he discovered an office named White Wolf Investigative Services. When he checked the website, it showed Cameron as one of their investigators."

"And David is still with the agency?"

"He is."

"Get flights for us out now. You and Hans are coming with me, and pick two others to accompany us."

"Yes, sir."

Now they were getting somewhere with this. Kintail hoped they weren't too late.

Chapter 23

At a garden center, Elizabeth and Sheri bought a couple of ficus trees to liven up the office foyer and some pots of ivy to give the bookshelves a nice warm outdoor appeal.

"Yeah, but you're going to have to keep them alive," Sheri warned her. "I overwater them or underwater them."

"I'll take care of them." Then they headed outside to look at the plants Elizabeth might want to put in her garden.

"Red roses for your grandmother for sure," Sheri said. "She loved them."

"I agree."

Sheri got a text message. She glanced down at it and ignored it, like she'd ignored a couple of others already.

Had she had a fight with Slade? Or was it someone from the pack back home? "What's up?"

"It's my brother. He kept texting when we first left Yellowknife, but then he stopped. I kind of figured he'd just given up when I didn't respond. But he's back at it now."

"So what did he say?" Elizabeth held her breath, hoping against hope it had nothing to do with Kintail.

"He said that Mom and Dad had disowned me." Tears sprang up in Sheri's eyes, and Elizabeth quickly hugged her.

"Don't believe him. You talked to your dad yourself. They understood, right? At least a little. *If* they disowned you, it was probably Kintail's doing. And that's a big if."

"I don't know. They might have changed their minds. I figured they would be happy for me if I was happy. But maybe with me leaving, I've only caused trouble for them."

"They're in Cancun for two weeks."

"Right, so Kintail can't be doing too much to them, yet. But he could very well have told them to disown me or else they could be kicked out of the pack."

"But he wants more pack members, not fewer," Elizabeth said.

"Still, he has to make an example of someone. You know how he is about having to at least look like he's in complete control. Besides, you and I are of pup-bearing age, and that's another reason he would be furious we both left." Sheri wiped away her tears and stuck her phone in her pocket.

"And you haven't talked to your parents since the last time?"

"No. I'm trying to get settled in here, work a job, and enjoy being with the pack. I'm not going back no matter what. If they want to disown me, I can't do anything about it. If it helps them in dealing with Kintail, then it's really okay." Sheri frowned at Elizabeth. "Did you put your home on the market?"

"I'm calling the real estate agent when we get back to the office. And we need to get new phone numbers."

"Why?" Sheri asked as they got into the car and headed back to the agency.

"We need local numbers, and...it might be better if we can get in touch with people in Yellowknife but they can't get in touch with us. At least for now." Which meant Bentley, Sheri's brother, and Kintail. None of them would know the new numbers. At least for a while.

When Elizabeth and Sheri arrived back at the office, Sheri was noticeably quiet. David hoped it didn't have anything to do with Slade. On the other hand, maybe that would be better. If it was something to do with Kintail, that was definitely worse. Not just for Sheri but for all of them.

David put it out of his mind for the time being, concentrating on helping Gavin with the Ms. Moore case. "Hey, Gavin, I found another instance of that business partner being accused of skimming off a company, but the charges went nowhere. Claimed it was a mistake in the accounting department and the feds weren't able to convict him. Either this guy falls face-first into a whole lot of bad luck or he's really good at covering up his tracks."

"Let me see that." David handed him what he'd found. Gavin looked it over and nodded. "It's looking more and more like this guy is dirty. I instructed Ms. Moore to have a forensic CPA go over everything. This guy might be good, but so are we." Gavin rubbed the back of his neck, his mouth tight. "What really sucks is the husband, he was dying of cancer, right? On all sorts of pain medication toward the end. And this guy, we know he borrowed heavily against the business, presumably getting Mr. Moore to sign off on it. What kind of person takes advantage of someone like that?"

"We'll get him," David said grimly.

Gavin nodded. "Hell yeah we will."

Elizabeth and Sheri continued to get their new life in order, working toward making Minnesota their official place of residence. That included taking a driver's test to get a new license. Using David's forged documents, they did the whole stand-in-line, deal-with-bureaucracy thing necessary to be official Minnesota drivers. After passing their tests with flying colors, they took care of getting new phone numbers. When they returned to the office, they shared them with the rest of the pack. Elizabeth felt free in that moment, like she'd finally truly cut ties with Kintail and the others. She should have done that right away, though no one had bothered to try to contact her.

The same wasn't true for Sheri.

"I'm glad we got that done," Sheri said as they settled back behind their desks, looking a little more at ease than she had earlier.

The phone rang, and Sheri immediately answered it. Her face went pale.

"What is it?" Elizabeth asked, her stomach clenching.

Sheri put the call on speakerphone, waving frantically for the others to come listen.

A low voice echoed through the reception area: "Imagine my surprise to learn you're answering Cameron's phone at the office."

Kintail. The office was deadly silent, every single PI focused on the voice none of them ever wanted to hear again.

"What do you want?" Sheri managed to say.

"You to return home. Your family loves and misses you. So does Bentley. Elizabeth has her own life to live," Kintail said. The line went dead.

Before a word could be uttered, two cars pulled up into the parking lot. Elizabeth didn't need to look to know who it would be. She'd smelled him even before she saw him.

Kintail and four other males, who looked like they were bouncers in a nightclub, walked into the lobby. At least there were no clients in the building at the time.

"So we meet again," David said, and if his hair could stand on end like a ridge down the top of his head, it would have. Everything about him screamed protective. Dangerously protective.

"I'm their pack leader, and neither of them told us they were leaving. Sheri's parents are worried sick about her," Kintail said.

"Leaving was their choice to make." They should be able to go where they pleased, and the pack couldn't hold them hostage any more than they could have held Owen and David against their will. "They came down here of their own free will. They're happy here. Let them be."

"I know better," Bentley said, stepping forward. "Sheri, I know you wouldn't have left if it wasn't for Elizabeth"—he sneered at Elizabeth—"and the others forcing you to hide that she was leaving us."

"That's Sheri's boyfriend," Kintail explained. "Bentley."

"She's happy to be working with us," David said. "And from what she has told us, the two of them are no longer seeing each other."

"That's a damn lie," Bentley said.

"She belongs with us," another man said. "I'm her brother, Hans, for your information. And we're taking her home."

Every single one of the pack members bristled. On both sides.

And Elizabeth knew the showdown she'd dreaded had just begun.

David smelled Sheri's nervousness. Elizabeth's too. But the Yellowknife pack, thankfully, seemed to be resigned to Elizabeth's new life.

Not so much Sheri's.

Kintail stood with his arms folded across his chest, a scowl on his face, trying to make himself as tall and as intimidating as possible. Hans, Bentley, and the others took their cues from him and maintained the same stance, each of them with a look of determination on their face.

David almost didn't blame them. If he'd had a sister and she'd left without a word, he might have been upset too, wanting to understand why she felt she couldn't come to him and talk before she just took off. But that was their fault, not Sheri's. Kintail had created such a toxic pack dynamic that Sheri really had no other choice.

But it was the boyfriend David was trying to get a read

on most of all. Did he really believe Sheri was meant to be his mate? Speaking from experience, David understood how powerful that feeling could be. It made some men do things they wouldn't normally do. Desperate things. Kintail himself had been known to commit horrific acts of desperation—David knew that from experience too—just to hold on to power, so it wouldn't surprise David one bit if members of his pack followed his lead.

The Yellowknife pack stood their ground, as if they were ready to strip off their clothes and fight to the death.

Finally Sheri said, "If I had wanted to mate you, Bentley, I would have stayed. I know all of you, know how you are, and none of you would have let me go, not easily anyway. And until now, I was still wondering if this place, these pack members, would truly be my new home. I love Yellowknife. It was…you were…my pack." They could all see her fight back tears, but David smelled something new now. It wasn't nerves or fear or regret. It was resolve. "But now I know what it means to be part of a pack that values me as more than a breeder. A pack who sees me for me, and not for what pups I can have. I'm sorry for the way I left, I am. But I'm staying here, and there's nothing you can do about it."

Elizabeth knew why it took Sheri so long to speak up. It wasn't because she wanted to leave; it was because she didn't want to put the pack members here in danger, should Kintail take this further.

"You have her answer," Elizabeth said, her voice strong. "She wants to stay here. And, Bentley, she broke up with you before she left. You need to let it go."

"That's the problem," Bentley said, looking growly. "She has always been too spontaneous. Only this time when she changes her mind and wants to come home, like I know she will, she might not have a home to come back to."

"She has a home with us," Cameron said. He'd been letting it play out, but stepped into the fray now. "She doesn't have to worry about that. Even if she left us to live somewhere else for a time, she would always be welcome back here."

That was what Elizabeth loved about Cameron and Faith's pack.

Hans's stance shifted a bit, his shoulders dropping just a little. "You are sure you want to do this? Dad is ready to cut you off from the family permanently if you don't return."

Elizabeth rubbed Sheri's arm with reassurance. She knew Sheri would feel bad about the rift with her family, but if she stayed with the Canadian Arctic pack, then what? She could be close to family and unhappy with the pack and not willing to mate Bentley, and possibly have no other potential mates up there. Or stay here, miss her family and enjoy her life, her new job, her new friends who felt no animosity toward her whatsoever.

"If that's what they want to do, that's their call. I would hope we could still see each other, even if they have to travel down here to do it, but this is where I want to live," Sheri said with assurance.

The door opened, and Elizabeth figured they had a client, but instead Slade walked in through the door, wearing his leather jacket and boots and looking like a hotshot WWII aviator, all smiles. "Hey, Sheri, I was going to—" He saw the newcomers and abruptly stopped speaking, his nose elevating slightly as he took in the aggressive scent spread throughout the room. "Sorry," he said, obviously guessing what was going on. Elizabeth knew, as did the rest of the pack, that Slade's presence—as an unmated wolf—would only make things worse. "Looks like I'm interrupting a meeting. Should I go?" He deferred to Cameron. If a fight were inevitable, he would clearly be an asset.

A low snarl came from Bentley. No matter how much Slade had tried to appear unthreatening, wolves always knew. Sheri couldn't help her reaction to him, and Bentley sensed it.

He took a step in the direction of Slade, and the entire room felt as if it were waiting for holy hell to be unleashed, but Kintail held up a hand, freezing the moment in time.

"We won't make the offer again," he said.

"You won't need to," Sheri said, her voice determined.

A potential client came into the office, breaking the tension, and Owen said, "I'll take it." He led the client into his office, shut the door, and that seemed to be the end of the discussion with the other wolves. Kintail bent his head in the direction of the door, and Bentley and Hans and the other two men left the building, Bentley's shoulders stiff in anger. Kintail stayed back.

"They need you more than you need them," Kintail said

to both Elizabeth and Sheri. "They're using you because they can't control their shifting."

"We're happy here. And I'm mated to David. We have the freedom to do as we want, and the pack is much more democratic. No bullying people about what they have to do," Elizabeth said.

"I expected it of you, Elizabeth, because of some misplaced loyalty to a newly turned wolf. But Sheri—" Kintail said.

"Because of my friendship with Elizabeth, I've been on the outs with the pack too. So don't act like you didn't know how I've been treated. I'm sure you were all for it. You've always punished those who don't see things your way," Sheri said.

Kintail shook his head. "Be forewarned, neither of you are welcome back. You're dead to me, you're dead to the pack"—he stared hard at Sheri—"and you will be dead to your parents." Then he stalked out of the building.

It was quiet except for the low conversation coming from Owen's office. Sheri took a deep breath, then another, and then dissolved into tears. Elizabeth quickly took her into David's office and hugged her. "This is a choice you had to make, unfortunately. Even though you shouldn't have had to make it. You should have been allowed to come here to live with us and return when you wanted to see your family. That's the problem with Kintail's rule."

"I agree." Sheri sniffled and wiped her tears with a tissue from a box on David's desk.

"Are you going to be okay?"

"Yeah." Sheri hugged her back. "I'm sorry I put everyone in a bind like this. If my parents really feel that way about me, then I guess cutting ties would be the best thing for us anyway." She sounded saddened by the prospect.

"Well, if the pack had different leadership, maybe things would change, and then you could see your family again. Especially if your family comes around to seeing this is what makes you happy."

David came into the office and without preamble said, "We're going to split the two of you up tonight. Sheri, you'll stay with one of the other families. Elizabeth, you'll stay with me. We want to ensure these men don't try to grab one or both of you, now that they know where you are and they're here. They could try taking Elizabeth, knowing you would try to go after her, just to have them release her." He gave Sheri a reassuring smile. "Just know we won't let anything happen to you. To either of you. As long as you want to be here with us, you have our backing."

Cameron and Gavin came into the office and added their voices to David's pledge.

Cameron said, "I'm going to alert our mates about the trouble we could be in for."

Elizabeth realized that Kintail might resort to grabbing one of the PIs' mates instead of either Elizabeth or Sheri, figuring they might be too well protected. What if they grabbed one of the kids?

That night, they all got together at Cameron's house. Even Slade was there, looking like he was eager to show Sheri he was glad she was staying with the pack.

Slade had always been a wild card, reckless, carefree, a fighter, and damn fun to be around. It probably stemmed from a life of growing up in the family business. Slade and Amelia's parents had their own seaplanes and sightseeing and canoe excursion service. Slade and Amelia had always been a part of that, and their parents were good people. Family-first wolves, which made them great pack members. Their children were no different.

And no matter how busy their parents were at any given time, or even Amelia and Slade, they were there for moral support whenever the pack needed it.

Slade said to Sheri, "I'm glad you stood up to Kintail and the others. Are we all running in the woods tonight?"

"We are," David said.

Cameron said, "We need to stick together. Sheri can stay with any of the families she wants to."

"I've got an early morning flight, but if you need anyone on guard duty, put me on first watch," Slade said.

"Will do."

His sister gave him a look that said he'd better get some sleep tonight.

"I'll be fine," he said, answering her unspoken question. "I don't crash planes like you do."

"I only did it twice and there were extenuating circumstances."

Gavin smiled, since he'd been in both planes that Amelia had crashed, not due to her own fault in either case. Luckily, they both had survived each of the crashes.

"So what do we do about the security of the homes

tonight? Maybe it would be better to stay in just two of the houses instead," Faith said. "Better security that way. I worry about the little ones. They would be the easiest to grab and hold for ransom. The ransom being Sheri."

David didn't want this to dissolve into a wolf battle. He worried about his friends, his family, getting seriously injured or killed if this ended up going sideways.

"Maybe they just went home," Sheri said.

"Do you really believe that?" Cameron sounded skeptical.

"I'm hopeful. You have the numbers," Sheri said.

"But we also have the kids to worry about, and the women," Cameron said.

Sheri took a deep breath, looking downcast. "Maybe I should have just gone back with them." Her comment seemed to take everyone by surprise as they stared at her in disbelief.

"No," Elizabeth said. "They can't bully you into returning with them. We will stick with you through all of this and beyond."

"But if anyone gets hurt because of me—"

"It wouldn't be because of you," David said, "but because of them. Because of Kintail."

Sheri smiled, but it lacked conviction.

"If this is something you seriously want to do, then we're backing you all the way," Owen said.

Cameron agreed. So did Faith.

"I don't want you to go," Faith said. "I just want to make contingency plans for the children."

"We'll do that." Cameron ran his hand over Faith's back.

Once they finished dinner, they all stripped, ready to run as a pack.

They tore off through the woods, enjoying the night sounds, an owl hooting to another, loons calling out to others, cicadas and crickets singing. The fresh scent of water in the air hinted at rain, but David still couldn't shake the feeling they needed to find Kintail and his men and set up surveillance on them.

Elizabeth bumped into him in playful fun, momentarily taking his mind off Kintail. Even Sheri and Slade seemed to be living in the moment, enjoying each other's company as they ran through the trees ahead of them. Everyone was watching the little ones, too, shortening their strides to make sure they stayed together as a pack.

They ran along the shore of the lake for some time until the wolf pups kept falling behind, tired—except for Corey, who kept moving off to chase night critters, forcing Cameron to nip at him to return to the pack.

Someday, David could see Corey running his own pack. Then he would learn what a job it was to keep the little ones in line. He smiled.

When they were afraid they would have to carry the worn-out wolf pups home, they all headed back. At Cameron's house, they ushered the slowpoke wolf pups up the steps. Even Corey was ready to call it a night. Then they got together to figure out a strategy for securing the houses against any possible attack by Kintail.

"Since you have the biggest family, I think we need to have more of our people stay here, for security purposes," David said to Cameron and Faith.

"I agree," Faith said.

"I'll help with the kids." Sheri sounded eager to make up for causing trouble for the pack, even though it wasn't her fault.

"Perfect, thanks. Cameron usually does reading time, so you and I can get their baths going," Faith said.

Before long, they heard water running in the tub, and then kids splashing in it.

"Okay, so who all is staying with whom?" David asked the others.

"Maybe we should all just stay here," Elizabeth suggested. "I know you thought it might be better if we were split up, but there's power in numbers."

"Slumber party," Amelia called out, and the kids all shouted with glee from down the hall.

Even David agreed they'd be better off staying together. He would have liked some alone time with Elizabeth, but they had years for that. Tonight, it was more important they were safe.

"We've got the couches that fold out as futons, an extra bedroom, sleeping bags, and comfortable blow-up mattresses. We can make this work," Cameron said.

In the old days, they wouldn't have had any trouble with sleeping arrangements like that. But today, with mates, it was a whole different story.

"We've got about everything you might need, but if there's anything else you need, go in pairs and get them. Toiletries, snacks, if we don't have them," Cameron said.

"We'll go in fours and pick up from each house," David said, wanting to make sure that everyone stayed safe.

David, Elizabeth, Gavin, and Amelia headed out while

the others stayed at Faith and Cameron's house, David's head on a constant swivel.

"Are you okay?" Elizabeth asked, rubbing his arm as they headed back to his house first.

"Yeah, I am. I was just wondering if there are more of them."

"Just the thought I had," Gavin said behind them as he and Amelia walked a few paces back. Seemed they were all worried about the same thing.

"We should have tailed them when they left," Elizabeth said. "I'd feel less like a sitting duck if we had some sense of where they were, what they were up to. I think we need to be more proactive."

David remembered Elizabeth helping them when they were desperate to join their friends and how she was a woman of action even then. Even returning to care for her grandmother showed that call to action was in her blood. Then coming down here to see him. Now dealing with her old pack leader.

"You're right," Gavin said. "I don't like feeling on the defensive like this."

"I've been thinking the same," David said.

Amelia cleared her throat. "I think we'll be all right for tonight anyway. I had to cancel my flights because of thunderstorms rolling in. I doubt they'll do anything in the middle of a storm."

"Oh, good." David breathed a sigh of relief. "Hopefully that gives us time to come up with a plan to go after them." Although he knew a little rain wouldn't have stopped him if someone had Elizabeth.

He just hoped Kintail didn't feel the same way.

Chapter 24

KINTAIL PACED ACROSS THE ROOM OF HIS RENTAL CABIN, furious things hadn't gone his way. Once Sheri had seen Kintail, that should have been enough to make her change her mind about not returning to the pack. And her brother, damn Hans, he should have spoken up and said more than he did. Even her boyfriend, Bentley, had been a lost cause. But what really bothered him was Sheri's lack of respect for him. He'd told her to come, and she refused.

She refused her pack leader. Made him look weak. Ineffective.

Made him look like he wasn't in control.

Kintail thought Sheri might capitulate until Elizabeth, the traitor, interceded on Sheri's behalf. And then some flyboy showed up and Kintail had been certain Bentley would step it up and do more to convince Sheri to come home with him. Instead, he looked like he was about to hit the pilot, and Kintail hadn't wanted that. Not there. Not then.

Sure, Bentley was angry with her—so was Kintail—but hell, Bentley hadn't helped the situation at all! On one hand, the pilot showed up, eager to see her, and glum-faced Bentley didn't even make an attempt to hug her in greeting, to show he cared for her, did nothing but glower at her. Hell, couldn't he have at least acted like he was glad to see her? And if he wasn't, then why the hell did he come, anyway?

He was surrounded by idiots and incompetents.

Kintail should have brought Sheri's parents with him instead. Except they were still in Cancun, and they weren't coming home over the damn situation to put the pressure on Sheri to return home either. Though they said they'd tried calling her and they couldn't get through. Maybe one of them would have convinced her to return to Yellowknife if they'd come with him. Hans telling her that her parents had disowned her wasn't the way to go. Kintail guessed he should have given the two men a script that told them exactly what to say, since they hadn't seemed to be able to come up with their own dialogue that had helped one bit.

Bentley stood at the window, looking out at the woods, running his hands through his hair. It was a nervous tic he had when he felt unsettled.

"I don't know," Hans said. "Sheri seems happy here. Maybe—"

"Why in the hell did I bring you here with me? Remind me," Kintail said.

Hans frowned. "You said she was coerced to come here. That Elizabeth and the others had forced her to leave with them to hide the fact Elizabeth was leaving for good. So Sheri wouldn't tell on her. But Sheri genuinely seems to fit right in here with Cameron's pack, and I don't think it's a good idea to take her home with us if she's happy here."

Bentley scoffed. "You were the one who was so gung ho on showing the newly turned wolves what a mistake they'd made in taking her in."

"I was when I thought she was forced to come and that she might have been hurt. Or at least threatened. Those were your own damn words, Bentley. But Sheri's happy here. I know my sister and that was no act. Do you think she'll be ecstatic to return home? You didn't even make an effort to hug her or smile at her or anything," Hans accused her boyfriend.

"Neither did you," Bentley said. "You were just as angry with her."

"Okay, look," Kintail said. "We need unity in this, not us fighting with each other. Both of you failed. Bentley, I didn't think I would have to tell you to greet her warmly in an effort to reassure her all would be well when she returned home with us."

"You didn't tell me I had to do that. I thought the whole point was that we were supposed to scare her into returning," Bentley said.

It took every ounce of control Kintail had not to chuck Bentley right out that window. "Only if we couldn't convince her otherwise," Kintail said. How dense could his wolves be?

"But *you* didn't act like that," Bentley said.

"I'm the pack *leader*. I'm supposed to be angry about it. You two were supposed to be eager to see her, grateful she was unharmed, excited to have her return to the pack. And if that didn't work, use the other tactic—threaten her with your parents disowning her, Hans, and you, Bentley, you were just supposed to be desperate to have her return home with us. The way you both handled it made her resolve to stay here."

"Yeah, but even if we did get her to come with us, she'd

be right back where she was. I know she wasn't happy back home. Not with her job." He threw Bentley a nasty glare. "And not with the selection of possible mates. I mean, compared to what this pack has to offer her—" Hans said.

"A bunch of dangerous, newly turned wolves that she would have to babysit all the time," Kintail growled.

"Right, but if they're not giving her grief like we're giving her," Hans persisted, "why *should* she come back?"

"Whose side are you on?" Kintail was getting ready to let Hans walk all the way home to Yellowknife, but he needed to keep them together as a unified force in case it came down to a fight.

"I'm on your side," Hans said.

"Good. I was beginning to wonder. You do realize if your parents finally get ahold of her, she'll learn they haven't disowned her."

"I'm not telling Sheri any different," Hans said. "And she won't learn any different. Our parents are upset and for good reason. She'll know that."

Kintail turned to Bentley. "Call her and—"

"I think she blocked me. I have been calling her and she won't answer."

Kintail let out his breath in exasperation.

Cameron's pack was continuing to create dissent when Kintail thought he had wiped his hands clean of them. Hell, all he had wanted to do was save David's life, but they'd had to turn Owen because he had been a witness to it. Beyond that, Kintail hadn't wanted to deal with the rest of them. If Cameron and Gavin hadn't gotten involved, Kintail would have succeeded in making David and Owen members of his pack and Elizabeth and David could have been together in Yellowknife, for all Kintail cared.

It was all for the pack. Always. Everything.

And as leader of the pack, it was on him to take care of this, once and for all.

Back at Cameron's, Elizabeth's phone rang, and she glanced at the caller ID. To her surprise, it was Sheri's parents, Fred and Georgia Whitmore. How the heck did they get her phone number?

"We want to know what's going on with Sheri. We know her friendship with you means the world to her. We understand that. We also know she's easily influenced, whether it's a good thing or bad. Living among wolves who have shifter issues can be dangerous. And we love our daughter. We just want her to be safe," Georgia said.

"You really need to talk to Sheri about this." Elizabeth didn't want to be the go-between.

"Please, Elizabeth. Can you just tell us if it's safe for her there? Is she happy? We don't want anyone to force her to return to Yellowknife, I don't care if it's the pack leader's wishes or not. Bentley's been insisting she was planning to mate him, and we just don't know what to think anymore."

"You should trust your instincts. You know Sheri, know what she's like. She wouldn't do anything she didn't think was right." No sense in whitewashing this.

"You did what *you* felt was right. And we understand that. You had your reasons, including a wolf who was waiting to mate you," Georgia said. "But Sheri *left* a wolf who wanted to mate her."

Elizabeth smiled at David, who'd been listening with interest. Then she let out her breath. "David and I have something really special going on between us. Sheri didn't have that with Bentley, no matter what he may think. And she's her own person. No one here is pressuring her to stay. Wolves help other wolves, that's how it should be, anyway. And these people are good people.

"If she wants to return home, and then come back here later, we will welcome her with open arms. It's not the same with Kintail's pack, and you know it. How much do you want to bet if she does return home, your pack will ostracize her for going with me in the first place? Plus she's building a life here. She signed up to work on a criminology degree so she can be a PI. Did you know that? She's happy. Do you want to take all that away from her?"

Silence.

"They're saying you've disowned her. Is that true?" Elizabeth said.

"What? We haven't disowned her. We would never do that." Georgia asked, "Fred, did you say we disowned her?"

"No, love."

"We didn't disown her. Who said that? Kintail?"

"No, your own son did. He's here with Kintail and his crew, and I don't think they're going to leave quietly either."

Silence. Someone was going to get in trouble when they got home, Elizabeth thought.

"Sheri's phone isn't working," Georgia said.

"We changed phone numbers because we wanted local ones"—not to mention they didn't want to be hassled by Kintail and his pack members—"but I'll ask if she wants to speak to you." Elizabeth padded down the hall to where Sheri was curled up in a sleeping bag in the kids' room. "Sheri," Elizabeth whispered. "Your mom and dad want to talk to you."

Sheri joined Elizabeth and they went outside on the front porch so they wouldn't disturb everyone, but David and Owen came outside with them to ensure their safety.

Sheri put the call on speakerphone. "Hi, Mom, Dad, I want you to know I love you both."

"We love you too, honey," Georgia said. "We want the best for you, and if that means living in the United States, then that's what you need to do."

"We didn't disown you," her dad said quickly, wanting to set her straight on that. "Like your mom said, we love you. Hans was wrong in telling you that we disowned you. We'll speak to him in a bit. If staying with the new pack is something you really feel you have to do, then you do it. Your momma went against her own pack to mate me and join mine, so I get it. You need to follow your heart. If your momma hadn't, we wouldn't have been mated and had two beautiful children."

"And we'll come to see you when we can," Georgia said.

Sheri scoffed. "If Kintail allows it."

"He's not going to stop us. He can try—" Georgia said.

"If he does try, you can count on us to step in," David said.

"This is David Davis speaking. You don't know me, but my pack has vowed to protect Sheri and Elizabeth in the event your pack leader decides to take aggressive action."

More silence.

"He wouldn't," Georgia finally said.

"Sure he would. I have firsthand knowledge of it," Elizabeth said. "He was furious when he lost David and Owen to their own new pack. He's still not over it. The notion that two more of his pack members jumped ship has made him even more angry."

"Has he threatened you girls in any way?" Fred asked.

"Kintail was pretty quiet, but you know him. He likes to try to get others to do his dirty work for him. I'm sure that's why he told Hans to say I was disowned."

"You aren't disowned, and we'll speak to Hans about it right after we finish this call. How do you feel about Bentley? Is there any hope for reconciliation?" her dad asked.

Everyone waited for Sheri to respond. She stuck her chin up. "No. Even if I never find a wolf to mate, I wouldn't mate him."

"Are there any male prospects there?" Georgia asked.

Elizabeth knew Sheri's mother wanted to have grandkids.

"Possibly." Sheri glanced at the door leading back inside. Leading back to Slade. "We'll have to see."

Elizabeth thought it was too much to hope for that Georgia and Fred, and even Sheri's brother, would join their pack, but Georgia was a midwife, and they could certainly use her. Fred built homes for pack members, and he would be a real help with the pack too. She wasn't sure Cameron and the others would want to increase the pack size that much, but if they did, all of them were royals, so that could be a good thing.

"Mate or no, I have a future here. Friends. A pack that needs me. A job. I'm going to be a PI... Can you believe it? I miss you both already, but this is where I want to be. I hope you can understand that."

That seemed to stun her parents into silence for a moment. Then Sheri's dad said, "That's wonderful. We love you so much. We're here for you, whatever you need."

They finally said their good nights, with Georgia saying, "And you keep her safe, David, you and your partners. We're counting on you."

He smiled. "We have every intention of doing so. They're part of the pack now."

"By the way," Elizabeth asked before they hung up, "how did you get my new phone number?"

"Kintail told us about the White Wolf Investigative Services near Ely, Minnesota, that Cameron and the others were running," Sheri's mother said. "We found Cameron MacPherson's number, called it, and a helpful little boy answered the phone, by the name of—"

"Corey?" Elizabeth asked.

"Uh, yes, and he gave us your number and Sheri's from his momma's list of contacts," she said.

They all looked at each other in laughing exasperation. That pup was lucky he was so cute, because man, he caused more than his share of trouble.

Chapter 25

David didn't know what he'd been expecting from the conversation he just heard, but it wasn't that. Sheri's parents clearly loved and supported her, of that he had no doubt. He even wondered if they might be open to coming to Ely to join their pack.

He wasn't going to act on that now—it would take the whole pack agreeing to it, and figuring out the logistics of such a move—but he definitely wanted to come back to that idea. It would be amazing to continue to grow the pack, especially with people who clearly loved and wanted the best for their children.

They headed inside, ready to settle back in for the night. David really hoped there'd be no more surprises.

"You know they want me to be mated though," he heard Sheri whisper to Elizabeth as they entered the house.

"We'll work on it," Elizabeth said. She and David watched her walk back to the room where she was staying, and then they slipped into the sleeping bag they were sharing.

"Maybe her parents will come to live with us too," Elizabeth said.

"Are you sure you can't read my mind? That was exactly what I was thinking too." Elizabeth snuggled against him, and he pressed against her, wishing they were in his bed and not in a sleeping bag, sleeping among his friends.

He was restless that night, and not just because he wanted to ravish his mate. Kintail, unfortunately, was never far from his mind.

But thankfully, they didn't have any trouble. Thunderstorms pummeled the area, just as Amelia had predicted, and lightning lit up the house over and over again, the thunder booming loudly, some of it shaking foundations. David never complained about his wolf hearing, but for once he wished he could dial it down a notch. As it was, the storm sounded as if it was on top of them more or less all night long.

The next morning, they all had a big breakfast together, everyone looking a little bleary-eyed. The storms partially cleared, though Amelia said they would return later that day. Everyone helped clean up and organize the sleeping bags spread out everywhere.

"I called my uncle Strom last night," Candice said, "telling him I would love to see him and that we have some new pack members, and I of course mentioned Kintail and his men."

"You know he'll be flying up here in his private jet in a heartbeat, right? With reinforcements?" Cameron asked. "And what if Kintail and his men leave without causing any further trouble? He will have come up here for no good reason."

"Ha! He's always looking for a good excuse to visit me. If nothing comes of it, fine. We get to have a big pack celebration for their visit. And we're always up for that. Besides, if my uncle didn't come and anything happened to any of us, he would feel terrible," Candice said.

"So he's coming?" Elizabeth asked.

"Do jaguars have rosettes? I imagine so. He didn't say he was for sure, but I can't imagine he won't be here as soon as he can." Candice shook out a blanket and started folding it up.

Elizabeth hated anyone else being put at risk for her, but if Kintail called for reinforcements, the wolves here could be at a disadvantage. It'd be good to have more backup, just in case.

"Okay, well, I have to admit, I called my dad in Portland and told him the same thing as far as wanting to see him, and that we had an issue with the white wolf pack that had turned us. He said he was going to confer with Leidolf and get back to me," Faith said.

Everyone smiled at the news, and David even chuckled.

"If we get reinforcements from the jaguars *and* the red wolves, Kintail won't know what hit him," he said, reaching over to rub Elizabeth's back.

"Well," Elizabeth said. "And here I once thought it was just our small pack against the world."

"No way," David said. "We're not like the gray wolf pack out of Seattle or your former pack. We help others out as much as we can. And sometimes, we get help too. We've got each other's backs, no matter what."

And hopefully their backup arrived soon, Elizabeth thought.

They all gathered at the office later that morning. The PIs were going to search the local rental agencies to see if they could locate Kintail and his men. Faith and the kids would hang out there until they could have more protection at home later. Reluctantly, even Candice went to the office to write on her book, sequestering herself in Owen's office since he wasn't using it, afraid she wouldn't get any writing done with all the distractions. But she closed his door and the blinds in his office window that looked out into the seating area, and they could hear her typing away on her laptop.

Cameron stepped out of his office, waving around a piece of paper covered in his writing. "Kintail rented cabin five, Big Pines Resort, for three days."

"I'll go check it out," David said.

"I'll go with you," Owen offered.

"Me too." Elizabeth was already headed for the door, not to be left behind.

"I'm going with you too," Sheri said.

"Gavin and I'll hold down the fort, try to get some casework done, and we can switch off with you in a couple of hours," Cameron said.

"Sounds good." David and the rest of his surveillance team headed out to his vehicle. When they arrived at the cabin, they found the same cars parked there that had been sitting in the agency's parking lot.

"I'll make sure it's them." David stripped and shifted in the vehicle, and Elizabeth opened the car door for him.

He lifted his head, checking to see which way the wind was blowing, and moved as close to the log cabin as he could without being seen. His nose immediately caught the scents of Kintail, Hans, and Bentley, and the other two men Kintail had with him. Fresh scents.

They were definitely still around.

He slipped back through the woods to the car, shifted and dressed, then stayed out of sight while they observed the cabin. He gave a call to Cameron. "Kintail and his men are at the rental cabin. The cars are still parked there, and I heard voices. Kintail is mad at Hans and Bentley. I couldn't make out what they were saying exactly, but the tone was clear enough."

"Okay, good job. Keep me posted."

A few minutes later, they watched as Hans came out of the cabin and ran his hands through his hair, looking totally pissed off.

Then a vehicle drove up and Hans got into it. Now what? Should they follow him to see where he was going? Or continue to watch the cabin?

"We should stay with the pack leader," Sheri said, reaffirming what David thought. "He's calling the shots. I'm sure my parents told my brother off, and he's probably on the outs with Kintail now too. He wouldn't like my brother to show any weakness when it comes to doing his bidding."

"Okay, we stick with them," David said.

Splitting forces might have made sense in a different scenario, but no way was he putting Sheri or Elizabeth at risk. Plus Sheri was right. Kintail was the real threat.

They'd been there for about a half hour when Cameron called them. They were far enough away that David felt comfortable putting it on speakerphone. "Hey, Hans is here at the office looking to speak with his sister."

Sheri's mouth gaped. "No."

"Yeah, apparently his dad gave him a dressing-down about lying to you about being disowned. So Hans is upset about that, and the pack leader is doubly upset with him for not standing up to his parents. Hans wants to talk to you in person. I'm coming to get you, if everyone else is busy with surveillance."

A couple of new cars pulled up to the cabin. David tensed. That couldn't be good.

"Uh, yeah, Cameron? Ask Hans if Kintail called in reinforcements to get more of his people down here," he said.

They heard Cameron ask the question, his voice muffled.

Hans got on the phone. "Listen, Kintail left me out of what is going on. I'm on the outs with him now. But I wouldn't be surprised if he called for backup."

"What do *you* plan to do?" Sheri sounded irritated with her brother for being mixed up in all this in the first place.

"I don't know, but I want to talk to you in person," Hans said.

Elizabeth and Sheri wrote down the names of the men they saw leaving the cars and entering Kintail's cabin. They were definitely called in by Kintail.

"They're some of the men who were on the bear hunt with you and Owen, David," Elizabeth said.

"I recognize some of them. Though some of them were wolves at the time," David said.

"Yeah, I recognize them too," Owen said. "So they've come to use brute force. Not surprising. They did the first time they tried to return us to the pack."

Sheri called her parents and put it on speakerphone. "Hey, Mom, Kintail has called up the troops to try and force me to go home."

Her dad got on the phone. "We're flying up there from Cancun."

"I don't want you to get mixed up in this."

"We are anyway. It's not right that Kintail thinks he can dictate whether anyone leaves the pack. Your mother is already getting a flight booked for us to come out right away."

"Thanks," Sheri said. "I hope it doesn't hurt your standing with the pack."

"Don't worry about that. We'll be there soon, I promise," her dad said.

"Okay, thanks, Dad." Sheri ended the call. "This is awful. I didn't want my parents to get in the middle of it." Sheri called her brother and put the call on speakerphone. "Thanks to you, my ex-boyfriend, and our pack leader, we've got a real crisis here. And Mom and Dad are going to be in the middle of it. You have a choice to stand with us or against us, but our parents are on my side."

"Hell, Sheri."

"Hey, if you all had left well enough alone, everything would have been fine."

"All right, damn it. I'm with you. I can't believe this. All because you followed your friend here."

"And *you* followed *us* here!"

"Fine. I know. Geez," Hans said. They heard a deep sigh, then he asked: "What can I do, Cameron?"

"Not screw this up!" Sheri suggested, as only a sister could, then hung up the phone.

David was glad she hadn't backed down. She was just like Elizabeth in that way. It probably didn't hurt that her parents were coming. He just hoped they wouldn't regret throwing their support behind him and his pack.

He also wondered if maybe they wanted to check out the new pack while they were at it. He suspected the way Kintail was, he would be as pissed off at them when they returned to the pack, which might increase the chances of them moving here too. He hadn't had a chance to talk to the rest of the pack yet, but he knew they would be welcome.

He just wasn't sure where that left Hans. But that was a problem for another day.

The phone rang again, another call from Cameron.

"We're going to switch out with you," Cameron said. "We don't want the women there now that Kintail has called in reinforcements."

"All right. We'll wait for you to arrive. They're all still inside. I'm sure Kintail has something planned."

"Okay," Cameron said. "We're on our way. Hans is coming with us."

"Can you trust him?" David asked.

"I think he's being sincere."

"Okay, gotcha. We don't want to hurt him and undo all the goodwill we have with his parents." David could just imagine that backfiring on them.

Not long after, Cameron and Gavin arrived with Hans. Sheri didn't want to speak with him, and he was just as irritated with her. But again, that was a problem for another day. Sheri's problem, not his.

David said, "Are you sure you don't want me to stay?"

"No, you and Owen watch over everyone else. We'll let you know when the men leave the cabin. I doubt they'll want to try anything until tonight though."

"Which is just what Kintail will think you'll believe," Hans warned.

David shared a look with Cameron.

Hans saw it and interpreted it correctly. "I'm on your side. Maybe not by choice," he said, "but I'm trying to do the right thing now." He ran a hand through his hair, the strands sticking up in every direction. "I *thought* I was doing the right thing before, what my parents would have wanted even, but they made it clear I was dead wrong." He turned toward Sheri. "It may not mean much now, but I'm sorry."

Sheri didn't seem quite ready to forgive and forget, and David suspected Hans's about-face was more that he was afraid his parents would disown *him* if he didn't come around, but if that's what it took, then fine.

And maybe the older couple could convince Kintail he was making a mistake. Unfortunately, it sounded like it might be a little while before Sheri's parents arrived, and all signs were pointing to the fact Kintail was putting a dangerous plan into motion as they spoke.

Chapter 26

David drove his surveillance team—Elizabeth, Sheri, and Owen—to the office. He'd barely sat down when he got a call from Gavin.

"Yeah, what's up?"

"Nothing with Kincaid. It's about the Moore case. The signature signing over the loan to the partner is a forgery. The handwriting expert reviewing it says it's definitely not Mr. Moore's signature. Seems Mr. Moore was savvy enough to understand something was up, medicated or not. Unfortunately, that might have been what caused his death."

"What do you mean?" David said. "His death wasn't natural?"

"Well, there is growing evidence that someone tampered with the dosage of his medication, and all signs point to the partner. I'd say yeah, we are looking at a murder case."

"Ah, damn it." David closed his eyes. He hated cases that took a turn like this.

"Yeah," Gavin said. "It looked like Mr. Moore wasn't dying fast enough to suit Cooper. I'm turning over everything we've found to Ms. Moore, and she's passing it along to the police."

"Okay, good." When they ended the call, David let Elizabeth and Sheri know what'd happened.

"Oh, wow," Sheri said. "Poor Ms. Moore."

"Poor *Mr*. Moore," Elizabeth added. "I guess you never know what you might dig up when investigating a case."

"Yeah," David said. "Sometimes it's really straightforward. Sometimes it's a shot in the dark. Then we see the light."

Candice came out of Owen's office smiling. "Heads up! Uncle Strom is arriving here in about fifteen minutes with old friends of ours, the Andersons, and some other jaguars in the United Shifter Force, and one human, Rowdy Sanderson, who was dying to meet us. They are bringing camping supplies if we don't have enough room for them."

Corey ran up the stairs to join them. "Granddaddy and Grandma are coming!" he shouted on repeat, making sure the whole office heard.

Faith and the other kids soon followed, and she ran her hand over Corey's hair. "My dad and mom and Leidolf and some of his men are arriving in a few minutes. He said they ran into the jaguars at the airport, and Leidolf, being the red pack leader, asked what Uncle Strom and the others were doing there."

"Had they not met before?" Elizabeth asked.

"Nope. Which is why Uncle Strom asked *them* what the hell they were doing there. And if they *were* Kintail's men, they'd better think twice about being there," Faith said.

"That's all we need: a big cat-and-wolf fight between our rescuers," Gavin said.

"Well, they figured it out, so it's all good," Faith said.

"So they're all coming in at the same time. Good show," David said. "We will probably need to pick up some more groceries when we can. Or pool what we have if we can't do that."

"And plan for sleeping arrangements," Faith said. "I'll begin working on that."

Faith and the kids went back downstairs, Candice returned to Cameron's office—since he was still with Gavin watching Kintail's cabin—and David and Owen took some time to review their other open cases.

A short time later, several cars pulled up into the parking lot of the agency. Everyone went still, and it was clear they shared the same concern: Were the jaguars and red wolves joining them? Or had Kintail and his men decided to come to the agency to force the issue with Sheri leaving them and not waiting until dark, like Cameron and the others thought they might?

Candice answered those unasked questions almost as soon as the first car door opened. "It's Uncle Strom," she said, coming out of the office. David and Owen hurried outside, smiling widely at Uncle Strom—everyone called him that—and Everett and Demetria Anderson, and Rowdy Sanderson—who David recognized from the search Elizabeth had pulled together to find him—and six other jaguars he didn't know.

As promised, Leidolf was there too. David recognized him right off the bat. He was joined by Faith's father and her mother, and five more of Leidolf's brawny red wolf men. Eighteen able-bodied jaguars and wolves, though Candice's mom and dad and Everett and Demetria would be better suited to helping Faith with the kids than fighting a wolf battle.

Faith and the kids hurried up the stairs from the basement and joined Candice as they all came outside to greet everyone. It was a huge extended family of jaguars and wolves, both white and red.

"Thanks so much for coming," Candice said, hugging her uncle.

Hugs were going around all over the place, except for Elizabeth and Sheri, who stood off to the side, smiling but not getting in on all the rest of it. They didn't know any of these people, yet they were the reason everyone had made the emergency trips here to help out the Cameron pack. David could see how the two women might feel awkward.

He stepped in to quickly remedy that, introducing each of their guests to both Elizabeth and Sheri, Elizabeth being his mate after all, and Sheri her best friend. They were as important to the pack as any of them.

David's phone rang and he stepped away to take a call from Cameron. "Kintail and his men—ten in number—are on their way to the agency. We're following them, but they don't know they have a tail. We'll slip around the back way so we're there when they arrive."

"The red wolf crew and the jaguar crew are here and ready to go."

"Great news. I know Faith and the kids must be so excited to see their family. If you would let them know to go into the basement for a time, I would be forever grateful," Cameron said.

"Doing it now." David hung up and announced Kintail and his men would be there in a few minutes. "Cameron wants his family waiting in the basement, if that works for you all."

"Yeah," Faith's dad said. "Let's go." He and his mate, Faith and the kids all headed inside.

"I'm going inside," Candice said before Owen or her Uncle Strom told her to.

David kissed Elizabeth and gave Sheri a hug, and they went inside too.

Cameron roared up in his car, and he and Gavin got out.

There were handshakes all around and more introductions. David smiled. Man, he felt good.

A few of the men headed inside to get familiar with the office, while Leidolf and some of his men and Uncle Strom and most of his jaguar friends waited with Cameron, David, and Owen outside.

It wasn't long before Kintail's car and two others were pulling up into the parking area. Kintail got out of his car, his gaze jumping from Hans to Leidolf. Kintail's head ticked to the side, sniffing, shifting his eyes to the other red wolves and the jaguars.

He had to understand, in that moment, exactly what he was up against: Hans siding with the enemy, David and his partners, all newly turned, standing as one with the established red wolf pack.

Kintail let his gaze return to Leidolf. He inclined his head in deference. "So we meet again. Still fighting Cameron and his friends' battles, I see."

"We're united by family, if you didn't know. Faith's father is one of my kind and mated to one of my wolves. Though even if we hadn't been united by family, I would have been here as their friend. Sometimes being friends with other packs is the only way to go. Isolationist packs are on their own when it comes to encroaching packs."

David was glad Leidolf had said so. There was a time when Leidolf—being royal—hadn't wanted David and his friends in his own pack. But in the end, they had been united with bonds that went beyond just friendship.

"So in other words," Leidolf said, in case he had to spell it out to the Canadian Arctic wolf pack leader, "we have their back in the event other wolf packs are giving them trouble."

"But not when they wanted to return to Seattle, I understand. A gray wolf pack wouldn't let them stay in the city, their home," Kintail said.

"No. The gray wolf pack had established roots there for centuries. Cameron and his friends were humans when they had grown up there. So it's not the same. Here, this is *their* pack territory, their rules," Leidolf said.

"You really don't want to get involved in this," Kintail said.

"Yeah, I do. Wolf pack boundaries are clear."

Bentley moved forward, all eyes turning on him because of his aggressive stance. "Sheri is *my* wolf."

Leidolf raised a brow.

David stepped forward, mirroring Bentley's aggressive stance. "Sheri came here of her own free will. She has plans to stay with us and is finished with you, as she has told you already. She's not interested in mating you. We don't want a fight over this. She's free to come and go as she pleases." He turned from Bentley, knowing who called the shots. "You can't force her to stay in your pack, Kintail. Think how this could impact your pack if Sheri is forced to return and she's unhappy. How do you think her family would feel?"

"They've disowned her. But if she returns, they'll accept her back," Bentley said, casting Hans a glower as he moved to stand beside David.

"But they haven't disowned her," David said, giving Hans a smile. "We know the truth. Sheri has talked to her parents and they're proud of her for taking a stand to do something she really wants to do with her life."

"We should never have turned you," Bentley said, growling the words.

Leidolf said, "But you did."

And now look, David thought. Now they'd lost two more of their people to Cameron's pack. And maybe even Sheri's parents and her brother, too, if they decided to join them.

"You don't want a fight on your hands," Kintail said finally, not backing down—surely a show for his pack to prove he was still the alpha—though he did glance in Uncle Strom's direction.

The jaguar leaned against one of the rental cars, his arms folded across his chest, looking relaxed and not like he would enjoy taking a bite out of Kintail.

It was a losing battle for Kintail; they all knew it. David just hoped Kintail knew it too. He needed to lick his wounds and return home before anyone got hurt. There were times to fight and times to give up the battle and live for another day.

To David's surprise, Elizabeth and Sheri stepped outside, joining David and Hans as a unified force.

"We're staying," Sheri said.

"She's right," Hans said. "We're staying."

David sensed the smallest ripple of surprise run through his pack. He sniffed, searching for a hidden agenda, a ruse, maybe a plan to infiltrate their pack and steal Sheri away when they were least expecting it. A wolf in sheep's clothing came to mind, so to speak.

But he smelled no subterfuge.

Proof of his sincerity came in Kintail's shocked expression, his lips parting, a scowl spreading across his face. "How do you think your parents will feel about this when they learn both you and your sister have abandoned them?"

Hans scoffed. "Mom and Dad are showing us their support and intend to join the pack."

David glanced at Hans. Hell, he'd better not be saying so if Sheri's parents weren't truly making plans like that.

But Sheri nodded, too, and Cameron said, "Yeah, it's true. Fred and Georgia asked if they could join the pack, and we are happy to accept them as one of us. Family sticks together."

Kintail's mouth gaped again; then he closed it and turned a hard gaze on Leidolf, who shrugged and said, "It's your own doing. Sure, we have to be in charge and show who's boss—especially to upstarts in the pack. But at some point, we have to know when to let go of pack members who are ready to spread their wings and do something new. Wolves in the wild do it all the time. It might not be a perfect situation, but you've helped to make this happen."

Leidolf spoke the truth. Whenever he had something to say, everyone listened. Even Kintail seemed to respect him.

Now it was left to see if Kintail would pay attention.

The fact of the matter was the packs needed to get along. All of them. To fight the rogue wolves together—and most important, to work together to keep their secret from humans. The wolf shifter packs shouldn't be fighting each other. But it was innate, David had learned, because of their wolf instincts. Especially for the royals. To preserve their territory.

For regular wolves, it meant having enough food to eat for the mated alpha pair's offspring and the pack. It meant the pack taking care of the pack leaders' pups to ensure the continuation of their pack. *Lupus garous* didn't have only one alpha pair in the pack, only one alpha couple leading the pack, and only the leaders having offspring. But the wolf shifters were still territorial because of the need to keep control of pack members who might stray from the rules. Someone had to "police" their pack members since they sure didn't want human law enforcement to get involved in their affairs.

"Who are you?" Kintail finally asked Uncle Strom, looking like it was killing him not to know why people who smelled like jaguars, not wolves, and one human were in on this too.

"Jaguar shifters from Texas, and I happen to be Candice's uncle. Candice is Owen's mate."

"But she's an Arctic wolf," Kintail said.

"Yeah, that's the way of the world, isn't it?" Uncle Strom said.

"What about him?" Kintail jerked a thumb at Rowdy Sanderson, the only human in the bunch.

"He works with us," Everett said. "The United Shifter

Force. We deal with shifters that cause the jaguars trouble." Everett gave Kintail a pointed look. "And Rowdy? He's a homicide detective. But if we have a fight here, I'm sure we could get him to look the other way. A few dead wolves from Yellowknife wouldn't really be in his jurisdiction, now, would they?" And that was one poignant threat and promise wrapped up with a neat little bow.

"Do you know what the pounds per square inch bite of a jaguar amounts to? Two hundred. That's a lot of damage. Believe me, you don't want to get in the way of their teeth," Rowdy added.

Kintail looked to Leidolf like he couldn't believe he would stand for threats against wolves, regardless of their pack, but Leidolf only smiled.

David's shoulders relaxed, tension easing out of him. They had won the match.

Kintail was still having a difficult time conceding defeat though. But he finally looked at Bentley and said, "Unless you can change Sheri's mind, she stays here." Kintail had to have the last word on the matter—at least with his own pack member. He'd played his cards with his wolves, hoping to show he had the power behind him, but he had been outmaneuvered. It appeared Kintail was finally capitulating and no blood had been shed—the best of all situations.

Bentley glowered at his pack leader, looking mutinous, but he didn't fight it, ever the loyal wolf.

"And, Sheri, I promise you that you and your family are welcome to return to the pack at any time, and no one will hold it against you," Kintail said.

David didn't believe it. The pack members would be loyal to the pack leader, and David figured they would treat Sheri's family—should they return—the same way they had treated Elizabeth: with disdain.

"Let's go," Kintail said. "Unless you have something to say to Sheri before we leave."

Bentley looked like he wasn't sure what to do. His own alpha posturing was taking a hit. He clearly didn't want to leave things the way they were.

David imagined his friends would give him a hard time if he didn't bring her home.

"Sheri, I want to talk with you." This time Bentley didn't sound like he was telling her what to do.

"Sure," Sheri said graciously. "In David's office. Elizabeth can come with me."

David and Kintail followed, standing outside the office, making sure Bentley didn't take his talk with her to violent extremes. It would reflect badly on both Kintail and Bentley if he did, though some of Leidolf's men were already in the building—and Cameron and Owen went inside too.

Everybody was quiet, shamelessly eavesdropping to hear what they could between Sheri and Bentley. They didn't want Bentley to say one thing and then say that he hadn't said it, or to twist Sheri's words.

Chapter 27

Sheri sat behind David's desk while Elizabeth stood near her, like a silent guard, and Bentley remained standing, not wanting to take a seat on one of the chairs in front of the desk.

"I'm sorry I didn't show you how much I cared for you when I first saw you yesterday," Bentley said, but the effort was belated, and he didn't sound sincere in the least.

"If you had truly cared about me, you would have handled this much differently," Sheri said.

"What do I need to do to make it up to you?"

Elizabeth was surprised he would even make the overture, though she didn't trust that he wouldn't be angry all over again with Sheri if she returned with him and didn't have Cameron's pack to protect her.

"If I ever decided to return—" she said.

He opened his mouth to speak, but she held up her hand to stop him.

"I would hope that we could be friends. But I don't believe I would ever return, given the way Elizabeth was treated. You were at the top of the list as far as giving Elizabeth grief every chance you had. She's my best friend, Bentley. How did you think I would feel about that? That it was okay? Well, it wasn't okay. And being mated to you would have signaled to her that I thought it was fine with me. I know it would be the same for me if I ever returned. Ostracized. I don't want that. I won't put up with it. It would be nice to feel that I could return for a visit because I still have some friends there, and I do still love Yellowknife, but I really doubt it would work. So I'm staying here."

"Then you're not changing your mind about us?"

She shook her head. "You and Kintail share the same beliefs. I love the way Cameron and his pack are so open to us. We can make decisions on our own and the pack agrees. David told us we could join the pack before he even talked to Cameron about it. It's like an open community here. Yet they're protective of and loyal to one another too. It's the best of both worlds. I wish you all the best, Bentley. But I've found a home here."

Elizabeth watched the play of emotions across his face, mostly irritation.

"Cameron and the others wouldn't welcome *me* to the pack," Bentley finally said.

"Maybe not. Maybe you would stir up problems within the pack on behalf of Kintail. Who knows? And even if they did allow you to join, which they might, I wouldn't date you anyway. It was never a sure thing between us. Once Elizabeth returned home from Maine and you treated her so shabbily, that cemented the deal for me. I didn't plan to mate you after that."

"That's why you kept putting off a mating? You were waiting for Elizabeth's grandmother to die and then you were going to leave with her?"

"I didn't know I was going to leave until the last minute. I had my own family to take into consideration, not to mention I worried going with Elizabeth could cause trouble if Kintail stirred up the pack members to come after us."

"Fine, I'll start seeing Olive."

Elizabeth and Sheri smiled. That would be news to Olive, another she-wolf in the Yellowknife pack, since she was already dating a wolf.

"Sure, that's a great idea," Sheri said. If it made him feel better to say he was going to date Sheri's friend, who cared.

Of course, Olive would have something to say about it. And the guy she was seeing would probably put a stop to that notion really quickly.

David was glad when it appeared Bentley was going to give up his wolf-driven need to claim Sheri as his mate whether she wanted it or not. He had to realize that unless she really wanted to go with him, he stood no chance of fighting the combined forces here today.

Bentley came out of the office fuming mad, despite saying he was dating some she-wolf named Olive next. David wondered if he'd been seeing her behind Sheri's back, or if he'd just made it up to rile her. Bentley went out of his way to bump into David, as if to say he would fight him wolf to wolf if he ever had a chance, but David just shrugged it off. Bentley wasn't worth his time. He hoped they wouldn't see the likes of them—Kintail and his men—again, unless it was on better terms. Which, at this point, David didn't think would ever happen.

One of Kintail's men smiled at Sheri in an interested way. David glanced back at Sheri and saw she was smiling back at the man. Who knew where Sheri would end up, but at least in the end it would be her decision.

A new car pulled into the parking lot, and Cameron hurried to speak to the driver.

A potential client? David hoped all the men standing about didn't scare the client off.

Before heading back outside, Kintail waited for Cameron to finish his business with the driver of the car, then the driver backed up and took off. Any of the PI partners could have concluded things with Kintail, but he seemed to believe Cameron was the only one he could do real business with.

"Sheri can return to the pack anytime she wants, Elizabeth too, without any repercussions from the pack members," Kintail said. "I guarantee it. But if they choose to stay here with you and your pack, I give them my blessing."

"And Sheri's brother and their parents?" David was thinking they would have to go home and straighten out their affairs.

Kintail gave Hans a hard look, but finally conceded. "Them too."

David thought it looked like it pained Kintail to say so. David wasn't sure if Kintail was softening his stance against the situation because he was afraid he might lose more pack members due to his totalitarian rule, or he was really coming around and wanted to effect some change in his pack. David hoped the latter, for his people's sake.

Kintail and his men departed, though Bentley cast David a killing look before he got into one of the vehicles and they drove off.

"Do you think it's over?" Uncle Strom asked.

"Maybe, but I doubt it," Leidolf said. "Kintail likes being in control. Seeing his people leave him to join another pack? Even the best of us wolf leaders can feel we're losing our people because we've done something wrong in governing them. We can't all be democratic like Cameron and his pack. They're unique because they have been friends for years. Cameron is just the emergent leader, but everyone has as much of a say in what goes on with their pack as he does. It works for them. The same isn't true for other packs. As wolves, the concept of pack leadership is innate but reinforced by pack behavior as the kids grow up. With Cameron and his friends, it's still a foreign concept."

"Well, I for one feel all this is a step in the right direction," Candice said. "Now that you all are here, it's time to have a celebratory feast."

But more than that. They would run as wolves, and jaguars, renew friendships, and show that sometimes change was good—and having friends was even better.

Hans lightly grabbed his sister's arm and said, "I'm truly sorry I sided with Kintail."

"You did what you thought was right as far as the pack goes. And maybe"—Sheri shrugged—"you believed I needed rescuing from Elizabeth. I know you. If you thought you could convince me to change my mind about staying here, you would have. Then you would have been in good stead with the pack leader, our parents—"

"But not with you. I could have made you miserable." Hans looked like he really regretted having come to force the issue of her returning with him.

"What about you, with staying here with us now?" Sheri asked, sounding genuinely concerned that he had made the right choice too.

"I can become a CPA, something I have always wanted to do. I can take care of the agency's taxes and financial records, maybe even start my own CPA business," Hans said. "Despite what Kintail says, there's really no going back to Yellowknife for any of us. I don't believe he will change overnight like that to accommodate just our family. So I'm going to set up a practice here and make it work."

Sheri hugged her brother. "I'm glad. Are Mom and Dad really staying here with us?"

"They are. They wouldn't stay in the toxic environment of the Arctic pack now that both of us have left. They'll be bad-mouthed for sure that they raised such traitorous children. I hope that Kintail is true to his word about allowing his pack members to come and go as he says, and we'll have to deal with leaving everything we owned behind and see if there's a way to sell our properties and change bank accounts and all that without returning, because I highly doubt he'll live by his word." Hans hugged her back.

"You can use my real estate agent," Elizabeth said. "And we know just where you can set up your bank account."

"And the pack will get you and Mom and Dad passports, birth certificates, everything you need to be American citizens living near Ely, Minnesota," Sheri said.

David was glad to see the sister and brother reunited. "By the way," David said, "what was the deal with the guy who was smiling so much at you?"

Sheri sighed. "He was suitor number two if I had dumped Bentley. I'm not in the least bit interested in him, but I figured it would irk Bentley if he noticed. Payback."

David hoped she wasn't really interested in the guy. He could just imagine the wolf coming to join them; they would be at issue with Kintail all over again for losing another pack member. Best to leave things the way they were already.

Even though the office was still open for the day, Faith was getting everyone to come to their home to have refreshments and go for a swim in the meantime.

He was glad she was taking charge. Sheri looked like she wanted to go with them. "Go," David said. "Have fun. You deserve it."

"Thanks, David. What about Elizabeth?" Sheri asked.

"I'm staying here until they shut the office down for the night," Elizabeth said.

"Okay. I'll see you later, then." Sheri hesitated. "Unless you need me too, David."

"No, we're good."

Even though Cameron and Owen had family among those who had arrived, and David knew they wanted to visit with them because no telling when they would see them again, Cameron said, "I've got a case I need to start working on."

"What is it?"

"A case of a missing donkey. It was all over the news that

you captured the llama and returned it to the farmer the week before you rescued Elizabeth and Sheri. Now a donkey goes on the lam, and the first one they thought of was you and our investigative agency."

"Do you want me to handle it?" David asked.

"No. I need to prove I can find missing farm animals too."

Owen and Gavin laughed just as the phone rang; Elizabeth immediately answered it. "A stray donkey was spied at a lake near here," she relayed. "Can't imagine there are too many missing donkeys out there, so I'm guessing this is your guy. Or girl."

"I'm on it," Cameron said, getting the location.

"Do you want me to go with you?" Gavin asked.

"Yeah, sure."

David and Elizabeth got to work on the cheating husband case. Elizabeth had taken a different tack and started searching whatever she could concerning the wife. And then she had it. "Hey, can we solicit work from someone who hasn't hired us to check on a cheating spouse?"

David smiled at her. "Not normally. Clients come to us, not the other way around. Why?"

"Okay, well, you couldn't find anything on the cheating husband, right? Seems like he's not cheating on her. He's a stand-up guy. He would make a decent wolf mate if he were a wolf. But his wife, on the other hand, has a lover. So to me, it sounds like she's either projecting what she's doing on him, or maybe she's trying to build a case against him so she can leave him for this other guy," Elizabeth said.

David went to her desk to see all the information she'd

collected on the wife. "Hot damn, you're already a hotshot investigator and you just started working here."

"Women's intuition. When Sheri and I were talking about the case, we got to wondering why the woman felt so strongly that her husband was cheating on her and had the brilliant idea to check what she was up to. And that was it."

"Well, you did it."

"So what do we do with the information?" Elizabeth asked. "I mean, if we were hired to learn that the husband was cheating, but it was the wife instead, do we tell her what we know? Or just tell her that her husband isn't cheating on her?"

"We tell the spouse there's absolutely no evidence of her husband cheating on her. If she wants, she can hire another investigator who will learn the same thing. In the meantime, we keep the file on hand, and if the husband ever comes in to hire us, we have the background evidence for it."

Just then a man with a trim beard and glasses walked into the agency. Elizabeth recognized him right away as the very husband they'd just been discussing. "How can we help you?"

"I need to speak with a private investigator about a personal matter," the man said.

David introduced himself and took him into his office and shut the door. "I'm David Davis. What do you need me to look into?"

"I believe you are familiar with my wife?" David didn't indicate one way or another, but apparently he didn't need to confirm. "I found this." He handed David his bank statement.

"I wondered what the retainer's fee was for and learned it was for this office. Normally, I don't bother with the finances. My wife handles all of that. But I was looking into the account because I had an overdraft and thought we had more in our checking account. I looked to see who the check was written to, and it was this agency. I'm sure your handling of a client's case is confidential. So fine. I'll just hire you to learn what it is she's investigating."

David smiled. "Sorry, that's not how it works."

The man smiled back. "No, huh? Then I'll go to a different PI agency and learn the truth."

"Okay, I'm going to ask you a question, and you speculate all you want on why I'm asking the question. Are you cheating on your wife?"

The man's eyes narrowed. "Of course not. And you've proven I haven't, haven't you?"

"I don't disagree with that statement. And that's all I can say about that."

"But she's been cheating on *me*. She lies to me all the time. Says she's out with her girlfriends, but when I run into them, they have no idea what I'm talking about when I ask how they enjoyed their ladies' night out. She spends money on things I can't account for. She dresses up to go out when she never dresses up normally, ever. The lack of intimacy between us—her lack of interest, not mine—is telling. If she's trying to dig up some dirt about me that isn't true, then it's the end for us."

"I can't counsel you one way or another, but I will tell you that we've decided to no longer pursue the case you reference due to lack of evidence." David let the man infer what he would from that as well.

The man sighed with relief and stood, and David stood too, shaking his hand. "Thanks. I feel better about this already."

Once he left, Elizabeth said, "I guess he can't have this." She waved around the folder with her findings on the wife.

"Just file it with the client's case. We can hold on to it. If he wants to hire us, we'll have it on hand. But he already seems to be well aware of the truth, and it looks like he's resolved to end things between them."

"Hopefully by divorce and not some other more drastic means," Elizabeth said.

That was the thing about marital relationships. The PIs never knew how something as simple as a private investigator's report could affect an outcome. Sometimes for the better, sometimes not.

An hour later, Cameron and Gavin came into the agency office, both smelling like a donkey.

"Hey, I know what we smell like. It took a few tries, but we managed to wrangle that donkey back home. You'll have to teach us again about lassoing an animal, though. I finally got it on the third try, but we definitely need more practice." He turned to Elizabeth. "If David didn't tell you already, he worked on a ranch in his youth to get away from his old man. And he learned to lasso horses and cows. It came in handy when he had to rope a runaway llama."

Elizabeth laughed.

"I told you I would handle it," David said, smiling.

"Yeah, next time," Cameron said, and he and Gavin headed home to wash and change clothes, their dress pants dusty and dirty and covered with grass stains.

When Gavin and Cameron returned to the office, David asked, "Did you ever find that standard poodle that went missing?"

"Yeah. Someone turned her in for a reward. I did an investigation of the individual who did and found he'd turned in a lot of dogs for reward money. There were all kinds of reports on him in the paper. So I handed the case over to the police," Cameron said.

"I never would have expected that," Elizabeth said.

"Good, at least maybe the guy will be held accountable," David said.

They worked for a few more hours, until they smelled the telltale scent of steaks grilling.

Owen smiled. "Bet the steaks are courtesy of our jaguar billionaire relative. They must have gone out to get them."

"And I smell hot dogs grilling," Cameron said. "The favorite food of our little ones."

"Hey, I'm off to meet up with Amelia," Gavin said. "See you there."

"We're coming too," Owen and Cameron said, following David and Elizabeth out the door. It was time to celebrate.

Chapter 28

On their way to the barbecue, David got a call from Jimmy's dad saying he didn't have any issues with shifting right now, and he and his son wanted to come in and thank him for all he and Elizabeth had done.

"Hey, we're grilling out with a bunch of friends and family. Why don't you join us? We're on a lake, and you can go swimming too. And for a run later with us, if you think you would like to." There was no better time to introduce them to the pack than when they were all together, including jaguars and wolves from Texas to Oregon to Canada.

"We'd like that. What can we bring?" Mel asked.

"Just yourselves. And have fun."

"My wife, Jane, is working at the hospital, but I'll bring my son and daughter, Cass."

"Good. We'll be just behind the agency building at the homes on the lake."

When David ended the call, he filled in Elizabeth about the new additions to the celebration.

"Oh, that's wonderful."

They walked up to the barbecue and were immediately pulled into the controlled chaos, Elizabeth visiting with all the people she didn't know, everyone playing with the dogs and wearing them out, though when little Corey dropped his hot dog, Winston was there in a hurry to scarf it up. She hurried to fix Corey another before he had time to get upset about it.

Jimmy, Mel, and Cass finally arrived at the party, bringing with them the most delicious-looking cake Elizabeth had ever seen—one of Mel's very own.

Sheri took Cass in hand to get her some food, while David and Elizabeth brought Jimmy and his dad to the office to speak privately.

"I want to thank you," Jimmy's dad said, "for saving my life and my marriage. Of course, Jimmy had a big hand in that when he bit and turned me, but it renewed my wife's interest in me. She knew I would continue to age as a human does, and she knew she couldn't keep the marriage going because of it. She loved me, always had, and now? We've renewed our vows. Only this time, it will be forever."

"Yeah, I did something right for a change, huh, Dad?" Jimmy said, smiling at him.

"You sure did. We just wanted to thank you, both of you, and I want to pay for your services." He handed David a check. "I finally started a bakery out of my house, and my son is making deliveries and set up the website for my business. So I'm still working but for myself now and I couldn't be happier."

"I'm so glad for that," David said, Elizabeth agreeing.

"I can't tell you how glad I was to learn you're like me. Newly turned. It helps knowing I'm not alone in this. I just had to adjust to the idea."

David nodded. "You always have a sounding board with us. We know what you're going through, and we're always happy to talk to you about it. You'll be in good hands with your royal-wolf family, but if you ever have issues they can't relate to, just gives us a call or drop by."

"Thanks. I sure appreciate that."

"Why don't you come and meet everyone else? The big party we're having includes jaguar shifters also."

Both Jimmy's and his dad's eyes widened.

David led them back to the barbecue and began introducing them, though Jimmy had to go fill a plate with a steak and the works. Cass was already eating and talking with the little kids.

"So you're the one David and Elizabeth were trying to find," Gavin said, shaking Mel's hand. "Good to meet you."

"Our pack has just been for those of us who were turned and had been friends for a lifetime," Cameron said, "but it's been growing. Since you don't have a pack, you and your family are welcome to join ours."

"We absolutely want to. My wife is working at the hospital tonight, but she told me to tell all of you she couldn't be happier with the prospect of joining your pack," Mel said.

"Can we go swimming at your lake then?" Jimmy asked, plate in hand.

David smiled. "Yeah, you can drop by anytime. And when we have fireworks for the Fourth of July, or other celebrations as a pack, you're welcome to join us."

Jimmy looked at his dad and he nodded. "Do we need to pay membership dues or anything?"

"No," Cameron said. "We just help each other out when we can and enjoy the camaraderie with other wolves."

"It's a deal. I'll bring baked goods to the Fourth of July celebration," Mel said.

"Why don't you help yourself to some food," Owen told Mel. "And welcome to the pack."

Mel shook everyone's hand and then he went to get some food, talking away to his son.

Elizabeth chuckled. "For being just four male wolves and a she-wolf in the beginning when I first met you, your pack has grown exponentially."

"I'm so happy to be a part of it," Sheri said, joining them.

David would never tire of hearing how happy the pack made her. He hoped the same would be true for *all* their new members.

"Oh, and my parents said they're getting in tomorrow. I don't know how long all your guests will stay, but they hoped to meet all the families and see jaguars in their fur coats too," Sheri said.

"Some of the jaguars might head home tomorrow for whatever assignments they have to handle with their agency, but Uncle Strom will hang around to visit with Candice and Owen a while longer. And the Andersons might too," David said.

"Oh, good. I'll let my parents know that."

Several people who were done eating began going into the homes, and David wondered if they were getting ready to shift and run. He'd better eat in a hurry if so. But the next thing he knew, jaguars and wolves alike were leaving the houses, wearing bathing suits and heading for the lake.

David grabbed a quick bite, and then he and Elizabeth returned to their home—and he was glad to call it theirs—to change into their swimsuits. Which led to them being sidetracked in the most pleasurable way, with hot kisses and snug hugs, before they raced each other to the door.

Outside, the kids were swimming with a crowd of adults.

David hadn't expected to see jaguar babysitters, but Everett and Demetria loved playing with the kids, so they were keeping an eye on them while Faith and Cameron were still visiting with others on the shore.

Then Jimmy and Cass joined in on the swimming fun, and finally Mel did too. It would be nice when their mom was free so she could get to know everyone and they could all get to know her.

David and Elizabeth swam out a way and just treaded water, watching all the festivities. People were eating and drinking, someone had started some music, and others were swimming or just talking to each other.

Finally, it was time to run. After that, they would build fires in their firepits and if anyone was still hungry, roast marshmallows or have s'mores, or snack on leftovers. But for now, everyone was headed for the houses for a run. All except the little ones, who were headed for bed with a promise of running as wolves before dawn—if they woke early enough.

After a night of fun like this, David doubted they would wake that early.

The run was going great. David and Elizabeth were way ahead of the wolves, red and white, and the jaguars, who were doing some exploring on their own, when Elizabeth heard the sound of a bear snuffling in the shrubs nearby. Undoubtedly, the delightful aroma of food cooking on the grills had called to the cinnamon black bear, and he was eager to join in on the party.

She howled in warning, and David followed her howl with one of his own, a call to gather the pack to fight a menace.

Suddenly, the sound of wolves and jaguars—all normally quiet predators—crashing through the brush indicated everyone was coming to Elizabeth's and David's aid, ready to take on whatever threat they faced.

David and Elizabeth howled again to let their reinforcements know just where they were. And as the others joined them, they took off as one, wolves and jaguars running side by side, to hopefully make the bear realize once and for all he just wasn't welcome on this side of the lake.

They'd run about three miles when Elizabeth stopped and David returned to her. She licked his face. Some of the other wolves and a few of the jaguars continued on, but her intentions were clear. She wanted to return home to make love to her mate before they wore themselves out too much, and David was all for it.

Once home, they both shifted and she said, as if they'd just been having a normal conversation and not chasing down a hungry predator, "And tomorrow I want to go to the garden shop bright and early in the morning before the agency is open."

"We can do that."

"We have all kinds of people who probably wouldn't mind digging some holes."

David laughed and pulled her into his arms in the bedroom. "I can dig a hole."

"And with their help, it will be all done so we can be free to do more of this." She kissed him soundly and he reciprocated in kind. "And this," she added, grabbing his buttocks and squeezing.

"Hmm, all right." He moved her onto the bed.

"And maybe some of this." She wrapped her legs around him, pulling him in tight.

"Anything else?" he asked, grinding against her.

She nipped his ear, and he yelped. "You'd better believe it."

This was the life Elizabeth had always looked forward to. She was glad she'd had more time to spend with her grandmother in the end, but this was her time as a mated wolf, hers and David's, and she couldn't be more thrilled as they worked each other into a sexual frenzy and fulfilled their other needs of loving and caring, loyalty and protectiveness.

"I love you." She would never be able to say it enough.

"I love you," David said, the reverence in his voice matching hers perfectly.

David felt he was one of the luckiest wolves alive to have Elizabeth in his life again. She was helping him enjoy the job even more and made his life even better, chasing away the loneliness he had felt when they were so far apart, while his friends were all snuggled happily with their mates at night. She couldn't have come at a better time, and he was glad their friends and extended families had not only helped to show Kintail and his people that the newly turned wolves couldn't be beaten by his bullying, but had also helped free them from the danger posed by the rogue bear.

For now, though, David concentrated on making love to his mate, Elizabeth, the woman he'd lost and brought home—to a place that was truly his home.

After making love and napping for a while, they eventually heard the others return and conversations starting up again outside. David and Elizabeth finally dressed, though he was all for just staying in bed with her until morning.

"We'll regret it if we act like two old wolves who can't get out of bed to visit with everyone, especially because some of them will be gone tomorrow. You know Leidolf's leaving. He has a pack to run."

David sighed. "We are newly mated, not old wolves, and everyone will know the difference. But you're right." He smiled at her. "And then we can return to bed and more of this."

"Now you're talking."

They headed out to visit with the wolves and jaguars, all talking about the exciting evening they'd had.

"We don't get a chance to chase off bears in Houston," Uncle Strom said. "Man, that was a good run."

"That was a big black bear," Gavin said, hugging Amelia close.

Owen and Candice agreed. "More fodder for my stories," she said.

Slade and Sheri were sitting together on one of the stone

benches, roasting marshmallows. "Do you think we chased him away for good?" Slade asked.

"Only time will tell," David said, hugging Elizabeth close. "This is really great, isn't it?"

"Family and friends?" Cameron said, kissing Faith. "You bet."

The next morning, Elizabeth and David headed to a garden center to pick out whatever she needed. She'd joked about having the others help, though if anyone was bored, they were more than welcome. What they hadn't expected was for several wolves and jaguars to volunteer to go with them and help her pick out plants; she couldn't have been more thrilled.

By the time they returned home that morning, she had enough to fill her garden, with room for the plants to grow. She loved it because she wouldn't have to keep shopping for items. Now she had a ready-made garden.

After the guys chipped in to dig the holes, they planted, mulched, and watered everything. Then, with Sheri and David by her side, Elizabeth spread the rest of her grandmother's ashes on the memorial rose garden.

After they finished a late breakfast, David and Elizabeth went in to the office, and Gavin joined them. Amelia had left earlier on another flight, and the other pack members came and went so they could spend time with all their guests. They were still talking about all that had happened with the jaguars and wolves coming to their aid and enjoying some cinnamon rolls that Mel had baked and dropped off for the whole lot of them at the breakfast, just in appreciation for everything they had done for him and his family.

A new client came in and they were back to business, setting aside the wolf business for now.

The woman who came in said to Elizabeth, "Hi, I'm looking to buy a wolf, not a wolf dog, you know, for protection, and I was hoping that you would be able to help me locate the real deal. I haven't had any success so far and I've been looking for weeks."

David, Elizabeth, and Gavin all smiled at each other.

They could help her find a wolf, not a wolf dog, for sure if she wanted to be part of a whole wolf pack. Not that they were going to turn anyone into a wolf, mind you, but...that was what immediately came to mind.

Epilogue

Elizabeth had been torn between being with her grandmother and returning to be with David, afraid he would find someone else in the meantime, yet she knew she couldn't have done anything differently. That if he'd had a chance to find someone he'd loved during the interim, she had to let that happen, particularly since she hadn't known how long she would have to be with her grandmother until the end. She was glad beyond measure that David had felt the same way as she did about him. That she was the only one for him just like he was the only one for her.

And she was so glad Sheri was here with her, not just because she was her best friend but also because Sheri couldn't wait to help with Elizabeth and David's babies when they came.

Elizabeth was thankful for Sheri's family, too, that her parents and Hans had broken away from the Yellowknife pack after all these years and joined them, vowing to help the newly turned wolves anytime they needed assistance. It warmed her throughout.

Sheri's mom and dad had adopted both David and Elizabeth, and since Georgia was a midwife, she was eager to finally deliver some new wolf pups. Sheri's dad, being a building contractor, was busy having the house of his and Sheri's mom's dreams built farther away on the lake, but close enough they would offer any assistance the newly turned wolves would need.

For now, Elizabeth was just enjoying the peace of her new life. She and David sat on the back patio, looking at the snow falling on the lake, watching some of the other wolves of the pack dashing out of their homes for a late-night run while Sheri babysat for Cameron and Faith, their kids having gone to bed already.

Elizabeth put her hand on David's thigh to help herself up, and he quickly stood to assist her. "Did you want to run as a wolf?"

"Yeah, you know it." Because she was having twins, she felt more off-balance than usual. The kiddos were kicking like crazy, and she'd learned today she was having two boys.

David had been thrilled with the news, but she knew he would have been just as thrilled to learn they were girls.

He helped her into the house and began stripping her out of all her clothes. She felt like a beached whale, but she loved how he looked at her as if she were just a beautiful mom who was having their babies.

David never imagined he'd have a family like this.

He had always planned to free Elizabeth from her pack and mate her. He'd known from the first time he'd met her that she was the only one for him. She would be his family.

He'd never guessed her best friend's family would make him part of their family. And he'd even gained a brother. He was glad for their expanding pack of royals.

He was also glad Sheri's family backed her all the way on working on a degree in criminal justice. She and Elizabeth had been having so much fun taking the classes together, and when he and his friends were having shifting issues, they were there to run the office.

Kintail would probably never forgive Sheri, her family, and Elizabeth for abandoning the pack for good. Maybe he would learn from the experience and be a better leader.

David smiled at Elizabeth as she rubbed her bare belly, and he was glad Sheri's mother could deliver her—most likely as a wolf. At least Elizabeth didn't have shifting issues—since the babies were due during the full moon. He wrapped his arms around her and put his hands on her expanding belly, loving her and the babies. They were his whole life.

And then they shifted, and were off on their run, no worries about the cinnamon black bear, who had vacated their territory for good.

Their whole pack couldn't be happier with all the additions to their numbers and the new friends and family they had now. And David and Elizabeth were the happiest of all.

Read on for more wild and sexy Arctic wolf adventures in

Flight of the White Wolf

Available now from Sourcebooks Casablanca.

En Route to Big Lake, Alaska

The case just had to involve flying.

On his first day as a private investigator in Seattle, Gavin Summerfield had gotten a case that made him want to string the thieves up. Stolen pets had become a lucrative market for criminals. In this case, two male, champion-sired Samoyed pups, worth nearly three thousand apiece, had been stolen from their owner's fenced-in backyard. The woman and her two teen daughters were in tears.

"I vow I'll find Kodi and Shiloh and bring them home safe," Gavin told the trio. He hoped he wouldn't fail them. Sometimes, pets ended up in lab experiments or were sold to breeders or puppy mills. Sometimes, the criminals who stole them were looking to return them for a reward.

Soon after he left the family's home with pictures of the

pups and their favorite fetch toys, he had discovered that a white van had been sighted at the owner's house and also in the vicinity of four other dognappings. One of the neighbors had captured a photograph of the Alaska license plate on the same van parked in a friend's driveway when the friend wasn't home.

Then Gavin had gotten a lead that the dogs had been flown to Alaska.

Now, he was trying to settle his stomach and pretend he wasn't flying high above the world on his way to see London Lanier, a retired police detective in Big Lake. Gavin's fear of crashing wasn't just a figment of his imagination. Six months earlier, while he was still a Seattle cop, he'd survived a plane crash after jewelry-store robbers had taken him hostage.

The Alaska-bound plane hit more turbulence, and his stomach dropped. He closed his eyes, telling himself he wasn't going to crash. Not this time. That wasn't the only reason he hated to fly. He liked to be in control, and flying left him with no control over anything.

At least he had a lead on the pups. He wanted more than anything to return them to the family, safe and sound. The Samoyeds' pictures reminded him of the dogs his family had raised when he was growing up. Their German shepherds had been as much family to him as his human family had been.

As soon as Gavin's plane landed, he picked up a rental car and drove to the town where his contact was located.

London Lanier was an animal rights activist, primarily concerned with the illegal hunting of wildlife in Alaska. Gavin had called to tell him the pups had been flown to his neck of the woods, and London had begun to check into it.

When Gavin met London at his Big Lake home, he thought the retiree looked like Santa Claus, with the white beard and hair, though he was a trim version of jolly old Saint Nick. He was tall, fit, and eager to take on hunters with his bare hands.

"You look like a cop," London said, shaking Gavin's hand.

Gavin took the remark as a compliment. Now that he was a PI, his hair wasn't as short as when he was on the force. Today, he looked more like a SWAT team member, with a black T-shirt, black cargo pants, and heavy-duty black boots. He was in a no-nonsense mood and ready to take the bastards down.

London served them both cups of coffee, and then he got down to business. "From what I've learned, a home near here has lots of dogs barking all day long, and then a few days later, most of them are gone. Shortly after that, they have a new batch of dogs. Some of their neighbors are suspicious. Since I don't work on the police force anymore, you'll need to do some canvassing. If you learn anything that proves they really are involved in trafficking pets, let me know, and I'll call the police. I'm still friends with several on the force."

London handed Gavin a hand-drawn map, saying, "I talked to the locals, but everyone knows who I am. Maybe a new guy, just looking for his pups, could convince someone to share something they didn't tell me. Or maybe they've seen something new or remembered something they hadn't thought of before. Good luck."

"Thanks, London. I'll let you know what happens. And I owe you."

London smiled. "Never know when I might need a PI.

Besides, if you can help us take these bastards down, you've done me a favor."

Afterward, Gavin headed over to the Big Lake housing area with its high-income homes, lakefront property, trees all around, and large yards for hiding a slew of runs for stolen pets.

He pulled into the driveway of the home three doors down from the suspect's house, parked, and went to the door. When he knocked, a gray-haired woman with bright-blue eyes greeted him with a smile.

"Ma'am, I'm a private investigator, searching for these two missing pups. They were stolen from the backyard while they were outside playing. Have you seen them? Or know anyone who might have them?"

"Oh yes, of course." Her eyes were rounded, and she licked her lips. "She's my next-door neighbor."

He frowned and glanced at his map. That wasn't the correct house. At least, not according to London. "Are you sure?"

"Yes. She has dogs all the time. Not the same ones though. I see her out walking them along the road in the late spring, summer, early fall. Even in the winter when we're buried in snow. Always different dogs. I figured she fostered them or something. I saw her with two of the cutest little Samoyed pups earlier, maybe six months old? Not sure. They look exactly like yours."

"Do you know her name?"

"Amelia White. She lives alone. Well, except for the revolving door of dogs. I never considered that any of the dogs could have been stolen."

"What about the people at this place?" Gavin pointed to the house on the map that London had targeted.

"Oh yeah, sure. Did London send you? He already asked me."

"You didn't mention Amelia to him?"

"No. She's so sweet. I really didn't think she could be involved in anything so nefarious. But she does have two Samoyed puppies. And that's what you're looking for, right? I hadn't seen them with her before yesterday morning."

"And the other people?"

"Oh, the Michaelses? Asher and Mindy? Yes, I wouldn't be surprised at all about them. Not sure what he does. They don't seem to have a regular occupation, just...money and lots of dogs. They don't walk them. The dogs just bark most of the time, and I've seen all of them rushing to the chain-link fence when I've taken strolls past the place. Different dogs all the time."

"What does Miss White do?"

"She's a seaplane pilot. Her family owns the business."

"Thanks." It would be easy to move stolen pets around as a pilot, wouldn't it? No paperwork hassle. Just fly them where they needed to go. What were the chances that both people were involved in the illegal trade of pets? Maybe Amelia took care of the overflow and the transportation. It would be convenient, with her living so close to the Michaelses.

Gavin drove to Amelia's house first, since she apparently had dogs like the ones he was looking for. He'd start surveillance on the Michaelses after that.

He parked and headed for the large, blue-vinyl-sided home, where he climbed the porch stairs. No dogs barked as he approached, and the front door was slightly ajar. That's when two curious little Samoyed pups poked their noses out, probably hearing his footsteps.

Before Gavin could stop them, they nudged the door open, and one raced down the steps. *Hell!*

The second pup ran to join the first, and Gavin was led on a merry chase. He managed to scoop up the one closest to him and finally reached the other, grabbing him up in his left arm. The puppies licked him as if this was just part of their playtime.

The problem was that Samoyed puppies all looked the same to him. These two were both white, identical to each other. And they looked just like the photos he had of Kodi and Shiloh.

One pup secure in each arm, he hurried back to the house, ran up the steps, and hollered through the open door, "Miss White? Your front door was open, and your pups ran off." If they weren't the right pups, he wasn't about to confiscate them and be accused of stealing *her* pets! On the other hand, he worried about foul play because the door was slightly ajar and no one was answering. What if something had happened to her?

Suddenly, a wet, naked woman streaked across the living room, glancing at him for a second as she ran, and disappeared down a hall. "Put them down, get out, and close the door," she called out.

Shocked, he just stood there, his mouth hanging agape, the image of the gorgeous blond in the raw still imprinted on his brain. She was in great shape, her hands covering her bouncing breasts as she'd dashed down the hall. He closed the front door so the puppies wouldn't run out of the house again and set them down on the hardwood floor. "I'm leaving," he called. "Sorry… Your door was open, and I was worried something might be wrong."

He needed to question her about the pups…maybe later. He started to back away from them slowly and had almost reached the door when they came bounding after him. He was trying to figure out how to keep them from dashing out again as soon as he opened the door, when suddenly the woman reappeared with a blue towel wrapped around her curvy body and a Taser in her hand—and shot him.

After taking down the man, who was unlawfully in her house, Arctic wolf shifter Amelia Marie White knew she recognized him—the uniformed, human cop from Seattle. The man who'd been taken hostage on the plane she'd been forced to fly as the getaway pilot. What angered her also was that the man in charge of the heist, Clayton Drummer, the gray wolf she'd been dating, had been a Seattle cop too. She knew now that he'd only been dating her because he wanted to use her to fly him out of Seattle after stealing the jewels.

Had the two men known each other?

Possibly. What if this one was really here to take her down for killing Clayton? Not arrest her, as she'd thought initially.

"Stay there. Don't move a muscle. I have another Taser all ready and fired up to use on you. And the police are on their way."

Not that the guy was moving. He lay prone on her floor near the door, watching her, groaning. *In her home.* He was half-dazed and looked like he was having trouble focusing. Maybe he hadn't seen enough of her to recognize her as the pilot of the plane that day. But if not, why would he be here?

Confident he wasn't going anywhere, Amelia rushed back to her bedroom, her foster pups running after her. She pulled on a T-shirt and a pair of jeans, then grabbed her phone to call the police.

Wouldn't you know, of all the times her front door hadn't locked properly, she'd stripped to take a shower, and the faucet handle had fallen off in her hand—probably due to mineral water corrosion. She'd had to use the guest bathroom and remembered only after she showered that she'd washed all the towels in there. Which were still in the dryer. And she hadn't brought clothes with her because she normally just walked from her master bathroom to her dresser.

When she'd heard the deep-voiced male calling out her name inside her house, shocking her, she'd had a split-second decision to make. She could shift into her wolf and scare the guy off, but she worried she'd scare her foster pups too. Or she could dash through the house naked, grab a towel and her Taser from the master bathroom, and take care of the guy. Dashing through the house as a naked woman had seemed to throw him off guard, at least long enough for her to tase him.

She'd hoped he would be gone by the time she returned. When he hadn't been, she'd had to take action.

Once the police were on their way, she hurried back into

the room where the guy was still lying on the floor, stunned. She wasn't sure if he was staying put because she told him to or if he really was still incapacitated. Too bad he wasn't a wolf, as sexy as he was.

"Who are you, and why didn't you leave when I told you to?" She prayed he didn't say he was still a cop and investigating her leaving the scene of a crime.

"Gavin Summerfield," he managed to get out. "Former Seattle police, private investigator now, looking into the theft of a pair of Samoyeds in Seattle, which led me here to Big Lake. And your place."

Now that she could really observe him—unlike the first time she'd seen him, when he'd been hustled into the back of the plane and she'd been forced into the cockpit, or when he was lying on the ground half-conscious after the crash—Amelia couldn't believe the hot-looking man she'd just tased was now a PI. Dazed green eyes, red hair, all dressed in black, his T-shirt showing off his nice muscles.

She'd really thought he'd been in on the heist, offering himself as a hostage as a cover. When Clayton had tried to kill him, she'd taken her boyfriend out, mainly for trying to kill the cop, but also because as a wolf, Clayton couldn't go to jail. And because Clayton had used her and would have killed her if she hadn't gone along with the program.

"Stolen Samoyeds?" What Gavin said wasn't registering because all she could think of were the jewelry heist and the downed plane. Sure, she was taking care of a couple of Samoyed puppies. She was fostering them, for heaven's sake. Just like she fostered tons of dogs until she could find them good homes.

Then she worried. What if Molly and Snowflake *were* the stolen pups he was searching for?

Two cop cars pulled into her driveway, and she met the uniformed men at the door. She prayed Gavin hadn't recognized her and wouldn't say anything about the Seattle business to them.

Brenham, one of the cops, began checking Gavin over and verifying his identity, ready to take him into custody.

"Call London Lanier, the retired police detective who worked in your department. He gave me the information about the pet theft ring in this area," Gavin gritted out.

The other cop called London to see if Gavin's story checked out.

"Do you want to press charges?" Brenham asked Amelia.

"No," she said. "He shouldn't have stayed in the house when I told him to leave, but he did return my pups when I could have lost them for good."

"I was working my way toward the door, and the pups were following me. I was afraid they'd dash out again," Gavin said.

She liked his deep, manly voice, though it was a little rough around the edges right now, different from when she'd first heard him talking to her from the foyer.

"*Was* your front door open?" Brenham asked Amelia, a black brow arched.

"Yeah, I'm having trouble getting it to seat properly, and though I locked it, apparently it wasn't shut all the way. I have a carpenter coming to check it this afternoon."

She couldn't believe Gavin hadn't told the cops who she was. Maybe he truly hadn't seen her face before, and he really was only here about the missing pups. If that was the case, she hoped he found them for the puppies' and the family's sake.

Brenham helped Gavin to his feet. Frowning, Gavin asked her, "Have we met before?"

Her heart pounded. The police waited for her to answer him. She quickly shook her head. "Everyone says that."

"You look familiar," Gavin insisted. "Have you ever been to Seattle?"

She felt light-headed all of a sudden and was afraid the color had drained from her face. "No." She hated to lie. Since she hadn't reported what had happened to her six months ago, she was afraid the police would believe she'd willingly been the robbers' getaway pilot. Especially if they learned she had been dating the dead wolf.

"Okay, my mistake. It's probably like you said. You just look like someone else." Gavin didn't sound like he truly believed that.

Which reminded her he was a former cop—like these two here who were watching her behavior. She was trying to look perfectly innocent. She wasn't sure Gavin was buying it.

Brenham began looking at the pups' photos that Gavin had, and then he carefully considered Amelia's pups. "The ones in the photo and the ones you have look the same to me. Are you sure the pups you're fostering hadn't been stolen before they were taken to the shelter where you picked them up?"

The police were thorough, so one got in contact with the animal shelter to verify her story. Especially since her neighbor had told Gavin the pups had arrived about the same time he learned the Seattle pups had been stolen.

Fearing that they might be, Amelia took the photo from the officer and really studied it. The Samoyed pups did look very much like hers. Except for one thing. The ones in the photo were wearing blue leopard-print collars.

She frowned at Gavin, who was leaning against the wall, still looking like she'd just tased him. "Are the two puppies you're looking for males?"

Once Gavin was feeling more like himself—though still having visions of a beautiful, naked, blond female streaking across her living room—he set up surveillance to watch Asher and Mindy Michaels's home, the place London had originally steered him to check out. Gavin still swore he'd seen Amelia White before—in the commission of a crime. A flashback of the blond wearing a blue dress flitted across his brain for a couple of seconds. The experience was like when he'd see a bank teller at the grocery store. Because she wasn't where he normally saw her, he couldn't quite make the connection. Yet due to having been both a cop and a private investigator, he was good at remembering faces.

Still, he needed to get his mind on his work and off the woman.

Early in the evening three days later, a new vanload of dogs arrived. Gavin quickly made a call to coordinate with the police. Once they were on their way, he went to talk to Asher Michaels, the man getting out of the van, to delay him until the police arrived.

"Hey, excuse me. You're Asher Michaels, right?" Gavin asked, stalking up the driveway and getting close to the man. He was dark haired and clean shaven, his square jaw tight with a cleft in the center of the chin. His hard, gray eyes narrowed at Gavin.

Gavin knew Asher wanted to secure the dogs pronto before anyone began asking questions. He kept looking back at the house as if expecting someone to come out and help him.

"I've got work to take care of. I don't allow solicitors on my property," Asher said.

"I'm not trying to sell anything. I'm just looking for these two little fellas. Kodi and Shiloh. They got out on me, and I heard you took in dogs sometimes. Your neighbor fosters dogs, and she thought you did too. Our family has been devastated by the loss. Can you look at the picture and tell me if you've seen them? Or have them?"

"Look, I don't have your dogs. Now get off my property."

Asher refused to look at the picture. Gavin shoved it under his nose, trying to stall him, but also wanting to get a reaction. "*Please*, take a look."

Asher did, only because it was hard not to since the photo was so close to his face. His eyes widened fractionally. Either he had a couple of Samoyeds he'd stolen, or he'd already gotten rid of them.

"I'm an undercover cop," Asher said. "Get out of here before you blow my cover."

Gavin hesitated, processing that information. Then he assumed Asher was spinning a tale to serve as a cover for his illegal business. "If you know anything at all about them, I'm willing to pay a big reward for their return," Gavin told him.

Asher moved his jacket aside and reached for a holstered gun. *Ah, hell.*

Gavin hadn't expected the guy to pull a gun on him. He grappled with the man, hearing the cops pulling up street side. Gavin was glad for his police training as he struggled with Asher, trying to wrest the gun away before it went off. He hoped the police didn't think he was assaulting Asher for just suspecting he had stolen the dogs.

Gavin called out to the cops, "He's got a gun!"

The cops ran toward them, yelling at Asher to drop the weapon.

Gavin finally managed to trip Asher and take the perp down. When a shot fired, just missing Gavin's head, he was thinking this PI work could be damn dangerous. At the same time, a woman raced out of the house and began beating on Gavin with her fists, trying to free Asher. Gavin wouldn't let go for anything. He was just glad the woman hadn't gone for the gun.

The police finally reached them and arrested Asher and Mindy, a petite brunette with catlike green eyes. Another couple of police vehicles arrived. The police officers hauled the couple off to jail. London even showed up with a list of dog thefts in Alaska to see if any of the dogs matched those that had been recently stolen.

"Hell, you need to come work for us," London told Gavin.

"I thought you were retired."

"Just got rehired to be on a special unit that deals with stolen pets and illegal hunting. Come on inside. Let's see if we can find those pups of yours."

"Asher said he was an undercover cop," Gavin told him as they found kennels full of dogs of every size and breed in the backyard. He would guess the Michaelses had well over a hundred, not including the ones in the van.

"Yeah, like I'm a strip-club dancer. He didn't fool you, did he?" London asked, smiling.

"No. I figured he thought I really was looking for my missing pups and he could convince me to go away. Then he must have realized I wasn't buying his story and thought a gun would change my mind."

Brenham, one of the officers who had gone to Amelia White's home to arrest Gavin, called out to him, "Hey, Summerfield. You might be interested in looking at a couple of Samoyed puppies in the bedroom up front." Brenham smiled. "They even have blue collars, just like the ones the pups in the picture were wearing."

Hoping they were the pups he was looking for, Gavin hurried into the house and found Kodi and Shiloh in a crate together. They were watching the other dogs being rounded up, excited, wanting to play. Gavin called their names, and they both turned, wagging their tails.

He checked them over. Their microchips had been removed, but he made sure they were both males. They were wearing the same blue leopard-print collars too. Thankfully, they were in good condition.

Gavin was glad to be going home with the two pups but found himself thinking about the naked woman who'd had two Samoyed pups. He hoped she'd hear that he'd broken up a pet theft ring so she knew he'd been completely honest with her.

After the terrifying plane ride back to Seattle and the return of the pups to their grateful family, Gavin went in to the PI agency, where his partners, all former police officers, were eager to hear how the agency's first case had gone.

He told his story, not leaving any detail out. Owen Nottingham whistled when Gavin mentioned the part about Amelia. David Davis laughed. Smiling, Cameron MacPherson slapped him on the back. "Hell, Gavin, you have all the luck."

Chapter 1

Nearly seven years later
Northern Minnesota

Gavin hated one thing more than anything else in the world—flying. And that's just what he was going to have to do for this mission.

Eleanor Dylan was a cosmetic heiress, though she also had other kinds of businesses, and she was certain her husband was having an affair. She needed proof to start divorce proceedings and keep her inheritance intact. "Conrad is going on a fly-in company canoe trip to the Boundary Waters Canoe Area Wilderness, the BWCA, and your agency is the closest to that location. They'll be in the wilderness, so you'll have to take a seaplane to get there. Well, I guess you could just paddle in, but it would take you too long to catch up to them. Wouldn't it? I mean, if you only have a day and a half to get ready and be there?"

"Yes, ma'am." Gavin grimaced, glad they were speaking on the phone.

"I would have called sooner if I had thought of doing this earlier. But it's the perfect way to catch them at it, I think.

They'll be there for nine days. The tour package includes food and all the equipment they need, so they won't be stopping for supplies anywhere. Can you do it?"

"Yes, ma'am. Our agency can definitely take care of it."

All of Gavin's PI partners and their mates were Arctic wolf shifters who had been turned a few years ago. As wolves, they had enhanced night vision, and their hearing was superior whether they were in their wolf coats or human form. They had settled in Minnesota and their PI business was booming, which meant Gavin was the only one available for this job. A trip to the Boundary Waters totally appealed. More so if he could have just paddled in.

"Not your agency. *You.* I've looked into your background already, and from everything I've seen, you've got an outstanding track record."

"Thanks. All of my partners are also well qualified." Gavin didn't want her to believe that they couldn't handle the case if one of them had to take over for him.

"You, or no deal."

"Yes, ma'am. I'll head up there and check it out." His pack had already reserved permits for him and two of his partners to go to the Boundary Waters later in the summer. He checked on his computer for the availability of a different entry point, and he found one. Some canoeists must have canceled their trip because of the bad weather expected over the next couple of days. Gavin was able to switch his time and port of entry without any trouble.

"Conrad gave me a copy of their trip itinerary in case anything happened," Eleanor said. "It shows their route and where they intend to set up camp. He'll never suspect a lone canoeist is doing surveillance on him, will he?"

"No, ma'am. Does he often give you the detailed itinerary for his trips?" Gavin couldn't help but think that if her husband were having an affair, he'd keep his wife *out* of the loop.

"Always. I would have been suspicious if he hadn't."

Okay, that explained it. Though Gavin wondered if Conrad would have given her a fake itinerary if he thought his wife was having him watched.

"Have you been in the Boundary Waters before?" she asked.

"Yes, ma'am. Several times." Especially once they had more control over their shifting. The wilderness had been the perfect, close getaway for them.

"Oh good," she said with relief.

"How many are on this company trip?" As a wolf, he could get up close to the campsite, and Conrad and his party would never know he was there.

"Four executives from various departments. Lee Struthers, the CEO, likes to chill out with her executives on adventure tours a couple of times a year instead of always conducting business in the boardroom. It's supposed to be a team-building trip. One of the executives is a woman. And the two sales associates going with them are women too."

"You suspect your husband is having an affair with someone in the group, then?"

"A top sales associate. She's in her late twenties. He's forty-five now. I know Orwell Johnston, who's also on this trip, is having an affair with the other sales associate. Conrad told me all about their antics. The long lunch hours at a nearby hotel. The gifts he gives her, even at work."

"How did you learn who would be going?" Gavin wondered why Conrad would tell his wife, if the guy was having an affair with someone at work.

"I asked. And Conrad told me."

That sounded like he was open about things with his wife. "Have you had other investigators checking into his activities?"

"Yes, before we were married eight years ago. I had inherited quite a large estate before I met him, and I wanted to make sure he wasn't marrying me just for my money."

"You must have learned he was a good prospect, since you married him."

"No skeletons in his closet. He worked his way up in the greeting-card business and is now one of their executives. I didn't suspect anything was wrong between us until he came home from the last trip. He acted distant and aloof, and he didn't seem to be his cheerful self for several weeks. I asked what was wrong, but he said nothing was. Which I knew was a lie. He wouldn't tell me what had happened."

"The sales associate had been with him that time too?"

"Yes. They seemed close when I attended the company Christmas party. She was sweet and got me refills on my drinks, and she was trying to be careful about not showing any overt affection toward Conrad. But there were coy smiles, and she patted his hand and ran hers over his back in a way that led me to believe there was more intimacy going on between them."

"How did he react to her attentions?"

"Like he was used to it. He didn't make her stop. I didn't see him treat her in the same way, but that could just mean he was being more discreet at the party because I was there. After the way he acted following the last team-building trip, and with Cheryl part of the group again, I want to know what's really going on."

"Okay, so anything else that raises your suspicions? Like he's taking more care with his appearance? Staying away from home later, leaving home earlier? Evasiveness? Defensiveness?"

"He has been working later. If you must know, our sex life is nil. He's always taken care of his appearance. Evasiveness? Yes, especially after the last trip. And defensiveness, yes. He's received calls he's secretive about. I haven't smelled a woman's perfume on his clothes though—and I haven't seen any receipts that would make me suspicious. Of course, he could be using a separate account that I don't know about for more…personal business."

"You have a prenuptial agreement, right?"

"Yes. If he's having an affair and we divorce, he doesn't get a cent from me. To be fair, if I divorced him and he wasn't at fault, he'd receive a settlement. I do love him, and I was willing to make that concession."

"Okay. I'll get right on this." Gavin didn't know what to think. If Conrad was telling his wife about his coworker's affair, was he trying to get a reaction out of her? Maybe. One of the cops Gavin knew on the Seattle force had done that. His wife thought it was amusing, until she learned her husband was having an affair with a nurse at one of the local hospitals.

"Thank you. I'm emailing you pictures of Conrad and Cheryl. I trust you'll be inconspicuous."

"Guaranteed."

They finished the call, and Gavin studied the photos Eleanor had sent, apparently taken at the company Christmas party. There was a Christmas tree in the background, and both Conrad and Cheryl were holding glasses of champagne.

Conrad was dark-haired, dark-eyed, and had a manicured, pampered appearance. He didn't appear to be the type who was ready to rough it. Cheryl had dark roots, but the rest of her hair was pale blond, and she had light-green eyes. She looked like the girl next door, sweet and innocent.

Gavin called Faith MacPherson, one partner's mate, to let her know he had a job and would be leaving as soon as he could. She managed the calls for their business while taking care of her six-year-old triplets. Her husband, Cameron, and their other two partners were out on jobs of their own.

"Oh, Gavin, I'm so sorry you had to be the one to take this particular case," Faith said.

He wished no one knew about his fear of flying. Faith had learned the truth when Cameron had needed his help to locate their missing friends, and he'd had to fly from Seattle to Maine to aid them.

"No problem. I'll let you know what's going on when I locate the group and tell you if I learn anything."

"Be careful."

"I will."

Like everyone else at the agency, Faith knew how things could go wrong at a moment's notice. Gavin called Adventure Seaplane Tours and got the owner, Henry White.

"Yeah, I had a last-minute sightseeing tour cancellation," Henry said. "Do you need all the outfitting equipment? Will it be just you?"

"Just me, and I'm bringing my own gear. Thanks."

"All right. Drive up here, and I'll fly you out. My son and I are taking a group out there a couple of hours before your flight. We'll be back well before you arrive. It's a popular time of year. Though a storm's coming in tomorrow. So we've had a few cancellations."

Gavin wondered if the earlier group was Conrad's. It would have worked out time-wise, from the itinerary Eleanor had, and Conrad's company was also using White's tour service. "Yeah, thanks. See you soon."

He was relieved he wouldn't be too far behind the company's canoeists, if that's who White and his son were taking. He'd be able to begin surveillance right away. Getting the job done meant he'd be available for another. He and his partners had accumulated lots of great reviews, and they believed that's why business had really picked up.

If time hadn't been against him, Gavin would have just paddled in from Ely and not bothered with the plane trip. But the group would only be out there for nine days, and a thunderstorm was rolling in the night after he arrived. By flying in, he'd be hunkered down well before the storm hit. If they didn't have too much lightning, the storm shouldn't hinder him much. In fact, it could provide him cover.

A day and a half later, Gavin loaded his canoe on his Suburban and finished packing his waterproof bags, cooler, and rain gear. He headed out thinking that, despite the storm and the fact that he had to fly there, he was going to enjoy this trip.

Amelia Marie White glowered at the group of male tourists who were waiting to take a plane up for sightseeing. One of the men had refused to go if a woman was piloting the plane. Was he a throwback to cavemen or what? She'd already had a day of it, so she wasn't in the mood for any more trouble. They'd loaded all their gear into her plane while she was away taking a call about placing a foster dog, so they'd thought her dad or brother would be the pilot.

The guy's arms were folded across his chest in a defiant way, his blue eyes narrowed in contempt. He was around forty, red hair cut in a short burr. He looked like he could be ex-military. Yet something about him seemed *so* familiar. She couldn't place where she'd seen him before though.

If they didn't want her to fly them, no problem. They could go somewhere else, though at this late date, the other seaplane services might be booked. Unless they also had cancellations because of the coming storm. Her dad wouldn't want to get bad publicity out of this though. The other two companies provided the same services and were already annoyed that her family had settled here and taken some of their business. She was certain they would jump at the chance to take these guys up and bad-mouth her company.

Her dad quickly took her aside to defuse the situation. "You know the other group canceled on me because of the iffy weather. Now I've got to take another paddler out to the Boundary Waters. You're scheduled to fly Winston to Saint Paul. Taking the paddler will give you more time to do that, and you'll be way ahead of the deadline. Just drop this guy off, take Winston to the shelter, and come back here—or stay there and do some shopping. I'll take these people up and see you the day after tomorrow."

Wishing he'd back her in telling the redhead either to fly with her or find another service, Amelia frowned at her dad.

"Listen, maybe the guy was involved in a plane crash where a woman pilot was at the controls. Who knows?"

"All right, Dad. It still irks me." Especially since she'd crashed a plane—on purpose—to give herself and the heist gang's possible hostage a chance to live. That still troubled her. No decent pilot should ever be forced to do such a thing.

Her father knew that was why the passenger's attitude bothered her and was empathetic. "I don't blame you. I have to take this group up and I'll just use your plane. If you have any trouble with anything, call me."

"Sure will." This was going to be one of those days, Amelia thought. First, she'd been running late because of car trouble. Then, while she was loading Winston's dog food in the car, he'd made a mad dash out the door of her duplex to chase a cat. She knew he'd just wanted to make friends with it—not that the cat would understand. She'd wasted a good twenty minutes chasing after him. Even her electric teapot had decided to conk out right before she had her first cup of tea. Now this.

Her dad headed out with his passengers, and she hoped the disagreeable man wouldn't give her dad grief. Her brother had already taken up another group.

Amelia was getting ready to pack Winston's container of kibble in the plane when a black SUV pulled into the parking area and the driver cut the engine. An orange canoe was secured on top. He must be the guy wanting the trip into the Boundary Waters. When a redheaded man exited the car and hurried to grab a couple of bags, her jaw dropped. *Gavin Summerfield.* In the flesh.

No way!

Her heart raced. How could he keep showing up in her life?

Was this karma or what? It was like the gods had decided she was going to have to deal with this man, one way or another. After the issue with her first wolf boyfriend, she always carried a Taser gun. So she was ready if Gavin gave her any real trouble.

He turned to ask, "Is Henry White here?" Bags in hand, Gavin stopped dead in his tracks, frowning, looking just as shocked to see her as she was about seeing him here.

Acknowledgments

Thanks so much to Darla Taylor and Donna Fournier for another great read-through and catching so many typos and such. And to Donna for keeping me straight on boating terminology for canoeing since I've done some of every kind of boating, but it's all just boating to me! I also want to thank her for taking me around the Boundary Waters Canoe Area Wilderness near Ely, Minnesota, to create the setting for this book. Also, thanks to Deb Werksman for helping to polish up the book and the book cover artists for giving us art that wows us!

About the Author

USA Today bestselling author Terry Spear has written over eighty paranormal and medieval Highland romances. In 2008, Heart of the Wolf was named a *Publishers Weekly* Best Book of the Year. She has received a PNR Top Pick, a Best Book of the Month nomination by Long and Short Reviews, numerous Night Owl Romance Top Picks, and two Paranormal Excellence Awards for Romantic Literature (finalist and honorable mention). In 2016, *Billionaire in Wolf's Clothing* was an RT Book Reviews Top Pick. A retired officer of the U.S. Army Reserves, Terry also creates award-winning teddy bears that have found homes all over the world, helps out with her granddaughter and grandson, and is raising two Havanese puppies. She lives in Spring, Texas.